TALES OF A MISSPENT YOUTH

Doyle Suit

TALES OF A MISSPENT YOUTH

Doyle Suit

Copyright © Doyle Suit Tales of a Misspent Youth 2020

All rights reserved. No part of this book may be used or reproduced by any means, graphic, electronic, or mechanical, including photocopying, recording, taping or by any information storage retrieval system without the written permission of the publisher except in the case of brief quotations embodied in critical articles and reviews.

This is a work of fiction. While some names, characters, places, and incidents are the product of the author's imagination, some are accurate, but used to further the story. The publisher does not have any control over and does not assume any responsibility for author or third-party websites or their content.

Mockingbird Lane Press—Maynard, Arkansas

ISBN: 978-1-64764-964-7

Library of Congress Control Number: Control Number is in publication data.

0 9 8 7 6 5 4 3 2 1

www.mockingbirdlanepress.com

Cover photos: provided by Doyle Suit
Cover setup: Jamie Johnson

My mother was left with five small children when her husband deserted her and disappeared, leaving us penniless. She managed to provide for us and inspired us to get an education and accomplish something with our lives. In her seventies, she took up writing, oil painting, and sculpture in stone. Hopefully, I've been blessed to inherit some small part of her talent and her iron will.

My wife of almost sixty years supported me by assuming more than her share of family chores to allow me time to write. Numerous friends and colleagues reviewed and critiqued my work. The book is fiction based on a true story.

I'm grateful for my editor, Regina Riney, and the folks at Mockingbird Lane Press for helping me prepare this manuscript for publication.

To Irene

Table of Contents

Footlog over a Flood 1
Home Brew 6
A Haircut to Remember 12
Saved by a Pig 16
Creative Ways to Get into Trouble 21
Sparse Cotton 29
Small Prey 34
Piper Cub Down 39
I Need a Parachute 47
The Sleepy Old Mule 51
Two Indians Carrying a Canoe 56
Coal Dust in Snowballs 61
Starting Over 65
Getting Acquainted the Hard Way 70
A Doubtful Christmas 76
Our Day in Court 81
A Lesson Learned 84
Wasps and Snakes and Such 90
It's a Cruel World 98
The String Ball 105
Paying our Way 111
Why Not Make Whiskey 118
Leaving Alive 124
Old Enough to Use a Gun 129
Firebreak 134

Brimstone and Bloomers	140
A House of Our Own	145
Can We Live Here?	152
A Pig for Sarah	158
Business Lessons	163
Grandpa's 'Possum	169
Coping with High School	174
The Road to Becoming a Sports Star	179
A Loose Sole	186
That Den of Iniquity	191
Buck Fever	197
Margie	204
A Better Job	212
The Big Bang	223
Twenty Dollars	227
Wheels of My Own	232
Intrusion of the Real World	242
Your Father's Peacetime Army	247
Fort Belvoir	252
NCO Rescue	257
Supreme Headquarters Allied Powers Europe	263
An Accidental Engineer	279
What Happened Next?	286
About the Author	287

Footlog over a Flood

Ellen stood silent, holding her shoes, measuring the slippery foot log with skeptical eyes. Spreading floodwater rose halfway to her knees. Earlier that morning her husband, Guy, left her alone to cross the shaky log over the flooded creek and visit his parents. The young couple sharecropped eighty acres of rocky fields nestled between the stream and the steep ridge that extended toward Pearcy Mountain. The isolation of their hardscrabble farm bred loneliness.

She'd smoldered with anger, stuck on this dreary hillside, knowing Guy's family had gathered to enjoy a visit and a fried chicken dinner.

Twenty-one years old and seven months pregnant, her gaze searched the sky that soggy spring day in 1934. Three days of rain had finally stopped, and the damp air smelled clean. The dense forest in the rugged Ouachita Mountains still shed water as it dripped from wet leaves.

It wasn't fair. She was stuck in this tiny shack, cleaning the single room while Guy's family enjoyed Sunday dinner together. She wanted the chance to visit Lydia, her mother-in-law, and catch up on news in the community.

Ellen weighed little more than a hundred pounds, but she'd been strong enough to do the work of a field hand. Her mother-in-law said the determined set of her chin clashed with her cheerful smile and soft brown eyes. She'd done acrobatics in school and had no doubt she could cross the log spanning the normally placid stream. Fish were usually visible in its crystal water. Not today. After the heavy rain, the flood raged ten feet deep. The swift current teemed with debris. Only a fool would risk trying to swim the turbulent floodwater.

The foot log rested on heavy wood blocks. Chains secured it to big oak trees on high banks at each side of the stream. The straight pine log spanned sixty feet without a handrail, rising above ground level at each end. When the creek wasn't flooded, the makeshift footbridge stood well above the trickling water, but today the sagging middle dipped into the torrent. Spray covered the smooth wood, making its surface slippery—treacherous footing to attempt a crossing.

She missed her parents. They scratched a living from the rocky soil several miles upstream and didn't often find time to visit. Guy wasn't always a friendly host, either. His welcome didn't sound convincing. She would have enjoyed the opportunity to visit with family. Instead, working the land consumed her time and energy. If she and Guy were to raise crops to pay the landlord and carry them through the coming winter, her labor was required. The Great Depression was an unforgiving taskmaster.

"I'm going," she huffed. The decision made, she dropped the broom and marched down the porch steps, following the trail to the flooded creek.

As she approached, the roar of rushing water enveloped her. The smell of damp earth reinforced the feeling of danger. The normally placid stream spread more than two hundred yards wide at the crossing. Only between the steep banks of this small rise was the flood channeled into a restricted path. At the water's edge, she stopped to remove her shoes. The foamy brown soup spread outward and swamped the approaches to the log. After hesitating, she lifted her skirt and waded in.

The shock of cold water sent shudders down her spine. Her bare feet felt like they were buried in a tub of ice. Fear seized her at the prospect of trying to maintain her footing on the shaky log. Fast moving currents could easily disorient anyone attempting to cross the unsupported span. If she fell into the churning torrent, she would have little chance of survival. But there was no other way to cross. The closest bridge stood several miles downstream through thick woods. It was probably under water, anyway.

Since she'd married Guy, Lydia had become a treasured friend, and Ellen enjoyed visiting with her. With all the farm work, she didn't get many chances to talk with neighbors. Guy should have taken her with him. Her strength and good sense of balance would carry her across. She'd walked the skinny tree trunk often when the creek wasn't flooded. It was only sixty feet long. She wouldn't yield to the temptation of looking down at the swirling water.

Ellen climbed the narrow steps to stand on the slick surface of the log and hold on to the sturdy tree, watching the tumbling waves of brown water rush downstream. The wood had been worn smooth by time and countless travelers, leaving its surface slick under her bare feet. As she watched it tremble from the impact of the current, she swallowed hard. The middle of the span would sway with her footsteps as she crossed. The need to maintain her balance and avoid looking down would be vital.

Tales of a Misspent Youth

A small tree, uprooted by floodwater, surged down the racing stream. Its trunk passed under the log, but branches slapped at the span with force that caused it to buck and sway. If such a limb hit while she crossed, she would be flung into the torrent. She paused for a long moment, frozen with fear, unable to release her grip on the big oak.

Finally, she gathered her nerve to take a tentative step. Bare feet conformed to the round log. Her frozen toes splayed to grip its slimy surface. The roar of rushing water pounded at her senses. Temptation to scurry back to safety threatened to overwhelm her. Stubborn resolve pushed her forward. Clinging to the shoes, she extended both arms for balance. Looking ahead, she maintained a steady pace, concentrating on the safety promised by the sturdy oak at the far end of the log. The flood pummeled the long timber and the earth that constrained it as she advanced along her water-slick support. Trembling and swaying from the swift current and her rhythmic footsteps, it threatened to dump her into the turbulence below.

A hard kick delivered by her unborn child reminded her of the added responsibility she carried. Guy would be furious. He'd just have to deal with it. Eyes locked on her destination, she refused to consider the possibility of falling.

After what seemed like an eternity, she reached safety and grabbed the welcoming tree. Drawing a deep breath, she wrapped her arms around its broad trunk, allowing her racing heart and trembling knees to recover. A moment later, she waded to dry land and slipped into her shoes. Smiling with relief, she resumed her trek up the long hill to Guy's family gathering.

The warm and inviting smell of fried chicken and blackberry cobbler greeted her when she pushed open the door to enter the crowded parlor. A flurry of astonished questions acknowledged her presence.

"How'd you get here?" Guy asked.

"I crossed the log."

"You should have stayed home." He waggled a work-roughened finger at her. "You're pregnant. Way too clumsy to keep your balance on that old log."

Ellen felt her face flush with anger. "You just wanted to go off without me."

He failed to meet her gaze. "You could've drowned."

"I didn't."

Lydia met her with a warm smile and a comforting hug. "Thanks for coming, Ellen. Sit here on the sofa. I'll bring your food."

A shiver of relief washed over Ellen as she settled onto the soft couch. Lydia's welcome made the ordeal worthwhile. She was safe here.

**

Looking back through a distance of many years, I find myself deeply grateful that Ellen succeeded in this risky adventure. Two months later, she gave birth to a seven-pound baby boy. I remember well when she told me this story of how the two of us crossed that treacherous span.

Home Brew

One Saturday, after we moved to a different farm, my father caught a ride into town with his older brother, Cleve. Uncle Cleve was a bootlegger who made moonshine in a dank little cellar dug under his barn. The trapdoor to enter the hidden still was kept covered by straw. Revenuers searched frequently, but they never managed to find it.

Cleve always wore bib overalls and a chambray shirt. His brogans were clean, and a neatly creased felt hat topped off his outfit. He always bragged he never sold whiskey where he hadn't bought the local law. The moonshine business brought in lots of money, and he used his profits to buy good farmland along the creek.

I was more impressed with the .38 caliber revolver he carried in his hip pocket.

Papa never worked up enough nerve to get involved with Uncle Cleve's operation, but he liked to drink beer. He brought home two cases of glass bottles, a gunnysack of crushed corn, and a couple of small packages one afternoon. A wide smile covered his face when he turned to Mama. "Got everything I need. We're gonna make us some home brew."

Mama dried her hands on her apron and grimaced. "Like there isn't anything else we needed more?"

It was the spring of 1938, and I looked forward to my fourth birthday. We'd moved to a bigger house on the side of Pearcy Mountain. I actually had a separate room to sleep in. The weathered plank building sat hidden in the deep forest, a mile from our closest neighbor.

My new pair of high-top brogans made loud thumps as I clomped across the porch, carrying sticks of split firewood. My age entitled me to a pair of real work shoes. Unfortunately, they came with a list of chores. I had to fill the woodbin by the kitchen range from the pile of split wood outside before Papa got home from the fields each day. Gathering eggs from our chicken house became my responsibility as well. I'd be in trouble if I broke any.

I also had to pull weeds from the garden while my mother cared for the new baby. The pigs thought fresh-pulled weeds were a delicacy, and they went after them with glee. I'd gather an armload, carry them to the hog lot, and toss them over the fence to the greedy porkers. Then I'd stand for a moment to watch them devour their treat. Weeds in the garden grew faster than I worked, so I earned a few spankings for failing to feed the pigs or keep the weeds out of the vegetables.

The big sow pushed the other pigs aside and grabbed more than her share. I made sure to toss a few weeds directly to a younger pig I called Fat Boy. He made a good playmate, following me around and grunting with pleasure when I scratched his back.

It didn't take long for me to learn that forgetting my chores would get me spanked. I liked to gather eggs from the noisy hens, but carrying stove wood wasn't much fun. Usually, I'd remember the chore when I saw Papa coming home from the fields, driving his team of tired mules.

One evening after supper, Papa cleaned out a large galvanized steel washtub and started mixing things in it.

Tales of a Misspent Youth

He didn't tell me what, but I saw crushed corn, yeast, sugar, and other stuff dumped into the tub before he added water. He gave me strict orders to stay away from the fermenting brew with the threat of another spanking.

Before long, I noticed a sour smell coming from the tub. Papa smiled and smacked his lips when he checked on the stinking mixture. I peeked a few times when he was absent, but I didn't find much to smile about. Grown-ups did strange things, and I'd figure it out in time.

Three weeks later, Uncle Cleve came over again to help Papa bottle the smelly liquid. After an hour, they had forty-eight bottles of homemade brew with a half-gallon jug left over to celebrate with.

Papa poured an inch of the liquid into a water glass and held it out to Mama. "Want to try some?"

She shook her head. "I can smell it from here."

Papa and Uncle Cleve carried the jug and a pair of water glasses out to the rockers on the front porch. Papa hung his straw hat on a nail, and Uncle Cleve shifted the pistol in his pocket so he wouldn't have to sit on it. At the front window, I watched them roll cigarettes from a can of Prince Albert tobacco and smoke while they took swigs of the brew. Finally, curiosity got the best of me, and I slipped out the screen door to join them.

Papa handed me his half-filled glass of the amber liquid and grinned. "Want to try a taste?"

I nodded, too curious to resist.

When I sniffed, it still smelled rotten. I took a big sip, and a terrible taste filled my mouth. Unable to swallow, I spit it out.

Papa laughed. "Go in the kitchen and have your mama put a spoonful of sugar in your cup. Maybe you'll like it better that way."

When I returned, Papa added another two fingers of the brew and stirred in the sugar. "Try this."

I took another cautious sip. It still tasted like spoiled apples with sugar poured over them. Making a face, I handed the cup back to Papa. "Tastes bad."

Dust flew when he slapped a hand against the leg of his overalls. "You'll like it when you get older."

After Uncle Cleve went home, Papa poured the sludge remaining in the tub into a big slop bucket. "Hogs will probably enjoy cleaning this up. Want to come watch?"

I tagged along as he carried the five-gallon bucket to the pigpen. He grabbed a stick to beat back the overeager porkers while he emptied the smelly mess into the hog's long trough. The fetid odor almost overcame the stink of the muddy hog lot. Not quite. All the pigs scrambled to dip their snouts into the soggy mix and get their share.

From the greedy way they ate, they surely must have liked it. The big sow snorted and swung her massive head to shove the competition aside. Fat Boy got a taste, but the sow pushed him away with a hostile grunt. Soon she had the trough almost to herself. The pigs darted in to scoop up a quick mouthful, but she wouldn't let them stay. She snorted and squealed as she slurped and chased the others away.

Papa watched and laughed. "She's gonna have one helluva hangover."

I felt sorry for the other pigs that only managed to sneak an occasional taste. That greedy old sow wanted it all.

Tales of a Misspent Youth

Papa stomped back to the house, and I stayed to watch. The sow began to stumble, and her feet slipped in the mud around the trough. Her legs wobbled, and she fell against the V-shaped vessel, continuing to suck in the slush. Other pigs grew braver and sneaked more frequent bites of the mash, but almost too late. Too unsteady to maintain her footing, the sow continued to chase the other pigs away. Finally, she rolled onto the trough lengthwise so her huge body covered most of it. Her head dipped, and she continued to swill the last remaining morsels.

With everything gone, the other pigs scattered to root in the torn up ground. The sow's head dropped into the trough, and her grunts diminished. She was soon asleep, her fat belly filling the long container. When I saw she wasn't moving at all, I began to worry. Maybe she was dead.

I clapped my hands and shouted, "Wake up."

No response.

Shouting louder didn't help, so I picked up the stick Papa dropped. My shoes sunk into the mud as I crept closer to poke her in the ribs.

The big hog gave a short grunt but failed to move.

I tried several times with the same result. The sow would grunt or snort when the end of the stick jabbed her, but she wouldn't budge.

When I returned to the house, I told Papa, "I think the sow's sick. She won't get up when I poke her with a stick."

He grinned at me again. "Most likely drunk. Don't worry 'bout her."

His quick glance took in my muddy brogans. "I just bought you those new shoes. Who told you to wade in the mud? Get outside and scrape it off."

Relieved that I'd escaped a spanking, I rushed to the porch to clean off the mud.

When I checked on the sow the next morning, she stood on four wobbly legs, looking unsteady and moving slow. The other pigs made an effort to keep their distance. Her grunts didn't sound happy, and I watched her blunder into a fence post without seeming to notice.

"Looks like she's in a bad mood," I mumbled.

I kept my distance from the angry-looking sow, too. That home brew and its leftover mash smelled bad, and it didn't seem to help that cranky old hog's disposition.

Home brew didn't appear to be anything I'd ever learn to enjoy.

A Haircut to Remember

This story was first published in Good Old Days Magazine, *September 2004, and later appeared in* Our Favorite Pets.

"Get up here," Papa shouted from the porch. "Time to cut that mop of hair."

I'd been in lots of trouble lately, so I drug my feet as I approached the house. He'd paddled me for being too slow bringing in wood for the kitchen stove and switched me with a peach tree limb for spilling milk at the supper table. To make matters worse, he'd been drinking home brew all afternoon. That usually made him touchy. Mama said he drank too much.

Coming up on four years old, I didn't always remember to do my chores without being reminded. Sharecropping eighty acres provided plenty of odd jobs needing to be done, and I had my share. Forgetting to do them on time got me spanked frequently. Coping with hard times kept the whole family on edge.

My feet slowed as I climbed the steps to the front porch. "Why do I have to get a haircut now?"

"Your mother's been chewin' on me all day. Grandpa's giving you a birthday party tomorrow." He popped a cloth he used to tie around my neck. "Dang right, you gotta get a haircut now."

Doyle Suit

I lifted the empty apple box onto the seat of a kitchen chair and climbed up to sit on it. Papa tied the cloth around my neck as he prepared to give me a haircut and blew a few stray hairs off the clippers. A red wasp buzzed around my head, and I turned to keep an eye on him.

"Keep your head still," Papa growled. "How am I gonna cut this hair with you wigglin' like a litter of pigs at feedin' time? Keep it up and I might cut your ears off."

"Yes, sir." I reached back to grip the sides of the box and looked straight ahead.

He put a drop of oil on the clipper's hand powered blades and squeezed the handles a few times. "Damn woman can't leave well enough alone. I got better things to do."

Afraid to move, I heard the clickety-clack of the clippers attacking my thatch of unruly hair. Papa paused to spit over the porch railing. He let out an evil cackle when he turned back to resume cutting. A moment later, he stopped and backed away. Then he handed me a small mirror.

"What ya think?"

I tilted the mirror to look at my ruined hair. "No!"

A strip of hair, the width of the clippers, had been cut to the scalp down the center of my head. It reached from front to back. The long, uncut tangle on both sides of the shaved strip looked freakish. I choked and my stomach turned over. My head looked deformed. I couldn't let anyone see me like this.

Papa laughed. "Don't you look fancy?"

Tears flooded my eyes. I heard the screen door bang, and my mother's footsteps approached. "Guy, how could you?"

Papa snorted. "It'll toughen him up. Guess I'll have to cut the rest of it off now."

Mama snatched the clippers. "I think you've done enough."

She put her arms around me and hugged me close while Papa stalked back into the house for another home brew. "There's no way to save it. I'll have to cut it all off. Don't worry. It'll grow back good as new before you know it."

A few minutes later, I looked in the mirror again to stare at my bald head. It looked awful. My life was ruined. Everyone would laugh at me. How could my father be so mean? What had I done to deserve this? I hid in a corner, unable to stop crying.

Later that afternoon, Papa's brothers, Henry and Claude, came by to visit. They found me sitting on the steps with tears streaming down my face.

Henry frowned and bent to look at me. "What happened to your hair?"

Mama told him.

The brothers stormed into the house. I heard an argument and the sounds of a tussle. Henry's voice rang out. "We can do this the easy way, or we can do it the hard way."

Moments later, they pushed open the screen door holding my father between them. Papa's face was red, and he struggled in protest, but they shoved him down in the chair. Claude stood behind, preventing the villain from escaping while Henry took up the clippers.

Within minutes, Papa's head was bald as mine.

Henry nodded with a look of satisfaction. "At least the two of you match now."

After supper, I managed to dry my tears. I still didn't want anyone to see me, but looking at Papa's bald head eased my pain a little.

When we met our neighbors, Papa was forced to explain why we were both bald. Grandpa was toughest on him. When he told Papa what he thought about my haircut, he made a fist and used a lot of words I wasn't allowed to say.

My hair grew back, but resentment stayed with me. That haircut lessened my respect for my father, and it became a major reason I eventually refused to accept guidance or correction from a man who could be so callous.

As I grew older, the sting of this haircut diminished. It was overshadowed by other events, both good and bad. I learned to laugh about it. Papa wasn't that mean or that stupid all the time. If I really concentrated, a few good things would come to mind.

On second thought, there weren't all that many good things to recall.

Saved by a Pig

The Ouachita Mountains north of Highway 70 consisted of steep ridges, narrow valleys, and an occasional peak that had survived countless millennia of erosion. Our house sat on an isolated slope of Pearcy Mountain on rented land my parents sharecropped. A narrow lane led to the house, a long way from the graveled road.

The weather-beaten dwelling was built from rough lumber, the interior unfinished. Plank siding and two-by-four studs stood visible from the inside. During its lifetime, the house had never been exposed to a coat of paint. There was no electricity or running water. An open fireplace competed with cold wind pouring through the cracks to maintain heat during the harsh winters. A hand-dug well that often dried up in midsummer provided our only source of water. The bathroom was an outhouse at the end of a footpath.

Having passed my fourth birthday, I figured that adult status couldn't be far off. Papa made me responsible for a list of chores, starting several months before my birthday. I kept the woodbin filled, fed the chickens, gathered eggs, and helped Mama weed the garden. Running errands for Papa frequently upset my opportunities to play.

Papa kept lots of animals on the farm—cows, horses, mules, pigs, chickens, dogs, cats, and sheep. Although they weren't welcome at the chicken house, wildlife abounded in the dark woods surrounding our fields. I tried to befriend any animal that didn't run away or threaten to eat me.

Buster was my first big pet, a wooly white sheep that jealously guarded his right to a small sample whenever Papa milked the cows. I taught Buster to drink from the rim of his tin can like a person drinks from a glass. Each time I carried a bucket of milk from the barn, I pretended not to notice him waiting for his treat. Buster would panic, retrieve his milk can, and chase after me, bumping my leg with the can, bleating his message of imminent starvation. After I reached the kitchen door, I'd pretend to notice the frantic sheep.

"Oh, you must be hungry. Why didn't you tell me?"

Buster bleated his eagerness and bounced with happiness when I stopped to pour him a cup of warm milk.

With no playmates nearby, I made friends with little pigs before the litter was weaned. One of them soon presumed to have as many privileges as the family dog. I named him Fat Boy. Too bad he was destined to end up as pork chops. Given a vote, I'd have kept him. We allowed the pigs to roam the woods, searching for acorns or whatever they could root from the rocky soil during the day. Since we fed them in the evening, they never forgot to come home.

Papa's proudest possession was a pair of matched mules, Bob and Ben, named after his brothers-in-law. Each mule weighed at least twelve hundred pounds. They were usually well mannered and worked together as a team. One summer afternoon, Papa returned from plowing the fields, hot, tired, and showing his bad temper.

Tales of a Misspent Youth

He interrupted my play when he pointed a finger at me. "The well is almost dry. If we water the mules, they won't leave enough for us. Take them to the spring. Let them drink their fill."

I looked at the huge animals with trepidation. "Are you sure they'll listen to me?"

"'Course they will," he growled. "Just be firm. Don't let 'em buffalo you. I'll take their harness off after you bring 'em back to the barn."

The mules towered above me, sweat-caked dust covering their backs. They moved slow, heads drooping after pulling a plow all day. The spring lay about six hundred yards into the dense forest, down a steep path, around a hill to a spot where water seeped from a rocky bluff and collected in a small pool. Tall oak, hickory, and pine trees stretched for miles, and I feared a wandering mountain lion might consider me a tasty snack.

With hands on his hips, Papa watched while I circled behind the mules to pick up the plow lines. "Gitty up, mules."

The big beasts lumbered down the trail, and my confidence soared. They were easy to handle as I held the reins and followed them to the spring. After they stood in the shade and drank their fill of the cool water, they stamped their hooves in the pool and took playful nips at each other. They didn't act eager to take instructions from me.

In my most commanding tone, I gathered the reins and barked out orders. "Gitty up, mules. Haw, Bob."

The mules ignored me.

Pulling on the reins to turn them toward the barn didn't work. The big animals had a different idea. They bolted in the opposite direction and charged into the thick woods. Jerked off my feet, I flew through bushes and briars, finally letting go of the reins to avoid being dragged as the mules tore through the underbrush. Fright overcame me as I watched the normally placid animals disappear into the forest. Papa would be furious if they escaped, so I chased after them despite my fear of the wilderness.

The rebellious mules plowed through the underbrush, catching their harness on briars and branches, breaking a few straps. Quickly outdistancing me, they disappeared over a sharp ridge. I stopped at the crest, out of breath, completely lost and frightened. The mules were no longer in sight. Then I wandered the hillsides for what seemed like an eternity, calling the unruly mules and looking over my shoulder for a mountain lion that might want to eat me.

As the sun sank in the afternoon sky, I began to lose hope of finding my way home. My voice grew hoarse from calling the mules. Tears filled my eyes. The shadows lengthened, and I imagined terrible creatures lurking in the gathering darkness. Fear overcame me. I stumbled and fell repeatedly on the steep slope with its snares of hidden rocks and tangle of branches and undergrowth.

Finally, a familiar sound over the crest of another hill caught my attention. I stopped dead still to listen.

"Oink, oink," I heard, followed by the rustling sound of fallen leaves being disturbed. "Oink, oink."

Tears forgotten, I sprinted over the hilltop toward the source of the sound. Sure enough, my pet pig roamed the woods, rooting contentedly in the leaves, searching for food.

"Fat Boy," I screamed, running to him, wrapping my arms around his broad middle, trying to give him a hug.

"Oink." He turned away to scoop up another acorn.

My fears faded as I stuck with the friendly pig while he wandered through the underbrush, confident now that I'd be home for supper. As the sun sank behind the hillside, Fat Boy picked up his pace and made a beeline toward the farm.

My footfalls grew lighter as I followed the pig back to his pen and the feeding trough. Fat Boy had never missed a meal. That day was no exception.

The mules stood peacefully munching hay from their rack beside the barn. Evidently, they had circled the hill and returned home while I got lost searching for them.

Papa charged out of the barn as I opened the gate for Fat Boy. An angry frown covered his red face. "Why didn't you keep hold of those mules? I ought to whip you."

My stomach tightened with fear. "They're too big. They ran away."

"They've broken their harness straps in a half-dozen places. It'll take me most of a day to patch them."

As I backed away seeking safety, Mama interceded. "The boy is only four years old. Those mules are a lot bigger than he is. Be reasonable."

Papa gave me a dirty look and grunted before he turned back toward the barn.

After supper, I rushed out to thank Fat Boy for guiding me home. Those crazy mules had caused all the trouble. Next time, I'd figure out how to control them.

Fat Boy stood still, allowing me to scratch his back. From time to time he let me know he was listening.

"Oink."

Creative Ways to Get into Trouble

From an early age, I excelled at finding novel ways to get into trouble. After all, that's how kids are supposed to learn. I must have learned slower than most.

Normally, I didn't have problems with Mama. Papa kept me in enough hot water for two parents. There were exceptions, though. When I was three, Mama left me on the back porch to watch my Uncle Howard build a rabbit trap. He's the one who complained to Mama I could talk the horns off a brass billy goat.

Howard left his tools on the floor when he bent down in a corner to fit parts of the long wooden box together. I grabbed the smooth hickory handle of his hammer and hoisted the steel head to make a few trial swings.

Not hearing any noise, Howard looked back over his shoulder. "Hey, put that hammer down."

I raised the heavy tool and took a step toward him.

On his knees and boxed in a corner, he raised his hands to protect himself. "No. Put it down. Don't you hit me with that..."

Smack! The hammer bounced off his upraised arm.

"Ouch, you little rascal." He grabbed the hammer.

I soon learned the consequences of my curiosity. After Mama paddled my backside, she delivered a lecture, and I delivered a tearful apology to Uncle Howard.

**

Tales of a Misspent Youth

My dog, Rex, was supposed to be a fiest, but he looked like he might be part beagle with a little collie mixed in. We were busy playing when Papa interrupted.

"I split a pile of wood. Carry it in the kitchen and fill the bin."

Bringing in firewood was a dreaded chore. I'd get splinters if I held the sticks wrong. The sun was hot, and I wanted to play with Rex. I carried a half-dozen small sticks on my first trip, and then I sat down on the chopping block to think about it.

Papa walked by the woodpile. "Get a move on. Your mother needs that wood."

That bin was huge. It would take half the afternoon to fill it. My feet dragged when I made a few more trips to carry the wood. After sitting down to rest again, I considered my plight.

"I never get to do things I want to do."

Casting a glance at the patch of thorny blackberry vines, an idea percolated in my fertile mind. I picked up a stick and tossed it into the berry patch. Life just wasn't fair. Another stick sailed into the tangle of vines. I had an idea. If the wood disappeared, I wouldn't have to carry it to the kitchen. Sticks began to fly into the thicket.

After all the wood had disappeared into the blackberry patch, Papa walked by again. "Did you carry all that wood in?"

I jumped up from my seat on the block. "Yes, sir. It's all gone."

He continued on toward the house. A moment later, he was back. "I chopped enough wood to fill the bin. It's not even half full. What happened to the rest?"

I scuffed my shoes on the ground. "I don't know."

Papa looked at the bare ground around the chopping block and peeked into the blackberry thicket. "How did all that firewood find its way into the berry patch?"

I squirmed and looked down at my feet.

"I want every piece of wood hauled out of those briers and put in the wood bin. If I find one stick left in there, you're in real trouble. Understand?"

"Yes, sir."

After he spanked me, I crawled into the thicket on hands and knees. Sharp thorns ripped at my skin, and the rest of my afternoon was spent finding the sticks and pulling them out, one by one, from the tangle of briars. It was really hot in there with no breeze, and my scratches burned when sweat filled them. Swarms of ticks found me. I'd have to pick them off later. Rex came by to console me, but he had better sense than to brave the thorns. Later, I filled the bin with wood.

Nobody felt sorry for me. Rex was the only family member to offer sympathy.

**

A week later, my scratches had healed. Papa and Mama decided to visit my grandparents, so we walked down the lane toward the creek. Rex and I lagged behind. He chased sticks until we tired of the game. Then he ran circles around me. Pine straw covered the oily, sharp-edged slate rocks in the path. The slippery surface invited a nasty fall.

Topping a hill, I spotted a bush filled with wild blueberries and stopped to taste them. Rex waited patiently while I gobbled the ripe fruit. Boredom inspired me to eat the berries like our horses did. Bending forward, I opened my mouth and bared my teeth to bite off a big clump. Another creature had the same idea, and I found myself nose to nose with a frightful, foot-long, green garter snake stretching to nibble the same treat. I suspect my sudden scream frightened the poor snake out of its wits, but I didn't tarry to find out.

Scrambling back to the path, I tripped on an exposed root and fell headlong on the straw-covered hill. The downhill slide on sharp slate hidden under the straw gave me a new set of scratches. I forgot the snake as I careened, face down, on the slope.

Rex joined the fun. He raced to overtake me and jumped in the middle of my back, riding me like a sled.

He barked with joy when we slid to a stop at the bottom. Lying still, I assessed the damage. Holes in my overalls and shirt showed the scratches underneath. This time, even Rex didn't offer me any sympathy.

**

My family moved to better farmland on the Ouachita River when I turned five. Shortly after we arrived, Mama invited a group of ladies to visit for a quilting party. They pinned the cotton batting and its cloth covers to a large rectangular frame hanging from the ceiling in the middle of our living room. The group gathered in chairs around the frame to sew the material and talk about absent neighbors.

I hid under the quilt to play and listen. Lots of good gossip flew across the quilt, but I finally got bored. Those women didn't even stop talking to catch their breath, so I yielded to a sudden inspiration.

Jumping up from my hideaway, I made my grand announcement. "We have an old mule named Tobe. He's twenty-seven years old, the same age as my mother."

Silence reigned for a moment, and then everyone started laughing. Mama's face turned red.

She pursed her lips and skewered me with an evil eye. Her arm went rigid, and a finger shot toward the door. "Outside! Now!"

Thinking I might have said something wrong, I stayed out of sight the rest of the afternoon. When the ladies left, Mama called me inside to discuss the incident. I didn't get spanked, but she left me dreading the possibility for the next few days.

**

My episode with the woodbin should have taught me a lesson, but I learned slowly. Papa tilled a plot of ground to grow field peas and drafted me to help plant them. He plowed long furrows while Mama and I carried buckets of seed peas and dropped them, one by one, into the rows. The sun baked me, and I got tired. My feet dragged in the plowed ground, and I complained. When Papa finished plowing, he helped us plant peas.

"I'm hot and thirsty. My back hurts," I said. "Can I quit now?"

Papa frowned at me. "Plant one more bucketful, and you can go play."

Tales of a Misspent Youth

Rejuvenated, I took off down the long row dropping peas in the furrow. Five minutes later, I returned with an empty bucket. "I'm done. Can I go now?"

"That was mighty fast," Papa said. "Did you plant all those peas?"

Suddenly scared, I hesitated before answering. "Yes, sir."

He walked the row to find the hole where I buried all the peas. "What's this?"

Silence.

After he warmed up my backside with a hickory switch, I planted peas under the hot sun for the rest of the day. Rex found a soft bed of leaves under a shade tree and took a nap.

"I never get to do things I want to do."

**

A wonderful opportunity to escape farm chores and Papa's harsh discipline presented itself the following year. I'd attend school and be unavailable for all the chores he invented.

It was a pleasant, one-mile walk to the plain little schoolhouse. The single room housed eight grades of noisy students and our kindly old teacher, Mr. Brown.

He gave me a textbook. "You'll soon be able to read if your mother helps you. With eight grades to teach, I can't give much individual attention to each student. You'll have to follow the rules. I don't have time to spend with kids who misbehave."

The best part of school was the morning and afternoon recess and a full hour for lunch. Lots of time to play. We climbed trees, ran in the woods, threw acorns at each other, and explored the red clay road ditch.

Back in class, Mr. Brown made an announcement to all the students. "Some of you tracked mud in the room after recess. Stay out of that clay ditch, and wipe your feet when you return to class."

Everyone looked attentive and nodded agreement.

During recess, one boy had an idea. "That ditch would be a great place to play. We could cut roads in the side of the bank and push our trucks without having to crawl."

It sounded like a good idea. "I'll bring a truck tomorrow."

The next morning, three of us brought push toys. At first recess, we headed for the ditch to walk on the muddy bottom and carve our roads high on the clay bank.

The oldest boy broke up a bunch of sticks. "We can play like we're hauling logs."

Soon we were racing along the bottom of the ditch, pushing our trucks on the mountain road we'd created.

"V-r-o-o-o-m," I roared, pushing my vehicle along the path.

The bell rang, announcing the end of recess, and it ended our play. We tramped back to the schoolroom and resumed our seats.

Instead of calling his first class to the recitation bench, our teacher strolled down the center aisle, looking at muddy footprints. An uneasy feeling invaded my stomach.

He walked back to the front of the room. "I see mud on the floor. Everyone, stick out your feet."

Scared now, I stuck my shoes out in the aisle along with the rest of the students.

Tales of a Misspent Youth

Mr. Brown checked all the shoes, and then he tapped my two friends and me on the shoulder. "Come up front."

We lined up at the front of the room, and our kindly old teacher brought a sturdy tree branch from the corner and warmed up the seats of our pants with all eight grades watching us dance when the stick landed on our backsides.

Mr. Brown then pointed to the door. "Go outside and clean your shoes. Stay out of that muddy ditch in the future."

This was the sort of thing that happened to me at home. Mr. Brown was as bad as my parents, but the spanking did improve my memory.

"I never get to do things I want to do."

"Sparse Cotton" was first published in Good Old Days Magazine, *September/October 2009.*

Sparse Cotton

I landed my first paying job the year I turned six. In the fall of 1940, the Great Depression still ruled the mountains of Southwest Arkansas. Money was scarce, and everyone worried about war.

My parents owned our livestock and equipment, but we sharecropped the land. Papa's team of mules pulled our wagon, loaded with the whole family, twelve miles to town for Saturday shopping trips—my favorite recreation. We'd tie up at the rail on the courthouse square and buy what we needed during the morning. In the afternoon, we'd watch a western double feature movie at the Roxy Theater. On the trip home, we'd stop at Cook's Ice Cream where I'd have a big vanilla cone for a nickel. If Papa happened to be feeling generous, he'd buy me a double dip for a dime.

With 120 rented acres of bottomland on the Ouachita River, we raised pigs, cattle, and a large corn crop. Papa even brought in a hired hand during planting and harvest seasons. He paid the man room and board, plus enough money to buy a little tobacco and moonshine whiskey. My biggest job was chopping weeds out of the corn rows with a hoe. Papa's big mules did most of the heavy work.

Tales of a Misspent Youth

Tobe, our elderly mule, did the lighter jobs like plowing the garden. He'd hang around with me, looking for an extra tidbit to eat. Tobe was my buddy. He'd cock his ears to listen when I told him my troubles. I trusted that mule.

In September, I enrolled in school—eight grades, twenty kids, and one overworked teacher. The term had barely begun when we were given a vacation so kids were free to pick the cotton that grew thick on the fertile flood plain of our river valley.

Since my friends all worked to harvest the fluffy white stuff, I didn't have any playmates. My family raised corn, and it wasn't time to harvest our crop. Papa said I couldn't sit around and do nothing, so he dreamed up plenty of chores to keep me busy.

When I realized all my friends earned money picking cotton while I worked at home for free, jealousy got the best of me. Our nearest neighbors, the Bakers, hired several workers to harvest their large fields. After I found the nerve to ask Mrs. Baker for a job, she told me I could work if my parents gave me permission.

I ran straight home to Mama. "Mrs. Baker wants me to pick cotton."

Mama frowned as she wiped her hands on a dishtowel. "Picking cotton is hard work. You're not big enough to pull a pick sack."

"All the other kids are working."

She shook her head. "Most of them are older than you, and they're working with their families."

"Mrs. Baker needs my help," I pleaded. "She'll pay a cent and a half a pound."

"I suppose you can try." She shook her head. "I'll make you a small pick sack. You couldn't pull one that's twelve feet long."

She sewed a strap on a cloth bag that once held fifty pounds of flour. The flimsy sack weighed almost nothing. Stuffed tight with cotton, it would weigh about five pounds. I reckoned I could carry that much.

The next morning, I joined the work crew at Baker's farm.

"Adults pick on the bottomland," Mrs. Baker told me. "Join Abner and Darren working on the hillsides. Cotton is sparse there. Adults want to work where they can make more money."

So I joined her two sons to pick the scrubby plants. Darren made fun of my tiny sack. The brothers had bigger ones, but they didn't get to choose where they would work, either. The sun baked us as we started down the long rows, grabbing wads of white cotton and stuffing it into our sacks.

Weeds had invaded the field. Cockleburs snagged my clothing and pricked my fingers when I tried to remove them. Dust rose from the trampled field, and I fought thirst, wishing I'd remembered to bring my quart jar of water. Cotton bolls split open when they ripen, and we had to get past their pointed ends to reach the fiber inside. My fingers soon bled from hitting the needle-sharp spines.

I quickly learned it took a lot of picking to make a pound of the fluffy white fiber.

Abner was older than me. He took advantage of his size and snatched the easy-to-reach bolls from the top of the plants in my row. I wound up bending to pick the

Tales of a Misspent Youth

cotton near the ground since we had to leave each stalk clean. It wouldn't have done any good to fight for my rights. I might have whipped Darren, but Abner was a fourth grader. He would have beaten me up if I defeated his little brother.

Mama had been right. Picking cotton was hard work.

After what seemed like hours of fighting sweat, bugs, and weeds, my sack was stuffed full. With dragging feet, I lugged it to the wagon where Mrs. Baker had set up scales. Adults carried a twelve-foot long canvas pick sack. They put a small rock inside a bottom corner. A wire hook was tied around the rock from the outside so both ends of the sack were supported when it hung from the scales to prevent it from touching the ground as it was weighed. Mrs. Baker deducted two pounds for the weight of the big sack when she tallied each bag of cotton.

She hung my little sack on the scales and adjusted the counterweight. "Five pounds," she said. "Minus two pounds for the sack, tallies three pounds."

I knew she cheated me because my little sack weighed almost nothing. However, I didn't know how to confront an adult, so I didn't argue. I hadn't been in school long, but the math wasn't difficult. On my way back to the hillside field, I calculated what I had earned—four and one-half cents.

On my next trip to the scales, my sack of cotton weighed four pounds. She tallied two pounds and added another three cents to my account.

After several days of stoop labor, we finished the job. Mrs. Baker paid all the workers. I counted my earnings to find that I'd worked for an entire week to earn a dollar and some change. I felt at least a foot taller when I brought home my pay.

Mama rolled her eyes, and Papa muttered some bad words.

During my life, it's possible I held a more disagreeable job. I can't remember one. Mrs. Baker did leave me a lasting impression of her generosity and sense of fair play.

Small Prey

Papa slammed the screen door after entering the kitchen on a clear Saturday morning. "Weather looks good and cool. Think I'll do me some squirrel hunting today."

Fall leaves were changing from green to shades of red and yellow, and I had the weekend free from school. "Can I go with you?"

He cocked his head with "no" written all over his face as he looked in my direction. "You're too little. You couldn't walk that far without slowing me down."

I jumped to my feet. "I'm six years old. I won't get tired."

Papa let out a deep sigh and relented. "Okay, but if you don't keep up, I'll leave you behind in the woods. You'd get yourself lost and make a good breakfast for an old mountain lion."

The cool, crisp days were perfect for tramping through the forest. The air smelled sweet under a clear sky. I swelled with pride to learn my dog, Rex, was good at hunting squirrels. Papa sometimes beat animals that didn't do what he wanted. Rex better find squirrels, I thought, or he might miss his supper.

Papa frowned like he did when he got serious. "Be quiet, keep up with me, and carry the sack of squirrels I shoot."

We slipped through the woods, moving carefully to avoid making noise, while Rex sniffed the ground for the scent of a squirrel. After he found a trace, he'd track the animal to flush it and chase it up a tree. The busy little critters liked the massive oaks and sweet gums for their height and thick foliage. Rex stood at the base of the tree, barking until Papa arrived to shoot the squirrel. Mama would clean and pan-fry them for supper. They made a welcome change from our steady diet of chicken.

I didn't like chicken.

Being proud of Rex, I hugged him and scratched his ears after he treed the little animals and stood barking to announce their location. "Good boy."

During the course of several hunts, Rex learned to associate success in finding squirrels with making me happy. That led to a change in his approach to the task.

Seeking my approval, he'd often stand under a tree and bark. Papa would come running, only to be disappointed when he failed to find the squirrel. After several of these episodes, Papa grew suspicious. He started paying attention to how Rex found, chased, treed, and announced his prey.

That's when he figured out the dog occasionally sat under a tree and barked without bothering to find a squirrel. "The stupid mutt's lying to me."

Rex yelped when Papa cursed and kicked him. The frightened dog ran to cower behind me for protection.

Hands on hips, I faced my angry father. "You hurt my dog."

"He lies to me once more, I'll kill him," Papa yelled. "If you don't hush now, I'll give you a whipping you won't forget."

I bit back angry words as I trudged home carrying the squirrels he shot. If I argued, he might hurt Rex again.

Tales of a Misspent Youth

Two days later, my dog failed to appear for his supper. Failing to find him, I asked, "Where's Rex?"

Papa speared me with a hard stare. "I sold him to a farmer who lives across the river. No sense feeding a hunting dog that lies to you."

Desperate to be alone, I slipped away from the table in silence and ran to the safety of the barn. Once there, I sat in the corner where Rex always slept. Papa wouldn't see me cry if I hid there.

**

The weather cooled, and leaves turned brown before floating to the ground. They crunched beneath my feet. The sun ducked behind Brady Mountain earlier each day. A cold wind whistled off the mountainside, and the trough where we watered the animals froze over. Cold weather hounded us for a whole week, and the ice thickened. A blanket of light, fluffy snow covered the ground when I woke on a bright December Saturday.

"Good day for rabbit hunting," Papa announced when he stomped into the kitchen after doing his chores. "They're easy to track in this fresh snow."

My ears stood at attention. "Can I go?"

Papa frowned. "It's cold out there. You'll freeze your toes off."

"I'll wear my boots," I promised.

He rubbed the back of his neck with a callused hand. "You sure you won't get cold and cry to go home?"

Mama gave me a quick hug. "I'll dress him warm."

After breakfast, she made me put on long underwear, overalls, flannel shirt, and a wool sweater. My feet were stuffed into two pairs of socks when I pulled on my boots. Next came my coat, gloves, and a stocking cap to keep my ears warm. I felt like an Eskimo as I waddled around the kitchen.

Papa took his Remington 12-gauge and a sack for me to carry the rabbits he shot. We left the house and headed across stubble-filled cornfields toward the river. Wading through the fresh snow and cornstalks was tough going. My layers of clothing made me waddle when I walked.

A number of quiet sloughs lay scattered along the swampy area of fields and forest bordering the ice-free river. Trapped water in the stagnant pools had frozen with a light covering of snow on top. Papa hunted the clear areas next to the swamps, and I tramped behind him, struggling to move my short legs fast enough to keep up.

He looked back and pointed a stern finger at me. "Keep quiet. There'll be rabbits along here."

Soon, he spotted tracks and followed them to a clump of brush beside a long, frozen slough. A cottontail sprang from the bushes and raced for safety toward the ice. Papa raised his old pump shotgun and fired. The rabbit tumbled and slid to a halt on the frozen surface covering the dark, cold water.

"Got him," Papa shouted. "He'll taste good for supper. Hide's bound to sell for at least a dime."

I stood silent, feeling sorry for the fluffy little critter.

"Go get him." Papa pointed toward the frozen slough. "Ice is too thin to support me."

Cold fingers gripped my chest, and I hesitated. The ice didn't look thick enough to support anyone. Afraid to defy Papa, my feet crept slowly onto the frozen body of water. The surface held. I moved away from shore another few yards and stopped, afraid to move when the thin sheet groaned beneath my feet.

"Hurry up," Papa yelled. "We don't have time to dawdle. Want to shoot a few more of them bunnies before it gets too late."

Biting my lip, I slid my feet farther away from the safety of shore to approach the dead rabbit. The ice beneath me creaked and popped. After halting in a momentary panic, I inched closer and watched a crack develop near the center of the big pond. Terrified, I dropped to my knees and crawled the final foot to snatch the rabbit and hold my breath as I scooted across the fragile surface to the safety of solid ground.

Papa grabbed the dead rabbit and stuffed it into his sack before handing it back to me. "Took you long enough."

Twice more I made terrifying trips onto the ice to retrieve rabbits he'd shot. When the sack held six cottontails we started home. My feet dragged. Drifted snow, stubble from cornstalks, and my clumsy sack of rabbits made it difficult to keep close.

Papa looked back and scowled as I lagged behind his long strides. "Get a move on. You told me you'd keep up."

As I struggled to run faster, I wondered, *just how had Papa known the ice was strong enough to support me?*

"Piper Cub Down" was first published in Storyteller Magazine, March 2006.

Piper Cub Down

The hum of the engine captured my attention before I saw the airplane. It skimmed the ridge on the far side of the Ouachita River five minutes after the sun dipped behind Brady Mountain. Then the little craft crossed upstream from our farm.

I held on to the net wire fence around our front yard at the end of a muggy summer day in 1941, watching the approaching aircraft. We didn't often see airplanes pass over our isolated valley. Having just turned seven years old, I'd read stories about them and even watched a few take off and land at the airport in Hot Springs.

The left wing dipped, and the bright yellow Piper Cub slipped into a gentle turn above the valley. It glistened in the last rays of sunlight when it passed overhead. The rain had stopped earlier, and the ground around me was already covered by the shadow of Brady Mountain.

"Mama, come look," I yelled. "An airplane is flying over our house."

She stepped outside, wiping her hands on her apron. The steep mountain ridges cast long shadows across our fields and the river.

"Why's he circling?" she asked.

Tales of a Misspent Youth

My feet couldn't stay still, and I jumped with excitement when it started around for a third time. It dropped lower as it passed over the farmhouse. I'd seen military planes flying high above our farm, but they never circled.

Two of my uncles were Army Air Corps pilots. One flew the B-24 bomber. Another flew the C-47 transport. When they learned how much I liked airplanes, they gave me spotter manuals from their training and taught me how to identify all the American, British, German, and Japanese aircraft. I learned lots of stuff about different kinds of bombers and transports by sitting in a corner and listening to my uncles talk when they came home on leave.

The Piper Cub continued to circle, losing altitude with each pass. The sky remained bright as I looked up from our yard, but I knew the pilot couldn't see much, looking down into the dark shadows covering the valley.

Papa joined us. "That pilot must be crazy. He's going to hit something, flying this low in the dark."

The graceful craft barely cleared the treetops around our yard. I could see the pilot inside as it passed over our house. He made two more low passes over the cornfield. The waist-high stalks and young leaves snapped and waved in the wake from its propeller. I held my breath as the pilot pulled up sharply to miss tall trees at the end of the field.

Papa took off his hat and shook his head. "He's in trouble."

As darkness descended, the pilot flew a half mile upriver and turned toward us. When the aircraft approached, I heard the engine change pitch. The nose lifted, and it settled toward the ground, heading straight for our cornfield. The wheels barely cleared the fence, and it sank into the half-grown corn.

The sleek little aircraft splashed into tender plants, ripping a path through the young stalks. The airplane bounced when it hit the furrows. It settled back to earth and slowed rapidly in the soft plowed ground. The tailskid bumped, and the airplane stopped in the middle of a gently waving sea of green leaves.

The Piper Cub was down.

Darkness covered the farm as we ran across the pasture and climbed through the barbed wire fence. I snagged my trousers as I scooted between the wires too quickly. The pilot killed the engine before we arrived. He sat in the back seat, staring into space, his hand gripping the control stick between his knees.

"You all right?" Papa called.

The pilot sat rigid, gazing straight ahead. He didn't move. Finally, he glanced around and noticed us standing under the wing, peering into the cockpit. The young man's face looked chalky white.

"I—I thought I was in the water."

Papa opened the cockpit door and helped him climb out.

The pilot's hands trembled. "This was my first cross-country solo. I got lost. It's all mountains. I ran out of fuel. When I found this valley, I was afraid to leave."

"Why didn't you land in the pasture?" Papa asked. "That's a better place."

"I couldn't see well enough to identify obstacles on the ground. The cornfield looked like a pond. It rippled like waves when I flew over. The chances of surviving a landing in the water looked better than hitting an obstacle on the ground."

Papa motioned toward the house. "Come on up. We'll get you something to eat and move the airplane to the pasture tomorrow morning."

"I can't leave it," the pilot said. "It's rented from the flight school. Would you call the airport and let them know I'm down safely."

"The nearest telephone is at the general store in Bear," Papa said. "That's five miles across Brady Mountain, and I'd have to ask a neighbor to take you there. The road's too rough and muddy to drive in the dark. We'd best wait for morning."

When my parents returned to the house, I stayed to talk to the pilot and ran my hands over the stretched canvas that covered the fuselage. "This is the first time I ever touched one. May I look in the cockpit?"

"Call me Tony." He helped me climb in the back seat.

"Why do you sit back here?"

"To balance the load. If two people were on board, I could fly it from the front seat."

"How do you make it fly?" I asked.

Tony laughed. "First, you'd need to put gasoline in the tank and start the engine."

"But what makes it fly?"

"The propeller spins to pull the plane through the air, and the wings hold it up."

What he'd said didn't answer my question. "How?"

"The shape of the wing makes the air go faster on top than it does on the bottom. The difference in pressure lifts the airplane."

I didn't see a steering wheel. "How do you make it turn?"

Tony showed me the flight controls. "The control stick and rudder pedals move parts of the wings and tail to make it change direction."

He answered lots of questions. After a half hour, I felt sure I could fly the beautiful machine if I got the chance. His story about the air going faster on top of the wing confused me, but I figured he knew what he was talking about.

I asked him again to sleep in the house, but he refused.

"I'm responsible for the plane. Someone might damage it. I'll sleep in the cockpit tonight."

Unable to persuade Tony, I returned to the house to spend the night dreaming of flying the bright yellow airplane high above the mountains.

The next morning, Tony agreed to come in and eat breakfast with us. Mama served biscuits and gravy with homemade sausage. Tony and I made it disappear fast.

After breakfast, I ran to Mr. Wilson's place and asked him to drive his truck to Bear and call the airport while we took down a section of fence and pushed the airplane into the pasture. I helped pick up rocks to clear a landing path. Then we chased the cows into another field.

Mama tore strips of cloth from an old sheet, and Tony set up little flags to mark a runway. Then we waited for help to arrive.

I moved closer to Tony. "I'm going to be a pilot when I grow up."

Tales of a Misspent Youth

He wiped a smile off his face. "You've learned a lot about airplanes. Maybe we can go flying together sometime."

That idea really started me thinking.

Soon, another Piper Cub appeared in the morning sky, following the river upstream. It made one pass over our farm, then landed between the flags and rolled to a stop beside Tony's plane. The pilot rode in the back seat with a five-gallon can of gasoline strapped in the front cockpit.

Tony introduced his instructor and told him the aircraft wasn't damaged. They walked around it, and the instructor looked at the tires, the engine, and all the control surfaces. After he finished his inspection, he emptied the gas can into the stranded airplane.

We moved away to watch the instructor start his plane and rev the engine. I smelled the hot exhaust and felt the windblast from the propeller as it began to move. Then it gained speed and swiftly rose into the bright sky. Tony waved to me and followed close behind. The two airplanes circled once and waggled their wings before following the river downstream to disappear behind the hills.

I spent another night dreaming of piloting a bright yellow fighter plane through the clouds, chasing a Japanese Zero with my machine guns blazing.

**

During breakfast, I decided to build an airplane like the Piper Cub. Designing it took at least thirty minutes of deep thought. Building the airplane came next. After gathering boards from the barn, I carried them to my construction site on our front porch.

My mother opened the screen door to check on me. "What are you doing?"

I gave her a serious look. "Building an airplane."

"Don't mash any fingers with that hammer." She turned back into the house.

Resuming my work, I chose a long board for the fuselage and nailed another across it for the wings. A shorter board across the back end served as the horizontal tail. Not sure how to attach a vertical tail, I split the short upright board while trying to toenail it to the fuselage. Frustrated, I finally decided the vertical tail wasn't needed because I didn't plan to make any turns on my first flight. Two long blocks nailed to the bottom of the fuselage served as landing skids.

My design wasn't big enough to provide a cockpit, so I devised a saddle made of rags behind the wings. My feet would rest on the trailing edge and provide roll control when I leaned left or right. Next, I nailed a short length of clothesline to the nose. Pulling up on the cord would control pitch.

The airplane was now complete except for a power plant. That took some thought.

A junk car behind the barn solved my problem. I borrowed Papa's wrenches from his toolbox and removed the radiator fan. After a twenty-minute struggle and one barked knuckle, I had my propeller. Then I nailed it to the nose of my airplane, verified it would spin freely, and pushed the craft to the launch area on the edge of the porch.

Tales of a Misspent Youth

The plank-covered floor stood about eight feet above the yard. I planned to sit on the saddle and scoot the airplane over the edge. My theory predicted it would fall at first. The airstream would spin up the fan and pull it forward, and I'd pull up on the line to raise the nose. Then it would glide across the yard and slide to a gentle landing on the soft grass.

I was ready for the test flight.

After spending several minutes rehearsing the control movements, I climbed aboard and pushed off the end of the porch.

The initial trajectory was exactly what I'd predicted. When I scooted past the edge, the nose dipped and the airplane started down fast. However, when I leaned back and tugged on the line to raise the nose to glide attitude, it didn't respond.

The total flight was eight feet and vertical.

A loud crash bombarded my ears as the airplane slammed into the hard ground. Sprawled in the dirt, amid the wreckage of my little flying machine, I wondered what went wrong. Lying still for a long moment, I nursed my bruises and counted the splinters I'd collected from the rough planks.

My Piper Cub was down.

I Need a Parachute

After my airplane's first flight crash, it took about a week for the cuts and bruises to heal. Mama used a sewing needle to dig out most of my splinters. She found the rest after they festered. A liberal application of Cloverine Salve covered the cuts.

She crossed her arms and frowned. "I hope you learned to be more careful."

My chin dipped to touch my chest. Mama had a point. "Yes, ma'am."

Papa wasn't gentle. "That must be the dumbest stunt I ever seen. Any kid with half a brain would know better."

He probably had a point, too.

I thought about my plane-building experience and tried to figure out what I'd done wrong. It should have worked. Building an airplane must be more difficult than I'd figured. Flying was tricky. Trouble happened fast.

My Air Corps uncles wore parachutes when they flew. I'd seen pictures in the training manuals they gave me. A parachute could save their life if an enemy fighter plane shot them down. Maybe I needed one before I built my next airplane. If it crashed again, I might get hurt.

That was it. I needed a parachute.

My first test model was in miniature. I tied string to all four corners of a handkerchief and used an oak stick for a miniature man. After tying the strings to the stick, I rolled the handkerchief around it. When I tossed the parachute as high as I could, it popped open and allowed the stick to drift slowly back to earth. Obviously, I needed something larger than a hanky to slow my fall.

Determined to be more cautious after my airplane crashed, I spent several hours figuring out how to build a parachute before I started work on it. I'd do it out in the barn where nobody would see what I was doing. An opened-up gunnysack looked like a good candidate for the canopy. It wasn't an exact square, but it was close enough. The burlap material was porous but sturdy. Good enough to carry a boy my size.

Lengths of clothesline lifted from Mama's storage closet made perfect risers. I cut four lines about six feet long and tied one end around each corner of the cloth. I had to figure out how to attach the other end to me. A strong shock would slow my fall when the parachute opened, and I wanted to cushion it.

Finally, I settled on a leather strap borrowed from Papa's harness room. It fit snug when I buckled it under my arms. A few long strips of rag wound around it made a nice cushion for my chest. After I attached the risers, I thought it should work as well as my miniature parachute.

I held my breath when Papa stomped through the barn. He raised an eyebrow when he looked over my spread out device. "If I catch you jumping off anything with that contraption, I'll warm up your rear end so you won't be able to sit down for three days."

"Yes, sir," I mumbled. I'd make sure he didn't catch me.

The catwalk at the peak of the barn roof looked like a good platform for a test jump. It stood seventeen feet above the packed dirt floor, high enough to prove the chute would slow my descent. Thinking back on my misadventure with the airplane, I spread a foot-deep layer of hay on my landing zone. The fresh-cut fodder still smelled good. It should help to cushion my fall.

I'd heard pilots were careful how they folded their parachutes, so I rolled mine up tight like my successful handkerchief canopy. When I was ready to test the device, I waited until Papa had taken the mules to work the fields. He wouldn't be home before suppertime. Holding the rolled-up parachute under one arm, I climbed to the catwalk and gazed at my landing area. The ground looked a long way down. Good thing I had my trusty parachute.

I hesitated a long time to work up my nerve before leaping into space and released the tightly rolled canopy as I stepped off the platform. The ground came up fast. I hardly noticed the light covering of straw as my legs collapsed and my body slammed into the packed dirt. The stink of trampled manure overpowered the smell of fresh hay against my cheek. New pains got my attention when I finally worked up the courage to move my arms and legs. My luck held. I didn't find any broken bones.

My chute lay beside me, partially unrolled. The platform hadn't been high enough for the wind to open it and inflate the canopy. I couldn't think of anything higher to jump from, so I'd need to make some changes to prove the device would slow my fall.

When I came inside for supper, Mama looked at me with a skeptical eye. "You look pale. Are you all right?"

I tried for my best smile. "Yes, ma'am. I'm fine."

At suppertime, I avoided limping and kept my bruises covered. A solution to the problem occurred to me as I lay in bed that night. *It'll open quicker if I don't roll it up.*

Tales of a Misspent Youth

I waited two days until Papa took his flat-bottomed boat across the river to pick up our mail from the general store and post office. He'd be gone for at least an hour.

I added another six inches of straw to cushion my landing and inspected the device to make sure all the knots were tight. Then I carried it up the ladder to the catwalk and strapped in. I left the canopy loosely folded on the platform behind me and peeked at the landing area. The floor still looked a long way down, but the parachute would surely open quick enough to slow my fall this time.

After taking a deep breath, I jumped from the platform. The packed dirt came up fast again, and I felt a mild tug from the belt as my burlap canopy inflated an instant before I slammed onto the hard ground. More bruises soon made themselves known. With an effort to ignore the pain, I tried to think of the experiment as a partial success. The chute had opened, and my body didn't hurt quite as much as it did after the first attempt.

In bed that night, I nursed my new collection of black and blue spots and decided to postpone building another airplane until I was older and had a parachute that worked.

"*The Sleepy old Mule*" was first published in Good Old Days Magazine, *December 2005*. *It was later reprinted in* Cuivre River Anthology, *April 2009*.

The Sleepy Old Mule

In the summer of 1943, I turned nine. My family left our farm and moved to the outskirts of Hot Springs, Arkansas. Papa took a job at a defense plant producing aluminum to build airplanes. To me, this town of 25,000 people was *the big city*.

Living in town opened up a whole new world. Always lots of stuff going on. Plus, we had electric lights, indoor plumbing, and a paved road. Instead of attending a one-room schoolhouse, I caught a bus to the consolidated school. Each grade had its own room and a different teacher.

Our house perched on a hillside by the railroad track, overlooking a switching yard to the west. The hobos called this tangle of tracks the jungle. Sometimes, I caught rides on freight cars when they were shuffled to assemble a train.

"Can I go with you?" my five-year-old brother, Jason, begged.

I shook my head. "You're too little to climb onto a boxcar. You'd get us caught for sure."

Tales of a Misspent Youth

The railroad detectives didn't nab me, but my mother became suspicious, and I lived under the threat of being skinned alive if she ever caught me playing in the jungle. She had taken over the job of riding herd on me after I attacked Papa with my fists each time he attempted to whip me with his heavy belt.

To the east, a neighbor's fenced pasture separated us from a local dump. We found lots of interesting stuff by poking around in its smelly piles of rubble. Wandering horses and small boys scavenging for treasure had made a well-worn path.

One Saturday, Jason and I took the trail across the pasture to search the dump for valuables. The early fall sun baked us. The piles of trash smelled ripe as a warm barnyard littered with rotten eggs. We spent the next couple of hours examining the endless variety of junk strewn about the site. Finally, we selected our loot and headed home. My treasures included a tattered Captain Marvel comic book and a store-bought slingshot with one broken rubber strap. I'd cut a replacement from an old inner tube.

We carried our loot along the path that passed under a large oak in the open field. Near the tree, two fat old mules dozed in the shade. I took my time, searching the close-cropped grass for bugs and lizards and avoiding the piles of horse apples littering the field. Jason ran ahead, keeping to the path, escaping my attention for the moment.

The mules looked like they were frozen in place as we approached. One stood in the middle of the trail with his rear end pointed our way. The tranquil animal appeared to be oblivious to everything around him. He must have weighed a thousand pounds.

Not wanting to wake the peaceful creature, I left the trail to walk around him. Jason had other ideas. He stopped about six feet behind the big mule, hands on his hips, indignant that the mule blocked his path. He gazed up at the lazy animal.

"EEEYIIIEEEE, MOVE!" Jason's shrill scream pierced the September afternoon. He waved his arms and stamped his feet.

The impact of this sudden blast of sound sent shock waves through the peaceful silence. My head snapped around to see what terrible thing happened to my little brother.

The mule panicked. His head and tail jerked erect. All four hooves tried to move at once. He swapped ends instantaneously while trying to identify the creature making such a terrible racket. Now facing the startled boy, his uncoordinated hooves flailed without moving him forward.

Confronted with the huge animal looming over him, Jason turned to run. The mule found traction and lurched forward. Churning hooves pounded the rocky soil until the beast spotted Jason in front of him. His front legs dug into the ground in an effort to stop, but they collapsed when his half-ton body continued on.

He toppled.

The mule's chest slammed Jason's back, driving him into the dirt and rocks. Sparse blades of grass provided the only cushion covering the layers of slate. Dust from the collision flew as the frightened animal scrambled to his feet and loped away to safety. Somehow, he avoided stepping on my brother.

Jason lay unmoving, face down in the dirt. After my initial shock, I raced to look at his body. He appeared to be dead. When I turned him over, his dust-covered face was laced with scratches from the sharp rocks. I was sure he was dead.

Finally, his eyelids fluttered open, and he moved a hand. Wide gray eyes stared at the sky without blinking. He didn't try to speak. He didn't cry. I was definitely more scared than he appeared to be.

My voice wavered. "Are you okay?"

Jason didn't say a word, but he finally nodded.

"Let's go home." I took his arm and helped him stand. Our treasures lay forgotten on the ground.

Jason's legs wobbled, and he started to move in the wrong direction. I guided him toward home, and he managed to walk out of the pasture. A barbed wire fence barred our way, but I spread the wires to help him climb through.

Mama cried out in fright when I opened the door. I told her what happened. She examined his battered face and removed his shirt. His chest was crisscrossed with the same scratches that marked his face. Deeper wounds covered his knees and elbows. Several dark bruises began to show, but his arms and legs bent where they were supposed to bend and nowhere else. He didn't appear to have broken any bones.

"Why did you go close to those mules?" Mama asked.

I hung my head without answering.

Jason looked better after a hot bath. His injuries turned out to be minor. Within a few days, he was good as new.

I got spanked.

**

Jason is a full-fledged senior citizen these days, slowing down a bit and drawing social security. He gets along fine with dogs, cats, and most other animals. However, for some strange reason, he never developed a fondness for mules.

"Two Indians Carrying a Canoe" was first published in Storyteller Magazine, *May 2003.*

Two Indians Carrying a Canoe

Our stay in Hot Springs didn't last long. The lure of better wages drove Papa to quit his job and move our family to a small town in Kansas.

Uncle Cleve loaded most of our belongings on his pickup truck and helped us move from our friendly mountains to the flat plains of the Midwest. Worn-out tires and a thirty-five mph wartime speed limit made it a long trip for a nine-year-old boy.

Papa took a job in a factory making gunpowder for the war, and we lived in a large village for the workers' families. Identical houses, made of concrete blocks and heated by a coal stove in the living room, lined the streets. Each structure had a big coal bin on the alley. Winter had arrived early on the windswept prairie. My coat wasn't quite warm enough.

Mama enrolled me in a large school with so many students they needed two rooms for each grade, a big change from my previous exposure to education. Our teacher, Miss Carter, and many of my classmates regarded me as a hillbilly. They let me know right off they didn't expect much of the new kid from the mountains of Arkansas.

During my first week at school, we studied the major rivers in Kansas. Miss Carter pointed out the "Ar-KAN-sas" River on a map.

I promptly raised my hand for permission to correct her. "The proper pronunciation is Ar-kan-SAW."

Miss Carter bit her lip and glared at me. I got the impression she didn't approve of my attempt to be helpful.

She pointed a finger at me. "My pronunciation is correct, and I don't need any interruptions. I'm your teacher, and you should remember your role as a student. You're here to learn."

Having not yet mastered the art of humility, I continued my determined effort to teach her the proper way to pronounce a word I'd known since learning to talk. Our discussion didn't last long, and I wound up in the principal's office where he pointed out that I'd failed to be properly respectful to my teacher. Because it was my first offense, he let me off with a lecture and detention after school.

The next week, several of the boys decided to play a new game. We all brought our cap pistols to school where we proceeded to have fun running in the small grove of trees adjacent to the schoolyard, playing cowboys and Indians with our toy guns. Miss Carter watched from a distance. She appeared to approve since she didn't stop our fun.

A few days later, it was my turn to be the cowboy as a group of Indians chased me across the playground. I turned to make my stand in front of the main entrance to the school building. A spirited gunfight between Indians and the cowboy erupted. I stood my ground as my pistol

Tales of a Misspent Youth

popped loudly. Smoke rose in small clouds from our blazing six-guns. Miss Carter's eyes looked wild as she ran down the steps, screaming for us to stop.

She promptly corralled our group of young gunfighters and led us back to the classroom where she collected our guns to be deposited in the trash. "I thought you boys were pretending to be hunters. Who started this horrible game of shooting each other?"

None of the other boys said anything. I waited politely to give them a chance to speak before attempting to calm our agitated teacher with a rational explanation.

"Everyone plays cowboys and Indians," I told her. "It would be silly to hunt wild animals with a six-shooter. Any fool knows you'd never get close enough to hit one."

Miss Carter's face turned red. When she calmed down and quit yelling, she marched me to the principal's office again. He listened politely and told me he understood the point I made, but he gave me another week of detention anyway.

After the Christmas break, we started art class. Miss Carter explained what we should expect. "An appreciation of art will benefit all of you. Have your parents buy watercolors and bring them to class on Monday. We'll teach you how to make paintings."

When my father got home from work that night, I waited until after he'd had his supper to tell him about the supplies I needed for school.

His face darkened as he pounded the table. "Watercolors? You don't need no such thing. Art class is for girls."

"We all have to study art. I'll be in trouble with my teacher if I don't bring what she asked for."

"No son of mine's going to spend school time playing with watercolors," he shouted. "They're just toys for sissies."

I continued to plead my case because I was already in deep enough trouble with my teacher. Papa finally relented. He allowed Mama to buy me a small package of crayons.

Miss Carter didn't appear to be happy with my efforts. She gave me a failing grade when I drew a simple outline in crayon for my first assignment.

After I explained the problem to Mama, she agreed to purchase what the school required.

"Don't tell your papa," she said. "He never had the opportunity to study art. If he sees the watercolors, we'll both be in trouble."

Miss Carter acted pleased when I brought the little package of paints and brushes to class. She gave me a passing grade for the next assignment. After practicing with the paints for a few weeks, I decided I liked making pictures with them.

For our next art class, Miss Brown brought in a record player and announced we would have the opportunity to create something completely original for a contest. "I'll play classical music, and you can make a picture of whatever the sounds inspire you to paint."

It was really sad music, with lots of fiddles and horns and other instruments I'd never heard before. It sure didn't sound anything like the songs on the Grand Ole Opry. I thought about the war overseas, and the music made me envision tragic happenings on the battlefield. I just sat and listened for a long time, an occasional tear escaping my eyes. Then I grabbed a brush and started to paint in a burst of energy and inspiration.

I visualized a wooded hillside with a quiet stream in the foreground. The late afternoon sun filtered through the trees, casting long shadows. A couple of large branches were shattered. Shell craters pocked the terrain. Two tired American soldiers tramped through low bushes along the bank of the stream. They carried their wounded buddy on a stretcher. Totally immersed in the event, I applied paint to my construction paper without hesitation, using broad strokes and somber colors to describe this tragic scene.

I finished my masterpiece quickly and turned it in to Miss Carter. She collected the artwork from our class and took it to the library where it was judged against the art from other classes. The teachers added captions and selected the winning entries.

At school the next Monday, our pictures lined the hallway. I was a little anxious and curious about how I'd done and searched for my painting, failing to find it at first. Finally, a small group of pictures taped to the wall by the principal's office caught my eye, and I rushed to see if my picture was there.

I found my painting with a blue ribbon affixed. My chest swelled with pride. The sign announced FIRST PLACE.

Then I recognized Miss Carter's handwriting on the caption—*Two Indians Carrying a Canoe.*

Coal Dust in Snowballs

Six inches of late January snow blanketed the ground. The brisk Kansas wind stung my skin as I trudged down the alley carrying a bag of groceries. The shopping task fell to me because Mama had a newborn baby plus three more preschool boys at home.

This shortcut took me down a dreary alley on my daily after school trek. Trouble found me when I spotted the gang of boys hiding behind coal bins. They'd been there every afternoon for three days, waiting to ambush me. I could anticipate dodging a flurry of snowball missiles packed tight with coal dust.

Papa brought our family to Sunflower Village to take a higher paying job making gunpowder for the war effort. Some of the kids at school started calling me Arky when they found out I came from hillbilly country in Arkansas. I didn't feel inferior, but being a bit hardheaded, it took me a while to adapt to their strange ways.

When I got within range of the ugly bins that stored coal to heat the homes on each side of the alley, an older boy stepped out and let fly a frozen snowball. Tugging my spiffy button-down cap, I tried to protect my face and neck behind an upturned coat collar. I couldn't fight them because Papa promised to beat my butt with his belt if I got careless and brought home a bag of damaged groceries. On that day, my bag held a loaf of bread, peanut butter, fresh vegetables, and a dozen eggs.

The rest of the gang joined in, pelting me from all sides. Dirty lumps of ice thumped against my coat. The snowballs stung when they hit. They left marks from the coal dust. Pride wouldn't allow me to run, but I walked faster, hoping to escape as quickly as possible.

"He's a sissy," someone yelled.

Another voice chimed in. "Arky can't stop to play. He wants to hurry home to see his mommy."

Head down, I trudged onward—frightened, but ashamed to let the rowdy gang know it.

Sam left the pack, trying to sneak up behind me. I recognized him from school. He was a year older, and he got in trouble even more often than I did.

"You scared of a little old snowball, Arky?" He launched a frozen ball of ice from close range.

It hurt when it hit my back, but I wrapped my arms tighter around the bag and kept marching toward home. Papa's belt would hurt a lot worse. If I fought him with my fists, he'd whip me twice as hard. That put me in a no-win situation.

When I didn't respond, Sam grew more brazen. He caught me from behind and yanked the new cap from my head. "Look what I found."

Surprised and outraged, I turned on him. "Give it back."

His whole attitude challenged me to react. Holding my cap at arm's length, he laughed as he dropped it into a puddle of filthy black water.

Stunned, I watched it float on the surface scum momentarily and sink into the icy puddle. With a ruined cap, I'd be in bad trouble at home. Rage replaced my fear of Papa. I dropped the grocery bag into a snowdrift beside the alley.

A red fog clouded my vision as I sprang at Sam with fists flying. He tried to fight back, but he couldn't match my fury. After wading through his feeble punches, I battered his ribs and face with both hands. His nose dripped blood, and he tried to run. Grabbing his collar, I threw him onto the muddy snow and fell onto his chest to put my weight into a flurry of hard punches to his face. Fresh blood stained the snow.

Sam quit trying to fight back and tried to protect his face with his arms. "Stop. I give up."

He couldn't cover everything at once, and I continued to batter him with all the force in my skinny body. It was already too late to avoid punishment at home. Papa would whip me, and I'd fight him and lose. Sam would pay the price for the beating I was sure to receive from Papa.

His high-pitched wail turned into sobs. "Don't hit me. I give up!"

I continued to land punches until the other boys pulled me off. They backed away when I turned to confront them. No one else offered to fight.

Sam scrambled to his feet and ran for home. He disappeared through a kitchen door, three houses down the alley.

My cap lay soaked in the black puddle. Dirty water dripped from the ruined fabric when I picked it up. It stank of black mud, coal dust, and garbage from leaky trash trucks. My rage increased when I looked at my bag of groceries. The brown paper sack had split, oozing slimy yellow egg yolks. Papa would kill me for sure.

Tales of a Misspent Youth

The crowd of boys disappeared, but I'd seen where Sam lived. Holding the ripped bag together as best I could, I left it on a snowdrift by his back step. Then I pounded on his kitchen door, refusing to stop until it flew open.

An angry lady, who looked like she might be Sam's mother, glared down at me. "What do you want?"

Too bent on revenge to be intimidated, I stared up at her. "Send Sam back outside. I'm not done with him yet."

Her reaction convinced me she might become violent, and I heard a lot of bad language not even the big kids on the playground used. In spite of my fury, I took a backward step to gain more space from her tirade. I figured she meant Sam wasn't coming out, and I'd best be gone before she called the cops.

My better judgment finally outweighed my rage, and I picked up the ruined sack to trudge home with reluctant steps.

Fortunately, Papa was still at work when I arrived. Mama listened to my halting explanation and cleaned up the mess. She covered for me, and I escaped with the hide on my rear end intact.

When I passed the coal bins the next day, carrying a dozen eggs to replace the ones I'd broken, Sam was nowhere in sight. The silent group of boys ducked behind the row of dingy bins. They didn't challenge me. During the rest of that cold northern winter, not one of them threw a coal dust-filled snowball at me.

Not even a soft, fluffy, clean one.

Starting Over

Blustery spring winds replaced winter's snow across the Kansas plains. My fourth grade school year ended. Miss Carter was surprised to find me near the top of her class in spite of my insistence on the proper pronunciation of Ar-KAN-sas. Hillbilly kids were supposed to be slow. Mama beamed and congratulated me when I brought home my report card. Papa grunted and turned back to reading the paper.

Frost marred the warmth of our home. Something had gone wrong. I didn't understand the problem, but my parents stopped talking to each other. Papa failed to come home at night on weekends. Mama didn't confide in us kids, but a long face replaced her usual smile. Once, I caught her crying.

"What's wrong?" I asked.

She dried her tears and pulled me close for a long hug. "Nothing you should worry about."

Mealtimes became an ordeal. Mama and Papa ate without speaking to each other. He snapped and cursed, threatening to spank my younger brother when he spilled his milk. He yelled at Mama to make the baby stop crying. When she asked him for money to buy food, he'd demand to know where she spent the cash he'd given her last week. I kept my worries to myself and remained silent, avoiding his rage, knowing he'd strike if I bothered him.

Freedom during summer vacation gave me time to find a way to make money. Mama didn't have enough to

Tales of a Misspent Youth

buy groceries. Borrowing a little red wagon from my younger brothers, I pulled it around the neighborhood to collect jars of bacon grease from our neighbors. The grocery store would pay for it because the defense plant extracted glycerin from the fat to make gunpowder for the military.

My first stop was the house next door. I knocked and waited for Mrs. Howell to answer. "I'm collecting bacon grease for the war effort."

She glanced at my wagon and smiled. "I think we have a full jar in the kitchen."

I put the sticky quart jar in my wagon when she returned. "Thank you, ma'am."

"You can keep the money," she said. "But they'll also give you meat rationing coupons. You must return them to me."

After I completed my tour of the neighborhood and sold the smelly jars of grease, I had almost a dollar in change and a wad of rationing stamps. Then I made a second round to return the stamps. Mama wouldn't need them because we didn't buy much meat anyway.

My route kept me busy and out of my father's way. I gave most of my earnings to Mama. Maybe she wouldn't have to beg Papa for money to buy food. Steering clear of his foul temper became an increasingly difficult challenge.

I turned ten during that summer. Blowing dust accompanied the soaring temperature, making me homesick for Arkansas. It didn't seem to get that hot in the mountains.

When I had no errands to run, most afternoons found me in the shade, reading or hanging out in a fort our gang of neighborhood boys constructed. Our refuge was built from a large wooden packing crate and scrap lumber we hauled from a dump. It decorated the lawn beside the telephone switching station next door.

As I headed for our fort one Friday morning, Papa cornered me. "You boys and your mama are going to Arkansas to visit your grandparents. Pack your clothes and be ready to leave tomorrow morning."

"Why?"

"Because I said so." He stalked off to his car and left for work.

We left hours before daylight the next day. Mama held baby Kevin on her lap in the front seat beside Papa. I shared the back seat with Jason, Dennis, and Ron, my three preschool brothers. Bags of our belongings that didn't fit in the trunk filled the floor between seats, leaving us no room for our feet. Nobody said much during the miserable, eighteen-hour drive. Papa stopped only for gas and bathroom breaks. Even my little brothers sat in silence. Well past bedtime, we finally arrived at my grandma and grandpa's modest log home to be greeted by their warm welcome.

Mama sat on a rocking chair in the living room while Papa ate breakfast the next morning. He prepared to leave without telling us where he was going or when he'd be back. All of us boys realized something bad had happened, but we kept our distance in silence. Mama didn't come outside to see him off.

My feelings flip-flopped between fear and joy that he'd be gone. I wanted to know more, but I wouldn't give him the satisfaction of ignoring my questions. He refused to look at me when he gathered his belongings and loaded

Tales of a Misspent Youth

the car. With a sense of foreboding, I watched the dust cloud settle after the old Chevy drove away.

Several days later, Mama sat the five of us down to talk. "Your father is not coming back. We'll live here with your grandparents until I figure out what to do."

My body stiffened with anger. "Why?"

Mama's chin lifted. Her brown eyes gazed into the distance. "He doesn't want to live with us anymore."

Trying to understand this treachery, I slipped away to be alone. Sitting on the chopping block at the woodpile, I pondered what had happened. Did I drive Papa away by fighting with him? Maybe it was all my fault. Maybe I should have accepted his fits of anger and frequent whippings without fighting back. Who would support our family now? Mama had me and my four smaller brothers to care for.

With no money and no way to earn it, our life wouldn't be easy. While idly throwing wood chips into the underbrush, I gave our problem some serious thought. I'd have to be the man in the family and take care of everyone. Mama was busy washing dishes after supper when I told her my plan.

She smiled and rumpled my hair. "School's starting soon. You can do your part by making good grades."

Papa had left all our farm equipment, the team of mules, a small herd of cattle, and much of our furniture with his parents when we moved to Kansas. Those possessions were the only things that kept us from being destitute.

A week after Papa left, my Uncle Bob's pickup truck stopped at the side of our road. He trudged slowly up to the house. When he spoke to Mama, his voice trembled with anger. "Guy sold everything you owned at auction. Then he took the money and disappeared. There's nothing left for you and the children."

Mama collapsed into the nearest chair. Her head drooped, and she looked suddenly smaller. Tears appeared in her eyes. After a moment she sat up straight and wiped them away with an angry swipe. "We'll find a way."

My grandparents gave us food and a place to stay. We'd have to start over and find a way to survive. Mama and I worked long hours in the fields to harvest crops and plant fall vegetables to provide our winter's food. My hands grew calluses and my back hurt, but I toughened up to do the work.

Even my younger brothers chipped in to help. We gathered wild grapes, nuts, and berries to be preserved. Working together, we put away enough food to see us through the cold weather.

When school started, Mama found a job as lunchroom cook at Alamo Elementary school. It paid forty dollars a month during the school term. That small salary bought our clothes and helped Grandma and Grandpa with the extra expense of providing a home for the six of us.

Grandma took care of the younger kids while Mama worked. Jason and I attended school. Fear, thoughts of revenge, and worry about our future troubled me. I forced myself to keep up a good front.

I'd not allow a treacherous father to defeat me.

Getting Acquainted the Hard Way

September arrived—time to start school. The shock of Papa leaving us diminished, and I looked forward to meeting kids who lived nearby.

On the first day, Jason and I stood by the roadside, wearing the western-cut shirts Mama made for us. The arrival of the big yellow bus at seven o'clock signaled the start of a new adventure at Alamo School. I'd enroll in fifth grade. Jason would start first grade.

Other boys on the bus ignored me. They'd sneak glances when they thought I wasn't looking. If I caught their eye, they shifted their gaze to the passing scenery beyond the windows. Gossip had spread the word of my family's problems.

After a twenty-minute ride, the bus delivered us to a large white building perched on a hill and surrounded by dense forest on three sides. White paint flaked from the siding. A large brass bell hung from a post by the entrance. The area in front had been skinned free of grass and covered with gravel for a playground. A lone basketball goal with no net stood near the center. The other students still didn't talk to me as we trudged up the hill toward the big double doors.

Most boys wore bib overalls, blue chambray shirts, and brogans. The girls' cotton dresses hugged their knees, and half of them had pigtails hanging over their shoulders.

Inside, we found two big classrooms, each with a large book storage closet. The smell of chalk dust and pencil shavings felt familiar. Jason appeared to be lost, so I took him to his room. His teacher, Mrs. Spencer, taught the first three grades. She quickly identified him as a newcomer and assigned him a seat.

Mr. Barnes taught the older kids. He stood a solid six-feet tall, wearing a necktie and striped shirt. His gruff voice and stern manner matched his height.

At the first recess, he asked me to stay inside for a moment. "Welcome to Alamo School. I need to explain a few of our rules."

I stood up straight. "Yes, sir."

He crossed his arms. "We don't have a janitor, so the older boys all help with chores to keep the school clean and warm."

"Yes, sir."

He nailed me with a hard stare and pointed to the corner of the room. "That stack of switches is for students who violate rules. I don't tolerate disruptive behavior or failure to turn in your assignments. Homework is due daily. Excuses are not acceptable."

A quick glance at his collection of switches convinced me he wasn't someone I should mess with. "Yes, sir."

Mr. Barnes leaned back in his chair and eased the tension with a friendly smile. "You'll take your turn sweeping the floor, filling the water jug, and carrying firewood. I expect you to apply yourself to your studies and stay out of trouble. We take pride in our students here and expect them to learn."

That sounded reasonable to me.

Tales of a Misspent Youth

When the lecture ended, I breathed a sigh of relief and escaped to the playground. A crowd of boys promptly encircled me, looking at me like I was a chicken they intended to kill and eat for Sunday dinner.

"Where you from?" a skinny tow-headed youngster demanded.

"Quapaw Valley, over on the Ouachita River. Lived in Kansas for a spell."

"Never heard of no Quapaw Valley. Must not be important."

A stocky kid spoke up. "Only a sissy would wear a stupid-lookin' shirt like that."

My face grew warm, but I didn't answer.

A younger boy cast a sideways glance my direction. "Bet you lived in the city."

I shuffled my feet in the dirt. "They had a big school in Kansas, but it was a small town."

"Want a home-grown plug to chew?" A chunky boy with patched overalls offered a brown wad of smelly tobacco. "I got loose stuff if you'd rather roll your own."

My stomach felt queasy from looking at his nasty offering. "No, thanks. I don't smoke."

"Must really be a sissy," the boy said. "Too good to chew home-grown."

I felt like a mouse being batted around a circle of cats. The situation didn't look like it would come to a good end. It didn't appear to be shaping up the way I'd wanted to get acquainted with my classmates.

A fat boy in bad need of a haircut pushed forward to get in my face. "Why'd your pa run off and leave your ma?"

I choked and felt my face flush, refusing to attempt an answer. It was obvious the boys wanted to provoke a fight, but trouble with Mr. Barnes on my first day of school didn't sound like a good idea.

The bell to end recess saved me.

During class, the boys pelted me with spitballs each time Mr. Barnes turned to the blackboard. Knowing I'd get in trouble if I retaliated, I tried to ignore them. When a classmate tripped me on my way to the recitation bench, I turned to glare at him. Then a sixth grader banged a thick geography book against the side of my head as he lumbered past my desk.

It took a while for the message to sink in, but I finally broke the code. Looked like there was no way I'd be able to avoid a fight. These boys were bent on learning how tough the new kid would be. I'd be a target until they found out.

During my fights with Papa and the beatings I'd endured, he usually hit me with his heavy belt or a leather plow line. After he ripped apart a book he caught me reading before I'd finished my chores, I'd rebelled and fought him with my fists. When I accused him of being mean to Mama, he beat me with one of his brogans.

For the last year, I'd fought back each time Papa whipped me. I tried to hurt him, but he just held me and hit. Refusing to cry was the only victory I earned.

I'd met the Baker boys' uncle about a month before we moved to Kansas. He was a club fighter, boxing in Hot Springs and Little Rock for money. He taught me how to fight. I learned to move and hit hard, putting my weight behind each blow.

Tales of a Misspent Youth

"A punch starts from your toes," he'd told me. "Your body uncoils, and you lean in to your opponent to deliver it. Don't waste time with pitty-pat licks. Convince the other guy he needs to quit. Do it fast."

Nobody at Alamo School could be tough as Papa, and I'd be sure to get in a few good licks if these kids forced me to fight.

During lunch break, the boys resumed their torment. They found new ways to ridicule me, and it didn't seem likely to stop. Resigned to my fate, I swallowed my fear and picked out the biggest kid in the pack. His name was Roland, and he hadn't really joined in the harassment. No matter if he was innocent, he stood a head taller than anyone else in the bunch. My stomach felt queasy.

I wandered over in front of Roland, looking him up and down, flashing a disarming smile. Then I hit him on the ear with a left hook and hammered a hard right hand to his belly. He expelled air with a whoosh, bellowed in surprise, and came after me. I dodged his charge and tagged his other ear with a straight left jab as he stormed past me. The boys yelled encouragement to Roland.

We stood toe-to-toe, trading punches until his big fist flattened me. Sharp pebbles bit into my back as I skidded across the schoolyard. One hundred-forty pounds of angry teenager landed on my middle and began to pummel me. His hot breath flowed over my face, and I smelled his rank sweat. Doing my best to squirm from beneath him, I tried but failed to slow the bigger boy by returning his punches. Unfortunately, my blows lacked power while I lay flat on my back.

Dust plugged my nose, and the copper taste of blood filled my mouth. Repeated punches to the head blurred my vision. I collected bruises, and my ribs hurt where he pounded me. A few of the boys began to cheer me on after they saw I wouldn't quit. Roland was beginning to mess up my face when the other boys pulled him off.

The fight was over. I stood with arms at my side, taking deep breaths, battered but still in one piece. Some of the gang gathered around me, helping me brush dirt off my clothes.

"Shake hands," someone yelled.

Both of us glared at each other for a moment. And then Roland stuck out his hand.

I looked him in the eye when we shook.

After the bell rang and we returned to the classroom, Mr. Barnes paused at my desk to look at my torn shirt and bruised face. Then he shook his head and called the fourth graders to the recitation bench for their history lesson.

During our afternoon recess, Roland approached me with a worn baseball. "Want to play catch?"

My face hurt when I attempted a smile. "Sure."

He slapped me on the back and grinned. "You don't fight bad for a little shit."

A Doubtful Christmas was first published in Thin Threads, Life Changing Moments Anthology, 2009.

A Doubtful Christmas

After Papa deserted our family, Mama scrambled to make a new life for us. My grandparents were not wealthy, but they provided us a home. We hustled to gather and preserve food to see all of us through the winter. Grandpa butchered an extra hog, and we planted a field of turnips. Not the greatest taste, but they fill your belly.

Papa had been abusive, but he'd always provided for us. Now, my brothers and I worried where food and clothing would come from. My mother stayed positive, assuring us she would keep the family together and safe from harm.

Relatives donated hand-me-downs, and the farm fed us. I milked cows before catching the school bus and did chores after I got home each day. The younger boys washed dishes, fed the chickens and pigs, and kept the woodbin filled. Six-year-old Jason and I manned a crosscut saw to cut firewood for heating the house during cold weather.

Our efforts paled in comparison to Mama's. At one hundred-five pounds, she swung an axe, wrestled heavy horse-drawn plows, hauled hay to feed Grandpa's open-range cattle during the winter, and harvested our food crops. Still, she found time to help us with homework, sing with us, and to say prayers with the younger boys. Her example taught us to work, be self-reliant, respect our neighbors and our church, and to appreciate music.

As Christmas approached, Mama's smiles became less frequent. Her face looked drawn when she gave me a hint of the problem she faced. "Santa might have trouble finding us this year."

I considered myself practically grown, so I hid my disappointment. An overheard conversation between Mama and Grandma increased my concern.

"I don't have money to buy Christmas presents for the kids," Mama said.

"You need to have something under the tree," Grandma replied. "Maybe you could wrap some of the hand-me-downs."

"The kids would be terribly disappointed to get old clothes. I have to do better than that. Maybe I can make toys for them."

Homemade toys didn't excite me, but I realized she couldn't afford to buy anything. Making the younger kids understand our situation might be more difficult.

One Sunday afternoon, my mother took a saw into the forest and returned with an armload of tree limbs. She left them in the harness room in the barn and refused to tell her curious children what they were for.

She worked on her project while I was in school, but I peeked when I had a chance. Pieces of wood had been cut into different shapes, then planed and sanded smooth. Later, I found a stack of discs cut from a round oak limb.

She'd also started to carve a long piece of hickory, but I couldn't figure out what it was for.

She hid everything and frustrated my attempts to snoop, but I could see that she used nails, glue, and paint from Grandpa's workshop. She had to be making gifts for us.

By Christmas week, Mama was her normal, happy self again. Her project was apparently complete, and she succeeded in keeping it secret. I looked everywhere without finding the results of what she'd done.

When school let out for the holiday, my brothers and I cut a Christmas tree in the forest and dragged it home through early snow. The tang of fresh-cut cedar made us more eager for the holiday to arrive. The whole family helped decorate the tree with ornaments, pinecones, and strings of popcorn. We gathered mistletoe and holly boughs to hang throughout the house.

While Mama and Grandma prepared food for the holiday dinner, I helped Grandpa with chores. The younger kids kept a diligent watch on the sweet-smelling peach, apple, and blackberry pies lined up on the cupboard shelves.

On Christmas Eve, we sang carols, and Grandpa read aloud from his bible. After Mama shooed us off to bed, I lay awake a long time, anticipating Christmas morning. Aunts, uncles, and cousins would come for a big dinner, and I was curious about my mother's project. I doubted that it would be anything elaborate, and homemade toys still didn't sound exciting. Nevertheless, I appreciated that she'd made a huge effort to have presents under the tree for us to open.

I was already awake when she tapped on our door. "Merry Christmas, boys."

We hurried into the living room to see that a stack of packages had magically appeared overnight under the tree. Before we were allowed to investigate what Santa had brought, Mama herded us into the kitchen for breakfast over the protests of my younger brothers. The boys dragged their feet, wanting to open their presents.

Later, we gathered around the tree, and she gave us each our gifts. My brothers opened newspaper-wrapped packages stuffed with brightly colored trucks, tractors, and trains. Those odd pieces of wood she'd made in secret were assembled and painted to form toys. The round discs made wheels that rolled, and the trucks and trains carried tiny logs and blocks. A tractor pulled a miniature wagon. The toys were beautifully made, and my younger brothers cried out with joy as they rolled the miniature vehicles across the wood floor.

I tore off the paper wrapping my present, and a smile lit my face to find the hand-carved bow and quiver of blunt arrows with straight shafts. I knew how to make them suitable for hunting rabbits by forging steel arrowheads in Grandpa's shop.

**

Looking back, Mama's determination and perseverance transformed our bleak prospects into a memorable Christmas filled with delight. The craftsmanship in those toys predicted her later accomplishments as an artist and sculptor.

Difficult years would follow, but I never again doubted my mother's ability to provide for us. That Christmas would have been a terrible disappointment without her skill and dedication. During the years that followed, we were never hungry. She kept us in school and monitored our progress to ensure we succeeded. By following her example, we learned to have faith in God and faith in the abilities He gave us.

That faith sustains me still.

Our Day in Court

We didn't hear anything about Papa for more than a year after he abandoned us, and Mama received no assistance from him. She eventually learned where he lived and sued for child support. The court set a hearing date and issued a subpoena for Papa's appearance.

When the case came up for trial, Uncle Bob drove us to town in his school bus. Mama brought all five of us kids to attend. We'd have our day in court, hoping to force Papa to support his family. We sat waiting in the courtroom for the entire morning while the judge disposed of other cases. The room filled with spectators and soon became stuffy. Odors of stale tobacco smoke, perfume, dust, and sweat filled the crowded room, competing with the rising temperature to make me uncomfortable.

Lawyers in dark suits shuffled papers and questioned witnesses while the judge presided behind his raised desk. My younger brothers fidgeted and squirmed on the hard benches as several other cases droned on at a snail's pace.

At midday, the judge announced a recess. "Court will now adjourn and resume at one-thirty this afternoon."

Lawyers shoved papers into their briefcases and disappeared. The crowd milled around a few minutes and scattered to find lunch. With no money to buy food, Mama led the six of us to a shady spot on the low rock wall surrounding the square. Noise from passing cars provided an occasional distraction. The smell of frying hamburgers drifted across the street from the restaurant. With growling stomachs, we settled in to wait for court to resume.

"Our case should be up next, so we won't have much longer to wait," Mama told us. "I'll fix a big supper when we get home."

Restless from the long morning spent sitting on a wooden bench, I wandered away to explore the grounds. The courthouse stood at the center of a large square. Its stone walls rose two stories high, looking massive and somber in the sunlight. Surrounding trees and shrubs softened the hard walls. Sidewalks led off in three directions from the steps fronting the broad double doors of the main entrance. A small jail with one barred cell hid in a corner behind the big structure.

Suddenly, a large figure loomed over me. The man wore a suit coat with matching trousers and a white shirt and necktie. A narrow-brimmed city hat shaded my father's face. His eyes didn't reveal any expression as he blocked my path.

He reached out with a callused hand, holding a folded bill. "Your mother and brothers are probably hungry. Here's five dollars. Take them to the restaurant across the street to get something to eat."

My body tensed as a cloud of emotion threatened to crush me. He didn't look threatening, but it felt as if a stranger had detained me. Temporarily mute, I looked up at my father's blank face and at the hand that had so frequently delivered punishment. It now offered money for a meal. Hunger made the offer tempting, but I couldn't force myself to reach for the gift he presented.

With a choked voice, I gave him my response. "I don't want anything you offer to give me. I'll take it when the judge forces you to pay."

I turned my back and walked away as he stood silent. When I rejoined the family, I decided not to tell them what happened. After the court reconvened, Papa pleaded guilty. The judge lectured him about his duty as a parent and ordered him to make monthly child support payments. Papa agreed, and the case was closed.

My heart leaped to know we wouldn't have to depend on Grandpa for what we needed to keep us alive. Mama's tiny salary as lunchroom cook at my school had stopped during summer, and we had no income. Her expression was calm, her face revealing no emotion, as we left the building. None of us looked back.

No child support payments ever arrived. We learned later that Papa left the state and neglected to leave a forwarding address.

I never saw him again.

A Lesson Learned

Mazarn Creek cut through the valley near my grandparents' farm. Although filled with rocky shoals and swift currents, it harbored numerous deep pools that made great places to swim. When we found an hour to spare, we'd visit one of them. I'd stay close to shore, dog paddling and struggling to stay afloat. I'd keep my head above water for a few seconds but invariably sank. It shamed me when several of the big kids made fun of my efforts. They all seemed to handle the water like they were half fish.

Our favorite spot was the Bluff Hole. Formed by a sharp bend of the swift mountain stream against the face of a thirty-foot cliff, it offered a deep pool of cool water. Older boys liked to jump from the top of the cliff. An underwater rock shelf protruded about six feet from the bluff. Divers had to jump far enough to clear the submerged rock.

A gravel beach occupied the other side of the stream, and I stayed close to the non-swimmers playing in the water near shore.

Several families visited the shaded pool regularly, especially for a quick bath after a hard day's work in the fields. While adults washed off the dirt from their labor and caught up on the latest gossip, kids enjoyed splashing in the clear water.

One bright Sunday afternoon in September, my uncle Ben joined us. He had joined the Air Corps and was on leave to visit my grandparents. He was a second lieutenant who had just completed flight school. Grandpa said he hadn't grown up yet.

He watched me struggle in the shallows for a while before commenting. "You're old enough to swim. Let me show you how."

Help sounded like what I needed. "Thanks. I'd like to learn."

He towed me across the deep water and stood me on the submerged shelf. "You can't learn much in shallow water. When you can't touch bottom, you'll be forced to sink or swim."

With that, he grabbed the seat of my cut-off jeans and launched me with a quick thrust. Surprised, I cannonballed into the deep water.

After coming up coughing and spitting, my arms flew. My cupped hands grabbed the water, clawing to stay on top. After a brief moment of hope, I sank again. My head surfaced for a few quick breaths, but I wasn't swimming. Uncle Ben had to haul me out and pound my back to get rid of the water I'd swallowed. After that, I stayed away from the creek until Ben's leave was over.

The school term and then a hard winter interrupted our swimming season, but the cold weather finally ended. Spring had arrived by the end of March. New leaves appeared on the trees, and the days warmed. Prolonged rain flooded the creek, and its banks overflowed. At the first sign of good weather, kids at school started looking for excuses to be outdoors.

A classmate, Billy Thompson, and I decided to slip off to go swimming. He was a better swimmer, but I couldn't admit it. His father had died the year before, and we cooked up a story that his mother hurt her back and needed someone to give her a hand with chores. They lived across the creek a half mile from school.

"You need to learn how to swim," Billy told me.

During our first recess, I approached my teacher, Mr. Barnes. "Sir, Mrs. Thompson hurt her back real bad, and she needs someone to help her with chores. They're almost out of wood for the cook stove."

He wrinkled his brow before speaking. "Who do you think should help her?"

"If Billy and I could get out of school this afternoon, we could cut wood."

Mr. Barnes hesitated, biting his lip like he was thinking about it. "You're both caught up on your schoolwork. I suppose I could let you off. Be careful, and be back in time to catch the school bus home."

I grinned. "Thank you, sir. We'll work real hard."

After lunch, the pair of us raced across the one-lane bridge to Billy's house to grab his axe and saw from the woodshed.

Billy took charge. "I'll saw the blocks. You can split them with the axe."

We'd barely started when Mrs. Thompson came out to the porch. "Why aren't you boys in school?"

Billy was quick to answer. "Mr. Barnes let us out to cut firewood for a half hour."

After we'd finished several armloads, Billy figured we'd done enough to cover our promise. We put away the tools and raced to the creek.

The stream was not normally deep enough for swimming this close to its source, but spring rains added a torrent of surging brown floodwater. In the big pool below the bridge, it was over our heads and muddy, filled with debris washed down by the flood. When I stuck a toe in the swift current, I discovered it was also cold. Not deterred by this minor obstacle, we scouted the area to find only about three feet of rushing water covered the rocky shoals below. This would be our safety net. In the event we were unable to swim across the flooded creek, the current would wash us downstream. We'd be able to regain our footing in the rapids and walk out for another try.

Satisfied with our plan, we ran back to the bank overlooking the wide pool upstream to shuck our clothes.

"Last one in is a teacher's pet," Billy shouted.

I undressed as quickly as possible, but Billy dived into the muddy torrent a half second before me. Competition to swim across the flooded stream erased all thoughts of drowning. Neither of us was a good swimmer, but Billy pulled ahead. The swift current took us, and we both failed to make it to the far bank.

The rolling current pummeled me, and icy water stung my naked skin as I struggled to keep my head above the surface. I tried without much success to advance toward shore. After taking in a few gulps of water, I coughed most of it up but managed to avoid panic until I washed up on the shoals. Collecting only a few bruises from the rocks, I clambered out of the foaming brown soup to escape.

Billy was right behind me.

Realizing I was in the lead as we started back, I sprinted upstream and shouted, "Last one in's a monkey's uncle."

Tales of a Misspent Youth

This time, I beat him into the water but failed again to swim all the way across. Billy pulled himself up on the far bank to watch me scramble to regain my footing on the slippery rocks below. After reaching shore, I started upstream for another try.

"Teacher's pet has to walk back," he taunted before diving in to swim to my side of the stream.

After several more attempts, I made it all the way across. Proud of myself, I repeated this feat several times. An hour passed, and both of us stood on the bank panting and shivering, happy to have mastered the challenge.

Sitting on a fallen tree trunk, we rested for a few minutes, and then we shook ourselves dry. The smell of clover and pollen from the oak trees set me to sneezing as we donned our clothing.

"We should get back to school," I said.

"Not until our hair's dry. We'd be in big trouble."

We tarried by the creek, throwing rocks into the torrent for a few minutes, and returned to school in time for me to catch the bus home.

A few days later, Mr. Barnes called Billy and me to the front of the classroom. "I asked Mrs. Thompson about her bad back yesterday, and she told me she didn't have one. Do you boys have an explanation for me?"

I sensed bad trouble. "No, sir."

Billy shuffled his feet. "We cut some firewood."

The entire group of students was given the opportunity to watch us get better acquainted with the stack of switches Mr. Barnes kept in the corner of the classroom. The red lines that marked where the switches landed didn't fade quickly. However, the experience did serve as a good opportunity to learn about consequences.

I no longer needed Uncle Ben's lessons, but the next time I tried a stunt like this, I'd look for a better cover story.

Wasps and Snakes and Such

Kids growing up in our mountainous backcountry missed out on entertainment available to city dwellers. We didn't have movies and ice cream parlors. No electricity meant no handy refrigerator. A bucket suspended in the hand-dug well kept our food cool. Buying ice for an icebox would have been nice, but it required a twenty-five mile trip to town. Unlikely for my family, since we didn't own a car.

Time spent listening to our battery-powered radio was rationed. Grandpa rubbed his chin with a callused palm. "Listening to the daily news with Gabriel Heater is necessary to stay up with world events, and we need to hear weather forecasts. Kids' programs are a waste of time. After you've finished your chores, you can do homework."

I protested. "But, you listen to *The Grand Ole Opry* on Saturday night. I want to listen to *The Lone Ranger*."

"The whole family can enjoy good music. Listening to *The Lone Ranger* drains the battery. A new one costs money we don't have."

Ah, but country kids learn to be creative in amusing themselves. I could think of lots of other ways to have fun.

I spent hours pretending to be Lou Boudreau, shortstop and playing manager for the Cleveland Indians. I'd toss pebbles in the air and hit them with my hand-carved baseball bat. Standing in the road where gravel was plentiful, my imagination would create a huge stadium that existed in my mind. Depending on where the pebbles landed, I counted singles, doubles, triples, and home runs to calculate the winning score. I even hit a few fly balls for outs just to keep the game fair.

When I got bored hitting home runs, I'd become Cleveland's best pitcher, Bob Feller. Dizzy Dean was the greatest when he played for the St. Louis Cardinals. He came from my neck of the woods, but he got too old and retired when I was a little kid. Feller was next best. A convenient tree became the strike zone, and my goal was to strike out the lineup for the New York Yankees.

Their shortstop, Phil Rizzuto, was a genius at getting on base. You had to throw strikes on the corners to get him out. Just looking at their stumpy catcher, Yogi Berra, struck fear in a pitcher's heart. Joe Gordon was a tough out with men on base. He was smart, and he hit with power. But their best hitter was Joe DiMaggio, the center fielder. He did everything well, and a pitcher couldn't intimidate him by throwing inside. I'd stand on the mound and imagine each hitter in turn. Round pebbles worked well for throwing fastballs. Flat slate rocks produced a devastating curveball. I had to throw sidearm to produce a satisfactory sinker. An occasional spitball kept hitters off balance, but my control wasn't very good with a slick rock. Lefties would be surprised by an occasional screwball.

During the season, I'd strike out the entire New York Yankees lineup several hundred times.

My cousins visited from time to time, and we all swam in the creek. Riding my horse or playing with the dog was always a good pastime. When I wanted to do something really daring, I'd fight wasps for fun—big, ugly swarms of angry red wasps.

After whittling a paddle from a piece of flat wood, I'd locate a nest of the bad-tempered critters. Feeling timid led me to choose a small nest. When I felt bulletproof, I'd select a large one. I'd find a suitable rock and choose an emergency escape route before disturbing the unsuspecting insects.

The game had strict rules. If I ran, I'd been shamed and lost the battle.

When the rock hit a nest, the wasps sprang up, looking for their tormenter. After spotting me, they swarmed at full speed to drive me away and save their home. Since their stingers hurt like the Devil's pitchfork, intelligent creatures don't hesitate to run from wasps. Standing firm was a test of bravery.

The enraged wasps arrived on target with stingers poised for revenge. It took sharp eyes to spot each of the speeding warriors as they dived to stab me with their venomous tails. I'd use the paddle like someone playing Ping-Pong, swatting each angry attacker as he arrived. They made a satisfactory splat when hit. My backhand improved quickly.

The fight was a challenge since these critters were quick, numerous, and motivated. If I missed one, he'd nail me. I never quit after a single sting, but if several of the nasty little dive bombers got past my defenses, I'd be forced to turn tail and escape.

I hated to leave the field of battle like that, since wasps flew faster than I could run. I'd usually collect a couple more stings before they quit the chase and returned to stand guard over their nest.

This game definitely proved that boys are superior to girls. I never saw a single girl who would stand and fight a swarm of wasps. Most of them wouldn't even come close to the nest. If they saw one of the round, cardboard-like hives, they would scamper away before a single warrior rose to investigate them.

One Sunday afternoon in July, three of my male cousins showed up, and a real brainstorm struck me. "I know where there's the biggest wasp nest you ever seen. Big as a dinner plate. Want to look?"

Without hesitation, the oldest replied. "Nests don't get that big. You got to be lying to us."

"I'll show you." I trotted off toward the barn.

The boys followed, intent on exposing my exaggeration.

At the barn, I led the way as we climbed the ladder to the hayloft.

After we reached the platform covering the harness room, I pointed out the nest. It was attached to a rafter and tucked into a dark corner. Hordes of big, mean wasps that didn't like to be disturbed covered the gray honeycomb structure.

My cousin leaned forward to get a better look. "Ain't quite as big as a dinner plate, but it sure is a big hummer."

The boys edged closer to examine the huge nest while I moved back a couple of steps. They didn't have any warning when I threw the dirt clod. It smacked the nest in the middle of its teeming mass of guardians.

Not waiting to watch what happened, I bypassed the ladder to leap from the platform. When I hit the ground, I rolled against the front wall of the barn. Knowing that wasps are attracted to movement, I froze in place.

In the loft, shouts of surprise and pain rang out. Three boys flew off the platform at full speed, scrambled through the gate, and raced down the dirt road with a horde of vengeful red warriors in pursuit. After about a hundred yards, the wasps relented and returned. The boys collected a few stings. I didn't move a muscle until the returning wasps passed over me to settle on their nest.

Feeling smug, I pointed out the wasps hadn't stung me even once.

My cousins didn't think it was quite so funny. I collected several bruises while the three of them expressed their point of view by pounding on me.

**

After the school year started, homework and chores consumed most of my free time. This routine robbed me of opportunities to amuse myself. Chores kept me busy before and after school, and I helped harvest our crops, but I chafed at being cooped up in a classroom all day.

A love/hate relationship with snakes had fascinated me for a long time. Poisonous ones like copperheads, rattlesnakes, and cottonmouth moccasins roamed the woods and hid out in our barn to help the cats catch mice. They frightened me, and I killed them on sight. My dog, Pudgy, agreed. He'd been bitten once, and it must have affected his brain. Hunting snakes became his favorite sport. He'd leave the dead critters on our front steps as gifts. I had to haul off dozens of the chewed-up reptiles every summer.

I tolerated other snakes and actually enjoyed catching little green garter snakes and playing with them. If I handled them gently, they didn't act scared.

One day, during lunch break at school, I caught a foot-long green snake and amused myself with it until the bell rang to resume class. Not wanting to give up my playmate so soon, I tucked him into my shirt where he was free to crawl around my waist. He circled my middle and explored the limited space for the next hour. Dry scales tickled my skin as he slithered through each circuit.

When the bell announced afternoon recess, I stayed at my desk to eat a peanut butter sandwich left over from lunch. Everyone else headed for the fresh air to enjoy a few minutes of freedom. I took out the cute little snake and held it close to my face.

"What am I going to do with you, little guy?"

He didn't bother to answer but squirmed and wiggled like he wanted to escape. I knew I couldn't keep him but hesitated to let him go. The friendly little creature made a great distraction from all that boring schoolwork.

A stray thought blossomed into an inspiration. What would happen if our new teacher, Mrs. Tucker, found the snake in her desk? An evil grin covered my face as I slipped to the front of the room to deposit the little critter in her middle drawer. Then I made a quick exit. Making sure the teacher saw me playing outside might keep her from guessing who put the snake there.

When class resumed, Mrs. Tucker called the fourth grade to the recitation bench to quiz them on math. I barely contained a snicker as I anticipated her eventual discovery of the desk's new occupant.

Tales of a Misspent Youth

The math lesson droned on and on while I waited for something to happen.

Finally, Mrs. Tucker opened the drawer and reached inside. A startled look covered her face. She took a quick step back.

"Oh."

Not understanding what the problem was, the students sat in silence, wondering what had startled the teacher.

Mrs. Tucker pursed her lips and glanced over the classroom.

I looked down, pretending to study my geography book, struggling to keep a straight face.

Reaching into the drawer, she pulled out the wiggling little green serpent. "Who put this in my desk drawer?"

Silence.

She stood there mute, not a tremble, not even a hint of fear. Her eyes swept the room, searching for a culprit.

She should have at least screamed. How was I to know she'd grown up in these mountains and knew more about snakes than I did? I examined the map of Europe like I might find gold there.

She walked to the door and placed the friendly little varmint in the tall grass. "Scat, little fellow."

Then she picked up a long switch from the corner of the classroom and looked at all the boys, tapping her open palm with the dreaded stick. "When I find the prankster, he'll get the spanking he deserves."

With that, she continued with the fourth grade math lesson.

My head stayed down, studying hard. Good thing she hadn't caught me. I'd seen her use those switches on a couple of the older boys. I didn't want to join that crew.

Thinking about how she'd handled the snake, I was forced to change an opinion I'd held for a long time.

Evidently, not all girls are scaredy-cats.

"It's a Cruel World" was previously published in Storyteller Magazine, *March 2010*.

It's a Cruel World

World War II had ended, but life in our backwoods community was still hard. My seven-year-old brother, Jason, and I climbed the pole gate and trudged across the pasture to pick blackberries, carrying several tin buckets to hold the fruit. At eleven years old, I figured being grown up was just around the corner.

As we meandered across the wide field of grass, I glanced at the herd of horses grazing peacefully in the shade near the tree line. While their teeth tore at the grass, bushy tails swished across their backs to drive away swarms of flies. Away from the herd, I spotted a large animal on the ground beside an isolated clump of bushes.

"What's she doing, Jason?" I squinted to make it out.

Jason looked up. "One of the horses is sleeping."

When we drew closer, it didn't look like the animal was asleep. Long legs stuck out straight, and the neck stretched at an odd angle. The chestnut brown mare lay about six feet from a tangle of bushes in the open pasture. Our new mule colt cavorted nearby, stamping its feet and tossing its head. The little fellow usually stayed close to his mother.

Flies buzzed around the mare's carcass when we arrived. Tears made the scene before me blur. "It's Lady. She's dead."

Jason ducked his head. "Why?"

I wondered how we'd take care of the colt. He was still nursing, and we didn't have another mare that could adopt him.

Swollen and discolored wounds marred Lady's head about four inches below her eyes, the obvious reason for her death. More than two inches separated double punctures on her long nose. The smell of death added fear to the oppressive heat in the open pasture. The mare must've been grazing near the isolated clump of bushes when a hidden snake struck her.

My stomach felt queasy as I turned to Jason. "Snake bite."

Jason's head swiveled to look in all directions. "Hope he's gone now."

Suddenly frightened, I jumped away and peeped into the tangle of weeds, briars, and shrubs. Then I grabbed a long stick and parted the leaves to search for the snake. Relieved not to find it, I examined the dead horse.

"Must have been a big old diamondback rattler." I wiped my eyes with a shirtsleeve. "I've never seen a snake with fangs that far apart. Had to be at least seven or eight feet long. She didn't take more than two steps before she fell."

Tears appeared in Jason's eyes. His voice trembled. "Poor little mule lost his mother."

Approaching the nervous colt with caution, I held out my hand and spoke softly. "Easy, boy. We'll help you."

He shied away at my approach and stared at me with big, round eyes. Each time I got close, he bolted. Once, he circled me to trot back and sniff at his dead mother, and then he galloped away again.

"He's too scared to let us catch him," I said. "We'd better go tell Grandpa."

We dropped our buckets in the field and ran home, sweating and out of breath. Grandpa was working in the harness room of our barn, using a large needle and thread to repair a torn bridle.

"A big snake killed Lady," I said. "We couldn't catch the colt.'

Grandpa looked up with a deep sigh. "She was our best brood mare. Leave her there, and I'll take care of it." He lifted his hat to wipe his forehead with a work-roughened hand. "You boys are late with your berry picking. Your mother is waiting for them. I know you like blackberry cobbler."

We hurried back to retrieve our buckets and picked the ripe fruit for the rest of the morning. Sunshine burned down on us. Briars and flies competed with ticks and chiggers to torment us. We tried to avoid the poison oak, but that was probably a lost cause. Sweat stung the minor scratches we accumulated. Worried about snakes, we banged on our buckets as we trampled narrow paths through the prickly vines to reach the ripe berries. I imagined each noise in the underbrush was a huge snake ready to trap me in the thicket of thorn-covered vines.

The sun climbed to the top of its arc, and we had filled five of the one-gallon pails with berries. We'd also eaten another quart, maybe two.

"We've got enough," I said. "It's time for dinner."

Jason's eyes were downcast, and his lips pursed. "Hope the little mule is okay."

When we passed the ominous clump of bushes with fearful steps, Lady's carcass was gone, along with her frightened little colt. I figured Grandpa had dragged the mare off in the woods for varmints to dispose of.

After we delivered the berries, the whole family gathered around the dinner table for our noon meal. When Grandpa finished saying grace, I asked him about the colt. "Did you catch him?"

He looked up from a plate of eggs scrambled in poke salad. "I herded him back to the barn and coaxed him into the front stall. He's scared. Fix him a bottle of cow's milk. Probably won't take it, but we need to try."

After we'd eaten, I filled a bottle and put a nipple on it. Jason followed me to the barn. The agitated colt paced in the stall, circling the enclosure, desperate to escape. When we entered, he pressed against the far wall, staring at us like we planned to eat him. The smell of his fear hung over the enclosure. Poor baby must have thought the world abandoned him. He'd have to trust me to take milk from my hand.

When I offered the bottle, he shied away. His hind legs flew backward as his tiny hooves battered the plank wall. I tried to persuade him we only wanted to help. No luck. Jason stayed close behind me, watching in silence.

After retrieving a length of rope from the hall, I knotted it into a lariat. Back in the stall, I waited for the little guy to stand still and tossed the loop over his head. He panicked, bucking and flinging his hooves at everything within reach. Pulling him toward me, I knotted a makeshift halter and held his head close to avoid his frantic kicks.

After waiting a moment, I tried again to calm the frightened animal, reaching out to caress his neck and shoulder. "We won't hurt you. You're hungry. Taste the milk, little buddy. It'll be good for you."

He reared up on his hind legs and tried to jerk the rope from my grip. I held tight and waited for him to calm down.

Finally, he stopped struggling and stood before me trembling. I offered the bottle again. Once more, he jerked his head away. Holding the halter close, I touched his mouth with the nipple. With a wild lunge, he tried to escape from the rope that restrained him. Nothing I tried appeared to work. The terrified colt simply didn't trust me.

The little guy couldn't survive without milk. I had to succeed, but when I tried again to touch the nipple to his muzzle, he broke into a fit of lunging and kicking. Frustrated, I backed away, pleading with the colt, convinced he'd injure himself before he'd allow me to touch him.

"Let me hold him," Jason said. "You can feed him the milk. Maybe he'll take it if you're not pulling on his halter."

It was a risk, but I let Jason take the rope. "Hold tight. We don't want him to get loose in here. Those little hooves could hurt you."

Jason glared at me like I'd insulted him. "I won't let go."

Softening my voice, I tried to find words to calm the little animal. Then I lifted the bottle slowly, tempting him to nurse. Instead, he lunged violently away and ripped the halter rope from Jason's grip.

Free of restraint, the colt wheeled and aimed a volley of kicks toward us. We split in opposite directions as flying hooves flashed overhead. Scrambling to avoid the lethal kicks, we found no place to hide in the enclosed space. The plank walls rang with repeated impacts from the panicked little animal's assault as we ducked and dodged to avoid his hooves.

Finally, I snatched the loose end of the rope and pulled him close. Jason dived behind me, sticking tighter than my shadow. Panting, neither of us found strength to talk for a moment. The colt eventually quit his protest and stood, head drooping, staring with frightened eyes. His look of despair tore at my heart.

I tied him to a post when we left his stall. The little mule stood head down, trembling. He didn't appear to notice as we slipped away. Outside, we looked back at the gloomy enclosure and breathed sighs of relief for escaping those sharp hooves.

Grandpa charged through the garden gate to investigate the noise and glanced at our ashen faces. "Looks like he won't take the bottle. I'll have to call the livestock dealer to come and get him."

Jason stuffed his hands in his pockets and shuffled his feet on the rocky ground. "Does the dealer know how to feed him?"

Grandpa looked away. "He'll take the colt to someone who knows what to do."

Jason's face relaxed in a smile.

I stumbled away without speaking, unwilling to hear more. My stomach turned over, knowing what happened to farm animals that were too old or too helpless to be useful. Tears formed in my eyes, and repeated blinking failed to drive them away.

The next morning, the khaki-clad livestock dealer parked his truck by the barn and talked to Grandpa. He pushed back his hat as he peered inside the stall. After a moment, he loaded the defiant colt into his battered old truck and snubbed him tight against the sideboards. After jumping down from the vehicle, he pulled his wallet from a back pocket and handed Grandpa a few dollars. Then he stepped on the running board and climbed into the cab. The engine roared to life.

The baby mule tried to jerk loose from his halter when the vehicle moved forward. Tiny hooves pounded the staked sides of the truck bed as it passed the mailbox where I waited and watched. His big round eyes speared me with a terrified look. Guilt crushed me as the vehicle gained speed.

Maybe I'd failed to try hard enough. There should have been some way to save him. My heart ached for the helpless little mule as the truck rounded the curve and vanished down the dusty road.

Even though I was nearly a man, I cried.

"The String Ball" was originally published in Sweetgum Notes, spring 2006.

The String Ball

Starting sixth grade meant I'd become one of the big kids at our country school. Never mind that I stood less than five feet tall and weighed about eighty pounds. The bus picked me up early, wound its way along a gravel road for six miles, and deposited me at Alamo School. From there, it continued nineteen miles through the mountains, hauling older kids to the consolidated high school.

In the fall of 1945, the school could barely afford to buy books. Playground equipment was nonexistent. Someone brought a baseball, and we used it until the cover came off and the strings finally unraveled. With no ball, the boys played war, throwing acorns at each other, and we did some bare-knuckle—no hitting in the face—boxing for amusement. I collected a few bruises and earned a reputation for being a tough fighter for my small size.

If we'd had another baseball, we would have chosen up sides for a game.

While helping my grandfather with chores around the barn, I'd noticed he saved the twine when he opened sacks of feed for his livestock. He always wound it around a stick and squirreled it away in odd corners of the musty old building.

Tales of a Misspent Youth

"Why do you save twine, Grandpa?" I asked.

"You never know when you might need a piece of string," he said. "It costs money. Saving it from feed sacks is free."

Nursing the germ of a new idea, I checked out his hiding places and estimated how much string he'd collected. After I liberated a small, hard rubber ball from a set of jacks that belonged to a cousin, I started the project.

On Sunday, after collecting the stash of twine, I borrowed a needle and thread from the sewing box in Mama's bedroom and slipped out to a quiet hideout under the big oak tree by the woodpile. The smell of fresh wood chips was comforting. A light breeze and the shade kept me cool as I worked.

I wrapped the string tight around the rubber ball, sewing it frequently to prevent it from unraveling. As it grew, I stayed out of sight so Grandpa wouldn't catch me wasting his twine. My dog, Pudgy, came by to sniff and check on my progress, but he quickly became bored and drifted away.

Bouncing my creation in my hand, I checked the size and weight as the pile of twine diminished during the long afternoon. It was almost as big as a baseball when I used the last bit of string.

After sewing dozens of long stitches to keep the ball from raveling, I made one more trip to Grandpa's workshop for a roll of black electrical tape. It made a durable cover when I wrapped it around the ball. My creation felt firm, and it was almost as heavy as the real thing. We'd have a game again on Monday. After slipping the homemade baseball into the pocket of my school jacket, I joined the family in time for supper.

An hour later, Grandpa returned from the barn to roar, "Who took all my twine?"

I was forced to confess. "I needed some string for a school project."

"You needed every piece of twine in the barn?"

"I'm sorry I used it all. I'll try to find some more."

"Every time I need something, it seems you kids have found a better use for it," he complained. His head gave a disgusted shake as he stalked out of the room.

The ball remained hidden in my jacket pocket.

Riding the bus to school on Monday, I took out my handiwork and admired it again. It felt good in my grip. I looked forward to a baseball game at lunchtime today. Then I tossed the ball in the air and caught it. When I tossed it a second time, a long arm reached across the aisle and snatched it away.

"Hey!" I yelled. "Give me back my ball."

Grover Smith, a senior at the high school, held it up and grinned from across the aisle. Grover was six feet tall and kind of scary. When I grabbed for my ball, he tossed it to the boy sitting behind me. I turned, and the kid threw it to the back of the bus. My anger mounted as the high school kids played keep-away. When it wound up in the hands of Annie Hawkins, a pretty junior, she held it up to taunt me.

"Give me my ball," I demanded.

Annie tilted her head and flashed me a wicked smile. "Come get it."

When I started to walk up the aisle, she tossed it out the open window.

"Oh, I dropped it." Her look was pure innocence. "Isn't that a shame?"

I stood in the aisle, crushed. The bus bounced along the narrow road beside a canyon. My baseball was lost forever. I'd gotten in trouble with Grandpa and worked all afternoon to make it. How could she be so mean?

I wanted to pound her, but I couldn't hit a girl. Kids on the bus all sat in silence, watching my face turn red. My fists clenched in helpless rage.

Then Grover laughed.

I looked down at him as he slapped his knees and guffawed. Still howling with amusement, he pointed at my red face while I stood there in shock.

"Sit down," the bus driver shouted.

A violet mist muffled Grover's ugly laughter. Something snapped, and I attacked.

Springing across the aisle, I launched a barrage of fists to his face and head. I got my weight into the blows, and they had to hurt, even if he was twice my size. Grover made the mistake of trying to stand up in the cramped space between the benches, but I drove him back into the seat with a flurry of furious punches.

Then he made a second mistake. Ashamed to fight back against a runt like me, he tried to grab my arms but failed as I leaned in to batter him.

The driver hit the brakes, and Grover made his third mistake. He pinned my left arm to protect himself from my fists. His grip prevented me from flying down the aisle as the bus slid to a stop on the gravel road. My right hand continued to batter him until the driver pulled me off.

"Okay, boys, what is this scuffle all about?" he asked.

Grover and I both looked at him with mouths clamped shut.

"If you can't explain it to me, you can explain it to the superintendent." The driver pointed a blunt finger at me. "Stay on the bus. You're going to high school today."

"Yes, sir." Still furious, I flopped into my seat.

The long ride to the high school seemed to take forever, and fear gradually replaced my anger. Mr. Steele was all business. Sweat dampened my shirt when the driver escorted Grover and me up the stairs and into the office. Neither of us said a word while we contemplated our fates.

Twenty minutes later, the secretary came out of the superintendent's office. "You boys can go in now."

Mr. Steele waved us onto a pair of chairs in front of his desk. "What happened?"

The wall clock ticked louder. The superintendent's glare didn't waver.

Grover remained silent.

"Nothing," I finally responded.

"So Mr. Allen brought you two in here to explain nothing?" Mr. Steele steepled his fingers on his desk and leaned back in the swivel chair. His hard stare threatened to nail me to the wall behind my back.

Silence filled the room until Grover finally answered. "We played keep-away with his ball, and someone threw it out the window."

Mr. Steele asked a few more penetrating questions. Little by little, he dragged the complete story out of us.

Eventually, we escaped from the office. Grover received an assignment to write a thousand-word theme describing how a senior should behave on a school bus, and he'd been notified that his next problem with behavior would most likely result in expulsion. Worst of all, he suffered embarrassment from his friends for allowing a little kid to beat him up.

I left with a lecture on my stupidity for endangering everyone on the moving school bus, and Mr. Steele promised a paddling I wouldn't soon forget if the bus driver caught me fighting again. My bruised knuckles hurt, my string ball was gone, and I spent a boring day confined to the study hall at the high school.

Annie Hawkins, the worst offender, wasn't even called into the office to explain her role in this drama.

I learned not to trust pretty girls who smile at me.

Paying our Way

Mama's job at the lunchroom didn't pay enough to support our family of six. Resourceful as usual, she gathered a large stack of textbooks and spent several weeks studying for a two-year college equivalency test offered by the state. After passing, she was awarded a provisional license to teach. In the fall, Alamo Elementary School hired her to instruct the first three grades. The position paid seventy-five dollars a month.

The job sounded like a dream come true. Mama rode the bus for transportation to and from school, and the job paid almost twice what she made as lunchroom cook. The man who taught the higher grades earned almost twice her salary.

The board's rationale for paying men more than women was that a man had to support a wife and family.

Several months into the school term, Mama, Jason, and I stepped off the bus on a brisk December afternoon to find a scene of total destruction. My stomach went queasy when I saw the smoldering ashes where the sturdy old barn had been. A few stray wisps of smoke still rose from the blackened remains. The lingering smell of fire hung in the air. It took a moment for me to realize what I was looking at—disaster. The barn held the winter supply of hay to feed Grandpa's herd of range cattle, harness and equipment for the horses, our tools, and supplies. Everything was gone. At twelve years old, I understood the enormity of this loss.

Tales of a Misspent Youth

Grandpa met us at the gate. "The boys burned the barn."

Mama's face turned white. "Are they safe?"

Three little faces peeked around the doorframe, answering her question. She dropped her armload of books on the ground and rushed to gather Dennis, Ron, and Kevin in her arms. The kids cried, and Mama held them close. Her children's safety outweighed the loss from the barn's destruction. I stood back, relieved my brothers survived and wondering how we'd feed the livestock during the coming winter.

When Mama had taken the teaching job, she left my younger brothers in Grandma's care. The oldest of this rambunctious trio had not yet turned five. The active preschool boys presented a bigger challenge than Grandma could handle. She already had enough work to keep her busy cooking, cleaning, doing the laundry, caring for the garden, and doing chores on the farm.

When we all gathered on the porch, the boys clung to Mama. Her lip trembled when she looked at Grandma. "What happened?"

Grandma wiped a hand over her graying hair. "I should've watched them closer, but they're so quick. I can't keep up with them."

The boys stood side by side like little stair steps, sadness and fear marring their pale faces.

Mama shifted her gaze to the children. "Tell me about it, Dennis."

"We found a box of matches in the kitchen cabinet."

She frowned. "The matches are on the top shelf, out of your reach."

Dennis looked at his feet. "I climbed on a chair. We wanted to play with them."

"Why did you take them to the barn?"

"So Grandma wouldn't see us."

Mama sighed. "Did you strike matches in the barn?"

Dennis glanced at his younger brothers. "After they burned, we dropped them on the ground and stomped out the fire."

I wanted to know more. "How did the barn catch fire?"

Dennis pointed at his brothers. "Somebody didn't stomp their match out."

Mama wrapped her arms around her body, fighting off the evening chill. "Didn't you understand that hay burns?"

Dennis raised his hands to protest. "We tried to put it out. I beat on it, but it got bigger and hotter. Then it climbed to the hayloft. We got scared and ran outside."

Mama shook her head. "Thank God you're safe."

After dinner, she turned to Grandma. "Dennis can come to school with me tomorrow. He's too young, but I'll enroll him in first grade."

"Ron and Kevin should be easier to keep track of," Grandma said.

Mama nodded. "You may have to let some of the work go. Busy little boys take lots of watching. I'll help you catch up when I get home."

Grandma had tried, but the little bundles of energy could outrun her. "There's too many places they can get in trouble."

Several days later, Grandpa bought a truckload of corn, and we converted our porch into a corncrib. With careful rationing, we just might get the herd through the winter. Corn wasn't their normal diet, but they'd eat it if they got hungry enough. I spent a lot of time shelling the grain and trying to convince hungry cows that eating dry cornhusks beat starving.

Replacing the barn would cost more money than we had. Grandpa sold a few of his cattle, and Mama gave some of her teaching salary to pay for building materials. Fortunately, she'd already bought our school clothes.

During the winter, my brothers had a bad bout with the croup. Mama had to call the doctor and pay for medicine. Another drain on our income.

When new grass sprouted in March, we turned the herd onto open range. The animals looked thin but healthy enough to attack the new grass like they'd been starved. We'd check on them from time to time, but they could find food and water on their own.

Grandpa bought stacks of rough lumber, cement, steel roofing, nails, hinges, latches, and other building materials. Two of my uncles took leave time from military service to build the new barn. Neighbors dropped by to work when they could spare the time. I missed a few days of school to help the men.

We hauled gravel from the creek and mixed concrete to pour a new foundation for the structure. Since the building rested on a hillside, it needed fill dirt to make a level floor, about four feet deep at the low end.

I wrestled with a large horse-drawn scoop to scrape dirt and rocks from a nearby field. The horses pulled the scoop to collect dirt and transport it to the site. I dumped the fill inside the foundation, using a shovel to level the piles of soil and rocks. The sun grew hot for the season, and clouds of flies swarmed to my sweat. Moving dozens of cubic yards of fill turned out to be a test of my stamina.

By the time I joined the crew raising the new building, the framework was already standing. Working wherever someone needed help, I wound up on a catwalk passing steel roofing sheets to the men nailing them in place. Balancing on the sagging planks of the high walkway, I lifted the sheets of corrugated steel up to the roofers. The big panels acted like sails in the blustery winds, threatening to send me flying off my shaky perch. I held my breath each time the breeze freshened, but I didn't fall.

We completed the barn, Dennis caught up with the other students at school, and Grandma still had trouble keeping track of my two youngest brothers. They proved to be ingenious at finding ways to get into trouble. Building the barn caused us to fall behind preparing ground to plant crops, and we worked daylight till dark to catch up. Most of Mama's salary went toward paying off supplies for the new building.

One evening after supper, Mama announced the decision she hadn't wanted to make. "I notified the superintendent I won't be available to teach next year."

Grandma rubbed her temple and frowned. "But why?"

"My children need me at home."

Grandma's knuckles paled as she gripped the arms of her chair. "I love those boys. It's not that much trouble to take care of them."

"You're already busy. Keeping up with two little ones is asking too much."

Tales of a Misspent Youth

Tears appeared in Grandma's eyes, and she dabbed at them with her apron. "I try hard, but they're so quick."

Mama hugged her. "You raised your kids. It's not fair to ask you to raise mine."

A week later, Dennis was thrown from a horse and broke his arm. After a trip to the hospital, he came home with a cast. Paying the medical bill took money Mama had intended to use for making payments on roofing and lumber.

She looked like someone had died the next day when she applied to the county for public welfare.

A lady from the agency soon showed up to interview her. "Can you explain why you need help from the county?"

Mama's voice cracked. Embarrassed, her fingers drummed the table. Her eyes were downcast. "I'm working, but I need to quit when the term ends. My preschool children are too much for their grandmother to handle. I'm afraid the boys are not safe without my supervision."

The welfare lady sat back in her chair with pursed lips and a frown, and then she nodded. "I'll approve a monthly check. You need to be home with your children."

I listened with a mix of troubled emotions. Mama worked all day teaching school and then half the night helping us with homework, sewing our clothes, washing and ironing, and doing farm chores. I was happy she'd be able to stay home. Welfare would pay us enough to live, but it was government money.

We'd be living on charity.

Kicking the ground in frustration, I walked away biting my lip, chin planted on my chest, overwhelmed by shame. This wasn't the kind of life we worked for.

Lazy people took welfare.

Why Not Make Whiskey

In the years following World War II, life didn't get much easier in our little corner of the mountains. Business boomed elsewhere as returning veterans went to school on the G. I. Bill. They married, bought new cars and built new homes, furnishing them with modern appliances. Good-paying manufacturing jobs were plentiful in some parts of the country, but not in the rough hills and narrow valleys where we lived.

Scratching a decent living out of these rocky hillsides was next to impossible on our subsistence farms. Lots of young people left to find good jobs in the city. Those who stayed were forced to tighten their belts.

A few hardy farmers eked out a living growing cotton or corn, but a lot of others went broke trying. Raising chickens on a large scale offered a chance to make a small profit, but it was risky. You needed a lot of money to start the business, and the market was uncertain. Most people planted crops to feed the family, and many of them made a little moonshine whiskey on the side. They were unlikely to be caught if they hid their operation back in the hills. Those who did this on a larger scale lived well. Nobody admitted to being a bootlegger in public, but everyone knew who they were. Grandpa never spoke of it. I sensed he didn't approve.

He ran a modest herd of beef cattle on open range for his primary source of income. The cows could find plenty of free grass all summer, and we grew hay to feed them during the winter. The farm produced food, but the family couldn't afford much else. Supporting six additional people was a bigger challenge than the land could meet. Mama couldn't spare much help from her meager welfare check, so I looked for ways to contribute.

A neighbor, Grady Pickett, contracted to supply fence posts to a mill that treated them with creosote and sold them. Grady also made a little extra money from selling an occasional batch of moonshine.

The Ouachita National Forest covered more than three-fourths of our county, and the rangers marked young pine trees that could be cut to thin out excess timber to make fence posts. Grady received seven cents each to cut and peel the bark from the posts. He cut them to length and hired kids to peel off the bark. I saw an opportunity to make money during school vacation. Making whiskey would have been easier work.

I visited Grady on a Sunday. "Could you use another hand?"

He gave me a skeptical look. "Think you're big enough to handle the job?"

I straightened to my almost five foot height. "Sure am."

"Okay, you can try. It pays a cent and a half each to gather, peel, and stack them beside the access road."

"I'll take it."

"Bring a drawknife when you start. I'll help you make a rack to hold the posts while you skin off the bark."

Back home, Grandpa took me to his forge to make the drawknife. He used an old crosscut saw blade, removing the teeth, bending it to a slight curve, and grinding the back side to a sharp cutting edge. After tempering the blade, we attached carved hickory handles to pull the springy knife that would remove bark from the posts. The sharp blade bent to peel a wider strip of bark than anything we could buy from a store.

The next day, I started work.

The six-feet, six-inch lengths of pine made a heavy and clumsy load to carry through the trees and underbrush to my rack. When I peeled off the bark, sap flew. The sticky mess covered me from head to toe, and the sharp smell of pine tar clung to me and refused to leave. More sap rubbed off when I carried the still-weeping posts and stacked them by the road. Other young workers suffered the same misery and provided sympathetic company during the long days. After learning how to do the work, I managed to earn about three dollars a week, sometimes even more. Most of my pay went into the family coffers. It helped, but we weren't likely to get rich from the job.

**

When school started, I had another brainstorm. I caught Mama and Grandpa together. "Some of the boys in the Future Farmers of America are buying dairy bull calves to raise and sell for beef. They're really cheap."

Mama cocked her head and made a face. "How would you take care of them?"

"I'll buy powdered milk, add water, and feed them from a nipple on a bucket."

She didn't look convinced. "When do you plan to do all this?"

"I'll get up early to feed them before school and again when I get home at night."

Grandpa added a caution. "They won't be as hardy as calves fed by their mother. Orphan calves are more likely to get sick."

"I'll build a shed to keep them warm and dry," I said. "We can put them in the little pasture where we have the honeybees."

I had to talk fast, but Mama finally consented.

I collected scrap lumber and part of a roll of tarpaper, plus nails and a pair of hinges for building materials. My younger brothers helped me build a shelter.

Two weeks later, a truck delivered five of the three-day-old calves. The buckets and powdered milk were waiting. Grandpa helped me neuter the reluctant animals. They all looked healthy. The patchwork shed wobbled in the wind, but it stood ready to welcome its new inhabitants.

My younger brothers competed for the opportunity to feed the little animals. The calves quickly became pets and responded to the attention. Five hungry critters met me by the fence each day to be petted and fed. They got more attention than the family dog. The rickety shed kept most of the rain off. The healthy young animals grew rapidly. Their feed and shots were expensive, but my little herd would bring about a hundred dollars each when I sold them as yearlings. A nice profit seemed like a sure thing.

November arrived with rain and brisk winds. The crude shed leaked. Cold air whistled through the cracks, chilling the wet animals. All the calves suffered and fell sick. Grandpa bought medicine while I tried to patch the big cracks in the walls to block the wind and blowing rain.

Tales of a Misspent Youth

We doctored the young calves, and Mama called my brothers inside at bedtime. I spent all night in the shed, plugging leaks and trying to care for my little herd. Their pneumonia couldn't be stopped. My tears flowed as the four largest animals died, one by one, in my arms. My fight to save them was futile, and I realized they might have lived if I'd taken better care of them.

The smallest calf survived, but its growth was stunted. I'd invested one hundred fifty dollars—more than two months' income from Mama's welfare checks—to buy the animals and pay for their feed and medicine. A year later, I sold the runt for seventy-five dollars.

My folly prevented Mama from keeping up with our share of the family's expenses for a time. Money was tight, and I knew Grandpa still made payments for materials we used to build the new barn. Loss of the calves loomed over me like a fortune that had been snatched away. Guilt nagged me because I wasn't able to recover my investment, and my family suffered the consequences.

I'd catch myself sitting in school, mourning the loss of the calves and worrying about how we'd live on our tiny income. Trying to find an easy out wasted a lot of time. In spite of my effort, I failed to think of any way to recover what I'd lost trying to bottle-feed the orphaned calves. One question nagged at me repeatedly as I searched for a way out of our predicament.

Grandpa and I were doing chores at the barn when I worked up courage to ask him the question. "Folks earn money when they make and sell whiskey, don't they?"

He pushed back his beat-up old hat and eyed me. "Yes, they do, but most of them don't make much."

"Don't they worry the sheriff might catch them?"

"Bootleggers usually hide their operation back in the hills. They're careful who they sell to and when they deliver it."

"You don't believe people should make whiskey, do you?"

Grandpa hesitated for a long moment. "The government allows people to make it if they get permits and pay taxes. Sounds to me like it's not considered bad if you pay the government. Lots of folks around here need the money. They hide their moonshine from the law, and they don't pay taxes."

I scuffed my feet on the rocky ground. "We need money. Why don't you make whiskey?"

He leaned against the barn wall, arms folded, looking me in the eye. "I could do that, but then we'd have to keep it secret."

I nodded.

He shook his head when he reached out to touch my shoulder. "I'd have to teach you children to lie."

Leaving Alive

The piercing note Grandma blew on her conch shell was her way of saying, "Breakfast is ready. Come and get it or I'll throw it out."

I wound up my chores in a hurry and ran for the kitchen. The family gathered quickly, and Grandpa sat at the head of the rough-hewn table. Grandma took the seat to his left, and Mama took her place on his right. We five boys filled the remainder of the table. As the oldest, I took the chair at the foot. Grandpa said grace, and we dug in.

After splitting my second biscuit in two, I looked down the table for the big bowl. "Pass the gravy, please."

My brother sitting next to me tapped it with his fork. "Get it your own self."

Flashing him a look that promised vengeance, I stretched to reach the bowl of thick milk gravy and pulled it toward me. I had just slathered the warm, tasty spread over my biscuit when the front door banged open. Heavy footsteps clomped across our living room linoleum. I looked up from my plate to see Travis Miller grab on to the doorframe to balance his wobbly body as he stuck his head into our kitchen.

He fixed his gaze on Grandpa. "Got any smokin' tobacco? I'm fresh out."

Since I sat closest to the doorway, his whiskey breath surrounded me and spread across the room. I looked down at my plate and tried to ignore him.

Grandpa pushed back his chair and rose. "I don't smoke. You might ask John Wallace. He keeps a can or two of Prince Albert. Smokes it in his pipe."

Travis stumbled as he released his support to enter the room. "Ain't askin' that cheapskate for nothin'. Tried to jew me down last time I sold him a quart of corn liquor."

Grandpa frowned. "Well, I can't help you."

Travis's unshaven face reddened. "You can hitch up your team and drive me to the store over on the blacktop."

"That would take most of the morning. I've got work waiting to be done."

"Sounds like you don't wanna help out a neighbor what needs somethin'."

Grandpa glanced down at our breakfast table surrounded by women and children sitting in silence. His thin frame was toughened by a life of hard labor, but he looked small beside the big bootlegger. Travis was one mean drunk.

Grandpa rose and took a step toward the door. "Let's go outside and talk."

I waited a moment before following the two men as they left the kitchen. Something seemed likely to happen. I didn't want to miss it.

Most of our neighbors were honest people—poor but proud. They spent a lifetime plowing their fields, paying their debts, and trying to raise kids who might achieve something better for themselves.

Travis was a different breed. Two men had died, and several had been injured in drunken brawls involving him. The valley had been a lot safer while he was in prison, but he'd been out for almost a year. Getting drunk

Tales of a Misspent Youth

and harassing people appeared to be his favorite activity when he wasn't actually making a batch of moonshine.

Grandpa maneuvered Travis out the gate and across the road for a private conversation. I knew he wanted to get the bootlegger away from the family to protect us. Hiding beside the well house, screened by a small bush, I stood close enough to hear everything they said.

Travis tripped on a rock and grabbed hold of the post supporting a salt block for our cattle. "If you was a friend, you'd haul me to the store."

"This isn't an emergency," Grandpa said. "I can't afford to waste half a day just to find you some smoking tobacco."

I knew that hill country tradition was to help a guy in need. It also tolerated selling an occasional batch of homemade whiskey. Folks didn't generally speak of it, especially to strangers. Most bootleggers were friendly and otherwise honest people.

Travis was different. People got hurt when he got drunk. Most of his profits went down his gullet. His family wore rags and endured hunger.

The morning sun began to heat things up. Grandpa pushed back his straw hat to wipe his brow. "I'm sorry to refuse you, but I've got to get my hay cut today."

Travis stuck his thumb against the side of his nose and blew a yellow gob into the roadside weeds. "Here I thought you was a good neighbor."

"I try to be."

Travis glared. "It's gonna get ugly if I don't get me some tobacco."

Grandpa extended both palms in a peacemaking gesture. "Old man Nelson chews homegrown. Lives just

Doyle Suit

down the road. Maybe a couple of twists would do you until the peddler comes by your place."

"Don't want no damned chewing tobacco," Travis snarled. His right hand brushed the ruler pouch of his denim overalls.

Rumor had it he kept a hunting knife with a five-inch blade in that pouch. He also carried a snub-nosed .38 revolver in a hip pocket.

Grandpa stood his ground. "The peddler will come by your place tomorrow morning. He carries tobacco."

Travis kicked some roadside gravel with a booted foot. "Ain't waitin' to get me a smoke. Ain't that much trouble if you was to take me to the store."

Both men looked up as a battered red pickup truck topped the rise and drove by in a cloud of dust. Uncle Bob waved from the open window.

Travis had turned back to Grandpa and stuck a bony finger in his face when we heard the truck slide to a stop with the brakes locked. The gears ground and popped as Bob shifted into reverse. His tires threw gravel, and the transmission whined as he backed the vehicle to our house.

The driver's door swung open, and my uncle stepped out in slow motion. His shirt was already wet with sweat from sitting in the hot truck. He wasn't very tall, and his stomach hung over his belt buckle, but his arms and shoulders were massive. At two hundred-fifty pounds, he was the strongest man around those parts. Grandpa and Travis stood silent to watch him approach.

Bob tipped his hat. "Mornin', Papa."

Grandpa nodded his acknowledgement.

Bob's jaw clenched when he turned toward Travis. "Mornin', Travis."

The drunken bootlegger straightened to his full six-foot height and glared down his nose at the shorter man. "Mornin'."

Bob turned back to Grandpa. "What's going on?"

"Not a lot," Grandpa said. "Travis wants me to take him to the store over on the highway to buy some tobacco."

Bob's eyebrows lifted. "Don't sound all that urgent."

"Travis seems to think I need to do it now," Grandpa said.

Bob nodded and turned to face the drunken bootlegger. "Travis, I'd sure like to do you a favor."

Travis frowned. His eyes shifted from side to side. "What kind of favor?"

My uncle commenced to smile as he moved close to the taller man. "If you leave now, you can leave alive."

The bootlegger's head snapped up. His face paled. His right hand hovered over the pocket holding his pistol as he backed away a half step.

Bob's fist doubled. He closed the distance and stared at Travis without speaking.

The bootlegger's hand stopped short of the gun. His face blanched. Then he commenced to shake. His tall frame seemed to shrink, and he turned away. He was stepping lively and mostly in a straight line when he rounded the curve leading away from our house.

Grandpa rubbed his palms on the seat of his overalls. "Coffee's still hot, Bob. Might as well help us finish our biscuits and gravy."

Travis never bothered us again.

Old Enough to Use a Gun

Being the oldest of five brothers, I couldn't wait to grow up, be taller and stronger than my skinny frame allowed. Necessity brought me more responsibility than most twelve-year-old boys, so I craved the recognition given to adults. Using a gun ranked alongside driving a car to hasten my transition to adulthood.

Grandpa's .22 rifle rested on two large nails driven in the wall over our front door. A box of long rifle cartridges set on the corner shelf supporting his grandfather clock. I'd been impressed when he shot a couple of 'possums and a few blacksnakes that tried to raid the chicken house.

Intrigued by the rifle, I asked Grandpa about it. "Why do you keep it here?"

He paused from chopping wood to wipe sweat from his brow with a shirtsleeve. "If a fox raids our chicken house, I don't have time to look for the gun in the back room."

Since we lived deep in the wooded hills, almost an hour's drive from the nearest lawman, the rifle also provided protection if anyone threatened our home. Fortunately, Grandpa hadn't used it for that purpose for more than forty years.

Squirrel season would open in the fall, and I envied my friends who were allowed to hunt. As Grandpa sat in his rickety, old rocking chair, reading a week-old copy of

Tales of a Misspent Youth

The Hot Springs Sentinel Record, I asked, "May I take the gun to go squirrel hunting?"

Grandpa chuckled. "You'd best talk to your mother. She may have some ideas on that subject."

I found Mama in the kitchen washing the breakfast dishes. "May I borrow Grandpa's rifle to go squirrel hunting?"

She frowned. "You're too young to take a rifle into the woods by yourself."

"Why not? Joe Miller gets to go hunting by himself. He's only ten."

She wiped a bowl and set it on the table. "Maybe next year, if Grandpa teaches you how to use it safely."

A few weeks later, Grandpa took the rifle down from its perch above the door. "How about we get acquainted with this today? It's a tool you need to respect."

He led me out past the woodpile to the big oak tree my uncles used to hang pieces of cardboard for target practice. Before he let me hold the weapon, he explained his first rule for handling a gun. "Never point it at anything you don't intend to shoot."

He handed me the weapon. "Press the butt to your shoulder and align the sights with what you're shooting at. Squeeze the trigger nice and slow."

I nodded.

"Remember what I told you. Let's see if you can hit the target."

I raised the rifle, pointed in the direction of the cardboard square, and yanked the trigger.

Bang!

"You missed the whole tree," Grandpa said. "Do it again. Do it like I told you this time."

During several more practice sessions, he stressed safety and the need to hit what I shot at.

After a few weeks of practice, Mama finally allowed me to borrow the gun. I couldn't wait to take it into the timbered hills and bring back meat for supper. Slipping through the trees on tiptoe, I looked for the busy little critters on every limb in the forest canopy. The first squirrel I found leaped to another tree and disappeared before I could shoot. The second dived into a hole near the top of a tall oak.

Finally, I spotted a small gray squirrel sitting on a limb. Raising the rifle, I squeezed off a lucky shot. The squirrel dropped at my feet. I carried it home in triumph. After I dressed the critter, Mama fried it for my supper, the best meat I'd ever tasted.

My second hunt sent me home empty-handed. On the next hunt, I managed to bag three of the tasty little critters in one day. I cleaned them, and we had meat for the whole family at suppertime. Everyone's praise made me feel like a hero.

Grandpa brought me back to earth. "How many bullets did you use?"

I cringed. "Uh, about six."

He shook his head. "Bullets cost money. If you're not going to hit something, you shouldn't shoot."

"Yes, sir."

"Besides, you need to shoot them in the head so you don't ruin any of the meat."

Squirrels are small, and they move quickly. I eventually became a better shot, but I never quite met his standards.

Tales of a Misspent Youth

The next spring, I plowed the ground, hauled manure for fertilizer, and planted a quarter acre of watermelons. Warm sunshine and frequent rains yielded a huge crop of melons. With no way to haul them to market, we ate watermelon every day, put up dozens of jars of preserves from the rinds, and gave some to all the neighbors.

Just before dark on several evenings, I noticed a group of boys, about eighteen to twenty years old, creep out of the surrounding trees. They climbed our fence and took all the melons they could carry as they slipped away through the woods.

I told Mama, "Some boys stole our watermelons."

"It doesn't matter," she said. "We have more than we can use."

After thinking about it, she was probably right. It wasn't a serious crime. We had more than we could eat. The boys probably thought it was fun to swipe them, but I still didn't like it.

Later, I walked through the field to find dozens of watermelons ripped loose from their vines and shattered on the ground. It looked like the young men had been throwing them at each other for sport. The more I thought about it, the angrier I became. I'd worked hard to grow that crop. It didn't matter if they took a few to eat, but it wasn't right to destroy them for fun.

After stewing about this needless destruction for most of the day, I settled on a way to handle the problem. *There might be a better use for Grandpa's rifle.*

During the afternoon, I took the sleek Remington squirrel gun from its perch and hid it in the barn. An hour before dusk, I chose a spot behind the big hayloft with a clear view of the field, waiting for the boys to appear.

Right on schedule, three of them slipped out of the woods and started thumping melons, looking for ripe ones. The range was over three hundred yards, too far for accurate shooting with a small-bore weapon. Sighting in on a likely target near the culprits, I waited. When the boys had chosen their loot and made ready to leave, I pulled the trigger.

The bullet slapped through a leafy bush near the boys. They spun around, looking for where the shot came from. My second shot landed slightly closer, plunking into a big watermelon.

One of the boys yelled, "He's shootin' at us!"

They dropped the melons and scrambled to reach safety in the trees. My third shot was aimed at the sky. The boys ran too hard to hear a bullet hitting leaves, anyway.

I had a good idea who the culprits were, but I didn't tell anyone about the scare I'd put into them. Mama would surely have taken some hide off my rear end with a peach tree switch if she learned what I'd done.

When I found time to think about it, I realized the boys couldn't be sure who was shooting. My grandfather might have been blamed.

After I turned thirty, I finally confessed to my mother what I'd done. She threatened to look for a peach tree.

I'm not sure the incident proved I was old enough to use a gun. However, we lived in the area for another five years.

And nobody ever stole another watermelon from my field.

Firebreak

Dead grass stood hip deep in the meadow as I waded through the dense stand of unwanted brown sage. The time was ripe to burn the worthless weeds and make way for new growth. The family had planned the burn for today, but Mama promised to visit a sick friend, and Grandpa had persuaded a neighbor to drive his truck and deliver a pair of calves he'd sold. My younger brothers had been ordered to get busy cleaning the house and pulling weeds in the garden.

Nearing the age of thirteen, lack of confidence wasn't among my long list of adolescent faults. I'd caught up with Grandpa before the neighbor's old truck left the barn. "I can burn off that meadow this morning. It's locked in with firebreaks, so I won't need any help."

Grandpa leaned out the passenger side window and shook his head. "Better wait. A burn can get away when you least expect it. We'll do it next Saturday. You might need help to stop it if something goes wrong."

"But I have baseball tryouts next Saturday."

"Can't be helped." Grandpa pointed to the corner of the corral. "You can load that manure pile onto the wagon while I'm gone."

When the truck disappeared down the gravel road, I kicked at the dirt. If I planned to make the team, I needed to show up for tryouts. Shoveling manure wasn't my first choice of how to spend the morning, and I didn't want to miss a chance to impress the coach by being absent. The cool air barely stirred as it trickled down from the rough, wooded hills surrounding our farm. Perfect day to burn that field.

Sighing, I trudged over to the corral to pick up a shovel and threw a few dozen scoops of stinking manure onto the wagon. Several minutes later, I reached a decision. Tossing the shovel aside, I made a beeline for the kitchen to gather a pocketful of matches.

"I'll surprise them. If I get that meadow burned today, I'll be able to play baseball next week." I glanced over my shoulder. "It took all winter for the cows to create that pile of waste. It can wait until I get back from practice."

Morning dew covered the tall brown grass. A faint breeze barely disturbed the clean-smelling air as the sun climbed a cloudless sky. I sucked in the smell of new grass springing up under cover of the dead sage. All around me, the land showed signs of waking from a winter's sleep.

A swampy area to the north and a cultivated field south of the meadow would channel the burn toward a farm road. The bare dirt path would serve as a firebreak. From the top of the hill, I examined the sage-choked field, making sure I hadn't overlooked anything that might spoil my plan.

On the other side of the hill, a partially completed pond intruded into the pasture across the beaten path, and the contractor's bulldozer stood on the raw earth of our new dam. Closer, a big tank of diesel fuel rested on an old trailer parked in the dry grass downwind from the farm road. When completed, the pond would provide water for our herd of cattle and horses.

Tales of a Misspent Youth

Young, second-growth pines dotted the rocky hillside at the far end of the pasture. I broke off several small limbs and stacked them by the road to contain spot fires that might jump the break. The bunched pine needles on my little stack of branches made an effective tool to smother flames. A barbed wire fence separated our land from a stand of mature trees on a neighbor's property to the east.

Satisfied I had everything under control for a successful burn, I tramped back upwind to begin the task. A handful of dead vegetation made a torch, and I set a series of small fires along the upwind side of the field. The flames fizzled in the wet grass, and I waited a few minutes for the sun to dry it. The timid breeze felt pleasant on my skin. My second attempt flared briefly, but it also failed to ignite the damp sage.

Persevering, I made a bigger torch as the warm sunshine and a pleasant breeze combined to evaporate dew covering the dead grass. This time the line of fires caught and converged along the western edge of the field to creep downwind.

Both sides of the fire zone held the moving line of flames in check while I ran along the barriers to make sure the burn didn't escape its intended path. Tongues of fire grew larger as it gathered strength, and a freshening breeze drove it eastward. Heat from the growing blaze dried the tall grass as flames leaped higher.

Racing to the road, I snatched the branches I'd prepared and stood ready to beat out spot fires that crossed the barrier. By the time the fast-moving burn reached the road, flames towered above me. A hot smoke cloud enveloped the hilltop. I stood firm, coughing, nose burning and eyes stinging, until heat from the advancing fire forced me to retreat.

Burning embers, propelled by the freshening wind, flew across the road. Flames sprang up in the dry grass as I scurried to extinguish them. That worked momentarily, but the line of burning sage stretched more than a hundred yards. New outbreaks multiplied faster than I could beat them out. Dirty brown smoke billowed to the sky while flying sprigs of flaming grass and heat from the approaching inferno scorched my skin and threatened to roast me. The monster fire jumped the narrow road without pausing and spread into the pasture, flames rising to twice my height.

My firebreak failed.

The violence of raging flames sent chills down my spine. Fear sapped my strength as I faced the blistering heat to swat at spot fires threatening to surround me.

A sudden vision of the trailer filled with diesel fuel jolted me into total panic. It sat in the middle of a dense patch of sage grass, directly in the path of the runaway burn. Images of the fuel tank engulfed in flames and exploding doubled my fear. The rig must have cost a fortune, and its loss would be my fault. This monster had to be stopped before it reached the vulnerable tank.

After a panicked retreat to the trailer, I set a semicircle of fire facing the oncoming inferno. When my newly kindled flames started to spread, I smothered those that approached the trailer. My backfire crept upwind toward the impending monster, leaving a burned-over area in front of the diesel tank. Leaping tongues of fire singed hair from my hands and arms as I fought to protect the trailer and contain the hungry wall of destruction racing toward me.

Smoke-filled breaths came in gasps. My pulse pounded. Wheezing and coughing from the acrid cloud, I flailed at the furious wall of fire. Sweat and tears obscured my vision, and my skin sensed the wind speed increasing. Crackling flames in the dry grass roared like an approaching tornado.

My puny backfire met the wind-driven inferno barely twenty feet from where I struggled to extinguish burning embers that jumped the break. I could only attempt to defend the area around the flammable trailer as the out of control burn swept past me on both sides of my narrow firebreak. At some point during the battle, the rest of the hair on my arms, over my forehead, and parts of my eyebrows disappeared.

With scorched earth in its path, the sea of spreading destruction dwindled to clumps of smoking embers around the diesel tank. One disaster had been averted. Fire swept past the trailer to roar into the swamp along the north side of the field. Standing water reduced it to isolated flames that quickly died.

The remaining fork of the blaze encountered sparse vegetation on the rocky ground. Its fury lessened, but the wall of fire continued to advance toward the neighbor's trees. If it reached the thick underbrush in the forest, it would devastate the stand of timber. Fighting exhaustion, my breath came in raspy sobs. Feeling totally alone, I raced to confront the threat.

Suddenly, Grandpa appeared at my side to snap off a handful of pine branches. Working together, we stopped the advancing flames before they reached the fence marking the neighbor's property. Another disaster averted. Relieved that we had stopped the burn, the condition of my blistered skin and my total fatigue intruded into my consciousness. A place to lie down and rest was what I needed. Instead, I followed Grandpa as we stumbled through the charred field to examine the ring of scorched earth around the fuel trailer.

Grandpa turned to look directly at me. "Good job with the backfire."

We tramped around the perimeter of the field and beat out patches of hot stubble that could re-ignite the fire. Grandpa moved slowly, making sure the fire had been completely extinguished. My knees shook. Pain from burns on my face and arms made itself felt.

Finally, Grandpa tipped his hat back and examined my smoke-blackened features. "Don't suppose I need to tell you that starting this job alone wasn't a good idea?"

I felt my scorched face flush brighter. "No, sir."

We made the short walk home in silence. My whole body ached and a persistent cough wracked my chest and throat. Movement made my face and arms hurt. My eyes felt like live coals, legs trembling from exhaustion, my shoulders slumped from embarrassment. I needed a cool bath and ointment for my burned skin. However, one positive thought penetrated my tired brain. I'd been lucky, and the firebreak had saved me from a complete disaster.

Furthermore, I was definitely smarter than I'd been earlier that morning.

Brimstone and Bloomers

My teen-age back ached from pulling weeds in the garden one muggy afternoon. My friend, Charlie Warren, interrupted the boring task when he stopped by with an idea to spice up our evening. "My parents are going to the revival meeting tonight. Papa said you could come with us. We can sit in the parking lot to watch."

I couldn't think of anything better to do. Chores were caught up, and my social calendar was wide open. Seemed like it had been open for as long as I could remember. All my friends called this church the "Holy Rollers." With the closest movie theater twenty-five miles away, most boys considered the revival service to be a prime source of entertainment.

"Sure," I said. "Some of those old ladies might get all excited and put on a show if the preacher gives a good sermon."

Charlie grinned. "Lots of girls gonna be there, too."

The small fundamentalist congregation held their annual revival in a large open arbor in the field behind the church. A freshly cut meadow provided ample room for parking if hadn't rained for a few days. Log posts supported the pavilion's corrugated roof. The floor consisted of well-trampled raw clay, and rough wooden benches filled the interior. Sawdust covered the bare ground. In case of rain, it prevented Sunday shoes from being ruined by the sticky red mud. Clouds of insects surrounded several bare light bulbs hanging from the rafters to illuminate the big shed.

Charlie's family hurried in to find good seats while he and I slipped away to wander about the grounds. The evening had cooled, and we only encountered a few hungry mosquitoes lurking in the weeds to ambush us. We met several boys we knew, and like us, the majority came to see the show. Most of the girls disappointed us by going to sit with their families. After all the cute girls left to go inside, we returned to Mr. Warren's battered old 1935 Ford sedan. The front fenders made excellent seats to watch what happened during the service even if we had to sit a little sideways to avoid the headlights.

There must have been a hundred people crammed onto the rough benches. The congregation waited quietly, waving cardboard fans from the funeral parlor to stir the humid air. Lingering heat and flying insects kept the big crowd sweating and swatting.

Charlie hoisted himself onto the left front fender. "We can see everything from here."

"Hope the preacher's not too loud. We're awfully close." I straddled the other fender, trying to smack a pesky bug that circled my head.

The out-of-tune upright piano rang loud and clear as an elderly lady in a big hat with flowers on it pounded the keys. The entire gathering joined in singing several of the traditional gospel songs. Charlie and I chimed in with uncertain voices and entertaining lyrics we made up from our perch outside the pavilion. Luckily, we didn't sing loud enough for the folks inside to hear us.

The visiting evangelist sweated freely in his black suit and tie. His pale skin looked like it hadn't seen the sun all summer. Over six feet tall and skinny as a fence rail, his dark hair billowed around a lean face dominated by a big Roman nose.

His strong and fervent voice boomed as he commenced a passionate sermon. I could almost feel the fire and smell the brimstone. He waved his hands in sweeping gestures, pounding the pulpit for emphasis. "Give up your sinful ways, ye of little faith. Follow in the paths of righteousness. Those who partake of carnal pleasures and demon rum will burn in everlasting hell."

Several in the congregation stood and shouted "Amen," "Hallelujah," "Praise the Lord," and "Tell 'em, brother."

The preacher's voice thundered as he hit his stride. Within minutes, he ripped off his jacket and rolled up his sleeves. Sweat poured down his face. The crowd was drawn to his vivid message like moths circling a flame. People leaned forward to look and listen. Several became more animated, surging to their feet, singing and clapping, as the minister evoked vivid images of the eternal fires of hell.

Finally, a fat lady leaped to her feet, screaming with joy, dancing into the aisle. Throwing her arms wide, she flopped backward into the sawdust. Shouting in tongues, she kicked her high-top shoes and flailed her limbs.

The spirit had possessed her.

A small group from the congregation filled the aisle around the woman, shouting, "Hallelujah" and "Pray for me, sister."

As she lay kicking, her long dress rode up over her knees. White legs shone in the harsh overhead light. Eager faces glistened as the group became entranced and pressed closer to the frenzied woman. Her voice changed pitch, ringing louder and shriller as she uttered her indecipherable words.

Charlie and I sat in silence on the hard steel fenders, watching with growing interest as the crowd became more intense. I sneaked a peek at a couple of the young girls. They gazed intently at the spectacle and didn't bother to look back at me. The din of hands clapping, shouts of encouragement from the congregation, and the woman's screams of joy rose to a deafening pitch.

Shattering the calm outside the pavilion, Charlie leaned forward and yelled, "I saw her bloomers."

"I don't believe it. It's your imagination. There's too many people in front for you to see anything." I stretched my neck, trying to catch a glimpse of the bloomers.

"Did, too. I saw her bloomers. They was white with a bunch of frilly lace around the bottom."

We argued for the next five minutes. We even cheered, hoping to encourage others to join the roll in the sawdust. I had the sinking feeling Charlie had seen something I'd missed. Unfortunately, nobody else was called to speak in tongues.

The evangelist raised his voice in a passionate plea to the congregation. "Brothers and sisters, reflect on the fate which awaits the souls of sinners. Come forward and accept salvation. Eternal joy awaits God's children. The torture of everlasting hell will be the destiny of those who choose to live in sin."

The preacher had me convinced that hell wouldn't be the most pleasant place I might choose to live.

The pianist resumed playing, and several people shuffled forward. The preacher made a big fuss over them, giving thanks for the souls saved. On Saturday, they would all gather at the creek to be dunked in the cold water for their baptism.

Many in the congregation probably received spiritual benefits from the revival. I doubted that Charlie and I had profited. I couldn't even figure out which had made the bigger impression on me—the brimstone or the bloomers.

Charlie and I failed to sort out what he had or had not seen, but we did agree on one thing.

The revival had definitely been more fun than staying home to play dominoes.

A House of Our Own

"He needs to be here, doing his homework," Grandma said. "Not running off to play baseball on the Sabbath."

I watched Mama bite her lip and frown. "His schoolwork is all caught up, and he went to church this morning."

"That baseball team is just a worthless bunch of young people with nothing better to do." Grandma gathered her knitting and left the room.

Mama shook her head and sighed. "Come straight home after your game. Your grandparents mean well, but it would be nice if I didn't get criticized for every decision they don't agree with."

Approaching my fourteenth birthday, I wasn't happy about being told what to do. "She just doesn't want me to play ball."

Mama's jaw tightened. "We moved in with your grandparents because we had no choice. I love them, but we need a place of our own. They already raised their family."

Grandpa and Grandma had always been caring and generous, but we lived in their home, not ours. We tried to pull our weight by helping with farm work. My aunts and uncles also expected us to watch after and protect the elderly couple. We did, but Mama valued her independence. Living like misers, we saved a little money from our welfare check. It wasn't enough to buy a house.

Tales of a Misspent Youth

During a summer evening, I talked to Mama again. "The Wallace place is for sale. It is forty acres of cut-over timber with a house that's falling down. I bet it's cheap."

"It's close, too," Mama said. "Your grandparents need to have family nearby."

The possibility of having our own home sounded good to me. "I could still help Grandpa with chores if we lived there."

Old man Wallace had died, and his family moved away two years ago. The place had been vacant ever since. They wanted to sell. The forty-acre farm was only three-quarters of a mile from my grandparents' house. All the fields were overgrown, and the house was going to ruin.

Mama drummed her fingers on the table. "They even sold the small pines for fence posts. It's mostly hills, and all the good timber has been cut. If I could borrow some of the money, we might make them an offer."

A few days later, Mama discussed our situation with Uncle Bob. "If someone would loan me a down payment, I know we could buy the place and pay it off."

Uncle Bob pursed his lips. "I'll see what I can do."

"I'd appreciate it," she said.

Bob talked it over with his brothers, and they struck a deal. They would contribute some of the money. The house was close by, so we could continue to look after my grandparents.

The Wallace family accepted Mama's offer, and we closed the deal.

Grandpa came with us for our first good look at the house. When we reached the overgrown yard, everyone stopped and stared. The crumbling old dwelling wasn't a pretty sight, with unpainted siding that had come loose in places. Several of the planks were missing, and decay was apparent in others.

None of the outbuildings had survived the neglect. Some were warped, leaning and sagging, and some had already caved in. We'd have to remove them and haul away the trash.

Grandpa tipped his straw hat back on his mane of gray hair. "We'll miss you at home, but having your own place might be best for all of us."

"We won't be far away," Mama said.

"The place needs lots of repairs. It's in sorry shape. You've got your work cut out for you. I can help with some of the big jobs."

The inside of the house looked worse. Smoke-blackened newspapers covered the interior walls. Sections of stovepipe for the wood-fired kitchen range lay broken on the floor. The fireplace chimney showed deep cracks in the crumbling concrete. Steps at the front and back of the house were rotted and unsafe. The kitchen floor sagged in one corner. I figured I could help grandpa repair the foundation and level the floor. Most of the windows were broken. Rusted screens were torn or missing.

Birds and rodents had moved into the vacant house, leaving evidence of their stay. It smelled like something had died in each room. The outhouse was ready to topple, and the yard had become a tangle of weeds and tree sprouts. Nevertheless, Mama's mind was made up. We'd make it our home.

Mama started work, and my brothers and I tackled the challenge. The job looked daunting for our small crew. Jason was next oldest after me. He was ten. Even the youngest, five-year-old Kevin, helped clean and repair the

Tales of a Misspent Youth

building. Days were long and the work difficult, but I didn't hear much complaining.

Mama listed things we needed to do before we moved in. She pointed to me. "Your grandpa will help us with major repairs. We can fix little things later."

"There's more," I said. "The water stinks. We have to clean the well."

She pushed back a lock of hair that threatened to escape from her scarf. "I'll ask your grandpa to bring his long ladder. You and I can empty it for him."

The next day, we used the bucket and chain to draw out all the water. It continued to trickle in from an underground spring. After lowering the ladder into the four-foot diameter hand-dug hole, I climbed down to the dark, cold bottom.

The source was obvious. "A dead squirrel is floating down here."

After removing the little animal, I scrubbed the rock walls as best I could. Mama and Grandpa manned the pulley and bucket. The ankle-deep water threatened to freeze my feet, and the work had me wet and cold all over within minutes. We emptied the well until it smelled fresh, and then we allowed it to refill.

Next, Mama gathered my brothers. "The house is too filthy for us to move in. You boys can help clean it. We'll strip the newspaper off and scrub the plank walls and floors. We want a clean house to live in."

A few days later, we loaded our belongings onto a wagon and hauled them to our new home. It still looked vacant. The house had no ceilings or interior siding, so we had a good view of studs stiffening the walls and rafters supporting the roof.

After we unloaded the wagon, I offered my opinion. "It still looks like whoever built this decided to quit work before they finished the job."

Mama laughed as she mussed my hair with her fingers. "This is our home. We'll live here if it's finished or not."

Everything we tackled was broken, worn out, taken over by tree sprouts, or missing. Mama became our planner and chief laborer. I started work on the yard while she and the younger boys cleared ground in the overgrown field for a large garden.

She redirected me. "The outhouse is not safe. You'll have to fix it first."

"Guess the yard can wait." I salvaged boards from the worthless old chicken house to shore up the decayed privy.

Later, Grandpa rode his ugly black horse to check on us. "You can have a young sow from my litter if you have a place to keep it."

"Mr. Wallace had a hog lot." I pointed to the overgrown hillside. "I'll have to patch the fence."

Three days later, the fence was ready for our pig, and Grandpa delivered it. I'd collected a few scratches from the wire and saw briars, plus a rash from the poison oak lurking there. We all went to bed tired at night, but we took pride in our new pig.

I made daily trips to help my grandparents with chores and brought home a jug of badly needed fresh milk—good payment for an hour's work.

Grandma occasionally added extra food she'd prepared. "I made too much. It would go to waste if you don't take it home."

When I was ready to leave after helping with chores, she often gave me a box of fresh eggs. "Don't you break them," she'd say. "That's all I have today."

The whole family chipped in to help my grandparents plant their crops. Since weeds seemed to grow faster than corn, we stayed busy using a hoe to remove them from the rows of plants we cultivated. We would share in their bounty at harvest time.

At home, we worked daylight to dark, making the house livable. We planted our garden and a few rows of corn, okra, peas, and beans when we found time. I even cleared a patch of ground to plant watermelons.

Three weeks after we moved in, the rain came. It started with a light sprinkle, just what we needed. The dry weather threatened to kill our garden before it had a chance to grow. We'd carried water in buckets to save the young plants.

The raindrops grew larger, drumming faster on the tarpaper roof.

Jason yelled from the living room. "It's leaking in here."

I scurried to bring a pan from the kitchen to catch the drip and spotted another puddle. Several more leaks appeared as we tried to contain the growing streams of water. Soon, we had a large collection of pans, buckets, and bowls scattered across the living room. I sent Dennis into the kitchen to find more vessels.

Suddenly, Kevin charged in from the bedroom. "My bed's wet. It's raining inside."

The downpour increased to a deluge, and we ran out of containers, trying to deal with water pouring inside from countless leaks. I looked in the other rooms to find all our bedding, our furniture, and our clothes completely soaked. Water streamed inside like the roof didn't exist. The house couldn't have been wetter if it had been dropped in the middle of the creek.

Eventually, all of us kids huddled in a corner of the kitchen, soaked to the skin and dejected. Water continued to pour in around the entire house. My brothers watched with downcast faces, but none of the boys cried. We stood together in silence, waiting for the rain to stop.

Mama wiped an arm across her brow. She finally gave up trying to save anything from the massive leaks streaming into the house and trudged slowly to our corner to stand with us.

She wrapped the five of us in a bear hug. "Don't look so sad. We'll fix the roof. Nothing will stop us from living here. This is our home."

Can We Live Here?

When the rain finally stopped, we carried our water-soaked belongings outside. Mattresses leaned against the porch wall. Bedding and towels hung across chairs set on the plank floor. The clothesline sagged under its load of wet clothing.

"Hang everything else on the fence," Mama said. "It won't take long for most things to dry."

I cast a sad look at the soggy mess and turned back to her. "Can we really live here?"

The determination in her eyes and her clenched jaw gave me my answer. "We *will* live here."

With no bedding, the family spent the next two nights sleeping on the floor.

"I'm scared." Ron's voice trembled. "Something might come inside to get me."

Mama laughed and patted his hand. "Don't worry. It's so empty and damp in here, even the boogie man wouldn't dare show his face."

The next morning, Mama contacted a neighboring farmer, George Atkins. He agreed to help us fix the roof for a reasonable price.

Barely fourteen years old and weighing about a hundred pounds, I climbed the ladder with George. We tore off the dilapidated roofing to find that much of the sheeting underneath had rotted. It needed to be replaced.

When we ripped out the decayed wood, we uncovered several damaged rafters beneath. It wasn't a pretty sight.

I turned to George. "Can it be fixed?"

"Sure." He raked a rough hand across his stubbled cheek. "Gonna cost money to buy new roofing and lumber."

"The hardware store will let me pay it off on time," Mama said. "We'll replace everything that's bad."

After George drove to town and brought back the material, we started work. Three days and one twice-mashed thumb later, we had a weather-tight roof.

I thought we were done, but George pointed to our fractured chimney. "You can't use the fireplace with that big crack in the cement. Might burn the damn house down."

Money was tight, but Uncle Bob found an old pot-bellied stove for us. I built a cover for the top of the chimney and used a hammer and chisel to chip holes in its cement face to run a stovepipe outside. Then I cleaned the fire pit and made it into a wood box. We set the stove on the hearth in front of the unused fireplace.

The roof repair took everything Mama had saved and more. George agreed to wait for part of his money. Our prospects improved when Grandpa showed up leading a milk cow he called Beauty. "Reckon you could find a place for this cow? We got more milk than we need, but you got to have some place to keep her."

Tears filled Mama's eyes when she said, "Thank you."

Grandpa and I used tarpaper and lumber removed from the roof. We spent the next two days cobbling together a small shed to hold hay and provide a stall for the cow.

Tales of a Misspent Youth

After that, each of my mornings started with milking the cow. I still did chores for my grandparents, but I no longer had to carry the jug of milk home every night.

Beauty drank several gallons of water daily, and we needed to irrigate new plants in the garden. Baths took water. On wash day, Mama filled several tubs to clean our clothing and linens. We'd empty the well, and then we'd wait for hours until a tiny trickle replenished it.

I asked George for help. "Would you take a look at our well?"

"Be there directly." He scratched an itch on his backside.

After dropping a ladder into the hand-dug hole, George climbed down to check it out. When he surfaced, he shook his head. "Whoever dug this, he got lazy and quit diggin' when he hit bedrock."

Mama bit her lip. "Can you fix it?"

"The water vein is only inches above solid rock, and the reservoir below it is too shallow to hold much. Don't refill fast enough in summer. Need to dig it deeper."

George spit a wad of chewing tobacco into a nearby patch of weeds. "It's colder'n a banker's heart down there. I'll need some dynamite, too."

The next day, George showed up with the dynamite and tools. We drew the water to empty the well and climbed to the bottom. The big farmer's two hundred pound bulk took most of the room. The four-foot diameter hole had narrowed as the digger encountered more rock. George handed me a star drill to hold and a pair of leather gloves for protection while he smacked the handheld tool with a short-handled sledgehammer.

"Rotate that drill a quarter turn every time I hit it." He paused for a moment before swinging the sledge again.

I wanted to pull back in fear each time the hammer fell. If George missed the drill, I'd get whacked with the sixteen-pound sledge. The steel drill rang as the heavy mallet kept up a rapid rhythm without missing its target.

When we had four holes drilled in the rock, I climbed to the surface while George set a quarter stick of dynamite in each one before he climbed out and we backed away. I sure hoped we were far enough. He used a battery to ignite the dynamite, and the explosion sounded like the war had found us. The noise was deafening. Smoke and black rocks belched from the opening and rained down on the yard.

After we shored up the A-frame supporting the pulley, we tied a sturdy tub to the chain and lowered it to the bottom. Grandpa's ugly black horse was hooked to the other end. George filled the tub with fractured rock and water before climbing out to avoid being hit if anything fell. I drove the horse to lift the load to the surface. Then we hauled out the remaining water and rock chips from the bottom.

"I'm getting tired. It's your turn." George handed the big sledge to me after we climbed down the ladder again.

Soaking wet and chilled inside the cold pit, I took up the hammer and gave the drill a couple of timid taps as the big farmer held it in his hand.

"You got to hit it," George roared.

"I'm afraid I'll hit you."

Tales of a Misspent Youth

He shook a gloved finger in my face. "Just keep your eyes on the drill and swing that hammer like you're mad at it."

The light was bad, and slimy walls didn't leave much room to move, but I finally mastered my fear and concentrated on hitting the drill. George didn't even lose any fingers. More dynamite shattered the bedrock. The next day, the bottom extended three feet deeper, and we called it good. The well never ran short of water again.

Mama paid George for the dynamite and his work. Then we ate corn bread and garden vegetables for the next month. We couldn't afford to buy anything.

A few weeks later, a nearby farmer had a huge field of peas ready to harvest. He offered work to all the neighbors, and we needed money. My mother and I plus two younger brothers joined a few farm wives and one older man who showed up to pick peas the next morning.

The farmer gave us our instructions. "Got sacks for each of you. Job pays a dollar a day for men, six bits for women, and fifty cents for a kid. Pick the rows clean, and dump your sacks in the wagon when they're filled."

Since I was almost as tall as Mama, he paid me the women's rate. Ron and Kevin sat on a quilt at the end of the rows. They'd been deemed too small to work.

"I want to pick peas, too," they cried in unison.

Mama answered in her soft and convincing voice. "You two need to stay here and guard our water jug."

The boys agreed, looking proud of their important role.

The rows stretched for hundreds of yards, the sun baked us, weeds grew thick, and an occasional snake lay waiting for a mouse attracted by the peas. The dried pods had sharp ends that pierced my fingers, and cockle burrs scratched me as they snagged my sweat-soaked clothes.

We finished the field four days later, and Mama brought home ten dollars. Later, I found a week's work peeling fence posts to bring home another three dollars.

Mama considered adding a few doodads to the old house, but its unfinished state made any decorations look hopeless.

She put our earnings to better use by ordering a load of eighth-inch-thick, four by eight-foot sheets of white cardboard. We used them for wallboard to finish the interior walls in the house. I even managed to complete the ceilings for our living room and half the kitchen before we ran out of material. We didn't try to cover the seams, but it looked better than bare studs in the wall. It also cut down on the amount of wind whistling through the cracks.

My chest swelled when we completed the job. My younger brothers looked equally happy. We'd all worked on the project, and the house looked like someone lived there after we finished.

Mama's smile revealed her pride when she brought out a pitcher of fresh lemonade. "This old house is beginning to feel like home."

A Pig for Sarah

The dog days of August wagged on, and there wasn't much to do on the farm except tend crops. School would open soon, and I'd start my freshman year. Plans to become a sports star and meet girls kept my head bouncing around the clouds.

Charlie Warren lived on the farm next door. He was a good guy, a year younger than me. We didn't get to spend a lot of time together because working occupied most of our days. We'd throw his baseball or football around when we got the chance. Charlie's sister, Sarah, would be a senior. She was turn-your-head gorgeous.

She had also failed to notice I existed.

Charlie's dad raised row crops like corn, beans, peanuts, and sorghum. Cattle and pigs were the biggest cash producers on the farm. The kids all worked in the fields, so we had limited opportunities to see each other.

The two of us leaned against his hog lot fence one Sunday, tossing a ball for his black and tan squirrel dog to chase. That didn't last long. Frisky wasn't all that frisky in the muggy heat. We'd found the shade of a big oak tree and stretched over the wire, trying to catch a glimpse of Mr. Warren's new litter of pigs. They snuggled inside their cozy hut, not yet ready to explore the outside world.

The ripe smell of hogs hung in the still air. I wrinkled my nose, but Charlie acted like he was oblivious to the foul odor.

"How many pigs in that hut?" I asked.

"Haven't got a count. Sow keeps them hid. Maybe a dozen."

"She sure is big." I studied the huge hog rooting in the torn-up ground.

"She'll top five hundred pounds." Charlie snapped a twig off a low-hanging limb and chewed it.

Sarah stepped outside the house and strolled over to join us. Her slim body was athletic and tanned from working in the sun. Playful brown eyes and a friendly smile interested me, but her big breasts in the tied-up cotton shirt dominated my attention.

"Would you boys catch a cute little pig for me?" She awarded us a come hither look. "I'd like to play with it."

"No way," Charlie said. "That old sow would eat anybody that touched one of her babies."

He flashed his sister a superior look and stalked off toward the house, leaving me alone with the young goddess.

She brushed a strand of long brown hair from her eyes and turned to me. "Charlie's just scared. I bet *you* could catch a little pig for me."

My heart raced, and I felt the warmth as my face turned red. When she moved closer with a pretty pout, I almost choked.

She gazed into my eyes with a look that said I reminded her of Superman. "You're not a scaredy-cat like Charlie."

Tales of a Misspent Youth

I had to clear my throat before I was able to speak. "Charlie says that old sow will protect her litter."

"But they're so cuddly." She stretched her long arms and wiggled. "I just want to play with one. I'll only keep it a little while."

After casting a quick glance at the huge sow rooting peacefully on the hillside, I tried to stall. "I don't know how to get it away from its mother."

Her voice sounded soft and sweet as she leaned closer. "You're a smart boy. I know you could catch a little pig for me. Please?"

This contest was a complete mismatch. No way could I resist that pleading voice and the promise of undying gratitude in her liquid brown eyes. Just being alone with her had me almost paralyzed. I surely couldn't admit I was scared. But snatching a baby pig from the sow didn't sound like a good idea. Unable to refuse, I scratched my head, trying to think of a way to catch one and escape without being eaten. Several ideas that would surely get me caught by the angry beast passed through my befuddled brain.

Finally, a flash of brilliance struck, and I grinned. "It just might work."

Sarah followed as I took several ears of corn from the barn and approached the lot. Frisky raised his head and lifted one skeptical eyebrow when I climbed the fence to creep downhill toward the brooder hut. The dog resumed his nap, and Sarah watched from outside of the fence.

My legs wanted to collapse, and the huge animal's stink increased close-up. It failed to completely mask the smell of my own sweat. The sow quit rooting when she spotted the grain and followed me to the far corner of the lot like a friendly puppy. I almost panicked when she pushed against me, trying to grab an ear of corn.

Mama hog didn't appear to listen when I promised I didn't intend to harm her brood. The sound of her powerful teeth crushing the rock-hard grain chilled me. Why had I listened to Sarah, anyway? Leaving the ears of corn on the ground, I tiptoed back to the little hut where the baby pigs nestled in their bed of straw.

One more glance back assured me the sow was occupied with devouring her unexpected treat. My knees shook. Sweat dripped from my brow as I approached the little hut. This wasn't a good idea, but there was no way I could tell Sarah I'd chickened out.

Finally, I closed my eyes to snatch a baby pig and dash up the hill toward the fence. The little porker's cry of panic shattered the summer day. He squirmed and squealed, kicking to free himself. The sow's snorted answer loomed ominous, and I almost tripped when she lunged toward me. This was definitely a bad idea.

After another dozen shaky steps, I glanced over my shoulder. The quarter-ton monster had already covered almost half the distance. Her pounding hooves and grunts of rage assaulted my ears and doubled my fear. Caught in the open with the baby pig, I'd surely be eaten before I could reach safety. How had I let a dumb girl talk me into this?

Desperate now, I sprinted. The beast had closed the distance, and the thunder of sharp hooves racing across the rocky ground surrounded me like an approaching tornado. I heard her long tusks snapping as her mouth opened and closed. Her bad breath clouded the air, making it impossible for me to breathe. If I survived, I'd never listen to a girl again.

Praying for a miracle, I dropped the squealing pig.

Fortunately, the sow stopped to check on her frightened offspring, and I reached the fence. Fright propelled me upward, and I cleared the wire with a running leap—my all-time best high jump by a wide margin.

Sarah's eyes and mouth opened wide as I flew over the top wire to crash land at her feet.

"Are you okay?"

I lay in the dirt, knowing my face had turned chalky white. Sweat covered me. My hands trembled, and my legs wobbled when I tried to stand. Dazed, I settled for resting on my hands and knees. The assortment of scratches and bruises from my hard landing began to make themselves known. Frisky rose to stretch and yawn before strolling over to sniff me with an air of disdain.

Gasping for breath, I gazed up at Sarah. "If you still want to play with one of those cute little pigs, you can climb in there and catch it yourself."

Business Lessons

Our monthly welfare check didn't stretch far enough to cover repairs we made to our house and farm. Mama had even gone into debt to the peddler who came by each week. Other than the Sears and Roebuck catalogue, the box bed on his truck held the only merchandise we had access to buy. She was making slow progress trying to repay the money we owed.

Knowing how badly we needed to catch up on our accounts, I scrambled to find ways to earn money. The market for fence posts lagged, so nobody would hire me to strip off the bark. After searching the ads in hand-me-down copies of farm magazines and the local newspaper, I rushed to Mama with a moneymaking idea.

"I know what we can do." I showed her the circled advertisement. "We can raise angora rabbits. Their wool sells for a fortune."

She studied the paper. "How much will it cost to build a proper hutch? Rabbits need lots of care."

"I can build it from sawmill slabs. They're free. I'll only need to buy wire mesh."

Mama pursed her lips. "The ad doesn't give the price for breeding stock. I've heard they're expensive. They're also prone to get sick."

I put on my most optimistic face. "The price for angora wool is so high we could make the money back with just a few pounds."

Tales of a Misspent Youth

She raised an eyebrow. "How many rabbits will you need to shear for a pound of wool, and where will you sell it?"

I wasn't able to calculate how many, but thinking about how much the wool weighed convinced me I'd have to shear a lot of rabbits. Maybe I needed to find a better way to make money.

Next, I scoured the papers for more opportunities and approached Mama with some exciting possibilities. "I could sell Wolverine Salve, or cutlery, or subscriptions to *Grit* Magazine."

She reminded me that very few people lived nearby and asked me to consider the potential market. "How much money would you make if half the people within walking distance bought something from you?"

Doing the math convinced me this wasn't a good way to get rich. But the thought of selling produce from our garden had me calculating profits again. At planting time, I added dozens of rows of vegetables we could sell to grocery stores. We borrowed a horse and plow from Grandpa for a few days. However, most of the work was done by hand, using a hoe.

Mama agreed with my plan. "Now that could make us some money."

Planting and weeding the crops took a lot of extra work, but my brothers pitched in to help. The weather cooperated, and the yield was more than I'd imagined. Saturday was the big shopping day in town, and we needed to bring our vegetables to the grocers before six a.m.

Our neighbor, George Atkins, agreed to haul our load of produce. Stores bought their fresh vegetables shortly after daylight so shelves would be filled when the doors opened. We planned to be there early.

On Thursday and Friday, we braved the weeds, heat and insects. The whole family picked green beans, peas, carrots, squash, onions, and cucumbers until we saw them in our sleep. My younger brothers complained of the heat and being tired, but Mama encouraged them to keep working. On Friday night, we loaded George's old Model A truck with boxes of produce. The night sky showed no hint of dawn when Mama and I joined him for the hour-long trip to Hot Springs. George fired up the little four-banger engine, and the truck clattered along the bumpy road toward town.

Halfway there, steam billowed from the engine compartment. George steered the truck off the road and opened the cover. "Radiator hose blew. We don't have a spare. Nearest garage is ten miles away, and it's not open yet."

"We can't afford to be late," Mama said.

George ran bony fingers through his mop of gray hair. "Do the best we can."

He found friction tape and baling wire hidden in his junk box. I walked a mile to the nearest creek for water to fill the radiator while he tried to repair the break.

When George started the truck, water trickled from the damaged hose. Five minutes later, we stopped at the creek for a refill. We added water three more times on the way to town. The smell of hot grease and oil wafted from the engine as we waited for it to cool before we finally arrived at a grocery store.

"Sorry, we already bought everything we need," the grocer told Mama.

Tales of a Misspent Youth

George added water to the radiator, and we drove to the next store. Same response. After our fourth stop, it became obvious we had a problem.

Mama's brow furrowed. "We'll sell everything door to door."

George drove us to a residential neighborhood and walked to a garage to buy a hose. Mama and I loaded paper bags and started down opposite sides of the street, hawking our vegetables.

At the first house, I carried several small sacks and offered my wares for half the grocery store prices.

The lady smirked. "Give you a quarter for a bag each of peas and carrots."

After a brief exchange, we settled on thirty cents.

The temperature rose with the sun, and we worried the produce would spoil. The load diminished slowly. George replaced the hose and helped us peddle produce.

As midday approached, we filled sacks to overflowing for the same price. I shook my head in disbelief when some people still wanted to bargain. We sold out by two o'clock and dejected we started home. Mama paid George for the trip, and we had eleven dollars and change to show for my grand plan. After subtracting the cost of seed, I calculated we'd earned about three cents an hour for our labor.

During the fall, Mama decided to raise chickens so we could become more self-sufficient. The pullets would lay eggs, and we would eat the roosters. The peddler would take any surplus eggs in trade.

Mama ordered a hundred baby chicks, and I built a brooder house on the hillside away from our dwelling. Young pines springing up around our fields supplied timber for a miniature log cabin with a dirt floor. We had roofing material left over from repairing the house so I could make it weather tight.

Baby chicks needed warmth. With no electricity, a tunnel dug deep under the little cabin solved my problem. I left two feet of packed clay above the pit. A small fire of hickory wood warmed the ground beneath the floor.

It worked great. The cute little chicks filled the cabin on their bed of straw and grew rapidly. I was already counting my eggs.

Since we needed a separate building for laying hens, my brothers and I cut pine posts for the basic framing. We used scrap lumber from Grandpa's barn and cheap sweet gum boards from a nearby sawmill to cover the crude chicken house. Leftover roofing completed the building.

On our first cold night, I built a larger fire to make sure the baby chicks stayed warm. Repeated heating had dried the clay, and it cracked. During the night, a tongue of flame passed through the narrow opening to ignite the straw. The next morning, I woke to find the brooder house had been reduced to an ugly square of black ashes. For weeks, I suffered from nightmares about the fate of my helpless little flock.

Undeterred, Mama bought another hundred chicks. She kept them in a tub in the corner of the kitchen until they were old enough to survive in the unheated chicken house. As they matured, the young roosters provided frequent meals of fried chicken, and the pullets grew up to become laying hens. We had eggs for breakfast and saved a few dollars by trading our surplus to the peddler.

When our sow delivered a litter of pigs, I watched over them and kept track of expenses. They stayed healthy and grew. Grandpa helped me neuter the males and the little porkers soon reached market size. We kept one pig to slaughter and sold the rest of the litter. After subtracting our expenses, I tallied fifteen dollars profit, plus enough meat to see us through the winter.

Business was booming. About time something worked out.

During the fall, a severe-looking lady from the welfare department arrived to monitor how we were spending our monthly check. Her dark skirt and jacket were cut to look like a man's suit. She carried a clipboard to take notes on everything she saw. Our new roof and the finished interior in the house caught her attention. She looked in the pantry, which was filling rapidly with jars of canned fruits and vegetables.

The lady smoothed the bun that collected her gray-streaked hair against the back of her head. She sniffed at Mama. "Looks like you don't plan to go hungry."

When I accompanied her around the yard, she remarked on the fresh cut grass and new steps. She made note of the milk cow in its shelter and the fat pig in its pen.

When she inspected the chicken house, she asked, "Do you sell the eggs?"

"Only what we don't eat," I said.

A few minutes later, the lady returned to the house and finished writing. She looked down her nose when she turned to Mama. "Everything looks clean and orderly. You seem to be quite prosperous. It appears the county is being too generous with you."

Then the mean old woman cut our meager welfare payments.

"Grandpa's 'Possum" originally appeared in My Dad is my Hero, *published in 2009.*

Grandpa's 'Possum

A marauding opossum searching for a midnight snack woke my grandparents from a sound sleep. The chickens squawked in protest when the thief entered their coop. Grandpa dragged his seventy-three-year-old body out of bed and grabbed his rifle. Wearing only his nightshirt and hastily donned shoes, he ran to investigate the racket. Chickens and their eggs provided needed food for the family, and he wasn't likely to share with varmints.

Grandma lay awake, awaiting his return. She heard a rifle shot, and moments later, a second one. Frightened, she scrambled from bed and ran to check on him. Grandpa was too thrifty with bullets to shoot twice. Something had to be wrong.

She found the dead 'possum, and then she spotted Grandpa lying on the cold, March earth, stricken by a massive heart attack.

His last words were, "Love you, Lizzie."

**

Tales of a Misspent Youth

Six years earlier, during the summer of 1944, my father left my mother and five little boys on Grandpa's doorstep. Then he disappeared from our lives.

The old couple had already raised ten children. Eight survived to become adults. Four sons served as military officers during the big war, and all their children had grown up and left home. Grandpa took us in without question and provided food and shelter necessary for our survival. I still recall the smell of dried fruit and fresh-baked bread mingled with wood smoke in Grandma's kitchen.

As the oldest child, it became my lot to help Grandpa with chores on the eighty-acre farm where he raised crops and ran cattle on open range. He was a thoughtful—sometimes impatient—teacher. I received a lesson on coping with a demanding world soon after we arrived.

A pasture gate had decayed, and Grandpa replaced the rotted boards with irregular sawmill slabs. We spent a morning patching the old gate. The work became tedious under the hot sun, and I soon convinced myself this was not the right way to run a farm.

"Grandpa," I said. "Why don't we buy a new gate and spend our time doing something to make money?"

The old man chuckled. "This farm doesn't run on income. It runs on lack of outgo."

He taught me how to handle his team of horses and plow a straight furrow. I learned to use the horse-drawn mower, buck rake, and the big turning plow before I turned eleven. His watchful eye monitored my use of an axe and saw to fell trees that supplied our firewood.

During the fall, we harvested a surplus of potatoes. A neighbor wanted to buy several bushels and offered a low price. He and Grandpa dickered for a half hour before reaching an agreement. The neighbor paid for the potatoes, and Grandpa promised to deliver them the next day. I filled each basket level with its top.

Grandpa checked my work. "You need to add more potatoes to round off the baskets."

"They hold a bushel when they're level full," I said. "He didn't pay for extra potatoes."

Grandpa lifted his hat to wipe sweat from his brow. "It's okay to bargain for a good price when you sell, but make sure to give a little extra when you deliver."

During the summer, we allowed our cattle to forage on open range. When a few of them failed to come home for salt, Grandpa saddled the horses, and the two of us went looking for them. Heat, flies, saw briars, second-growth brush, and rain took turns plaguing us while we rode the rough country. We searched for cows until we located the last one and knew they were safe. I learned about perseverance.

When his father died, Grandpa had been eleven years old. He took a job in a saw mill to support the family and promptly got caught in the big saw, losing parts of three fingers on his left hand. Later, he taught himself to play the violin using the stumps to press the strings.

He completed only two years of formal schooling, but he educated himself, passed state examinations, and taught school for several years. He served as a justice of the peace and was elected to the county council. With no access to a high school where he lived, he rented a house in a town twenty-five miles away. Living there and working as a carpenter during the school term while he

Tales of a Misspent Youth

tended his farm on weekends gave his children the opportunity for a better education.

He possessed considerable skill as a practical veterinarian for his farm animals and even patched up people on occasion when doctors weren't handy. Since we lived twenty-five miles from the nearest doctor and used horses for transportation, they were never handy. When I dislocated a shoulder pretending to be a circus acrobat, he popped it back in place and put me in a sling for three days. A week later, it was good as new.

His evil-tempered black horse carried him to church each Sunday. Nobody else could get along with the animal. He'd leave the ugly brute tied to an oak tree in the corner of the parking lot, and other members of the congregation would park their old Fords and Chevys some distance away.

Grandpa always arrived early enough to build a fire and make sure the church was clean. He taught adult bible class and served as the stand-in preacher about three times each month. As song leader, he taught me to read shape notes and sing during the service. When I managed to get hold of an old guitar, he encouraged me to play it.

He showed me how to shoot his rifle and took me squirrel hunting after I turned twelve. On my first successful hunt, I used more bullets than the number of squirrels I brought home. He taught me to aim before pulling the trigger.

He was a stern and unyielding taskmaster, but he allowed his sense of humor to show on occasion. He grinned when he admitted that, "Hindsight is better than foresight by a darn sight."

We failed to agree on some things. He didn't approve of dancing, and when I started high school, I slipped off to attend a neighborhood dance on Saturday night. I'm pretty sure he knew, but he didn't say anything. I felt guilty anyway.

Baseball was even more contentious. The community sponsored an amateur baseball team, and I wanted to play center field.

Grandpa had other priorities. "They play games on the Lord's Day. Your time would be better spent keeping the Sabbath."

I lost that argument and stayed home most Sundays. He got the blame when I failed to make the St. Louis Cardinals roster—or the high school team.

He was nearing seventy years old and suffered from heart problems when he took us in, but I never heard him complain that we were a burden. I missed growing up without a father, but Grandpa was always there for me. I haven't forgotten the example he set or the lessons he taught.

**

Seventy years have flown by since Grandpa took me under his wing and showed me how he lived his faith.

I'm blessed with a loving wife, stories to write, songs to sing, and grandkids that need an occasional nudge in the right direction. When my time comes, I hope I'm able to "kill my 'possum" before I leave this earth.

"Love you, Grandpa."

Coping with High School

After I turned thirteen, I left my country school to catch the bus for a twenty-five mile ride across the mountains to a consolidated high school. The place was huge. My class alone had forty kids enrolled. That equaled the entire student population at Alamo where the kids lived on small hill-country farms. Half the students in high school lived in town.

My homemade shirts looked out of place, and my shoes often smelled of the barnyard I tramped through before daylight to milk our cows. Plus, I saw a lot of things differently than town kids. Coping with high school meant I needed to adapt.

I'd done well at Alamo, and my teacher had promoted me two grades. I could have entered as a freshman, but I wasn't sure I was ready for algebra. I enrolled in eighth grade. Good choice. Eighth grade math was enough of a challenge without tackling algebra. Besides, the older kids already called me a runt.

My interest picked up when I joined the band. Music had always been something I liked. The bandmaster had me play the sousaphone. It was the logical choice since I couldn't afford to buy an instrument. The school provided the big horn. I also needed to prove my skinny frame was strong enough to carry it. When we marched on windy days, it proved to be a challenge.

I took up boxing for fun, and I showed some talent. The school provided two pairs of sixteen-ounce gloves for our physical education class, and nobody used a mouthpiece. I didn't even know they existed.

After the third time I failed to play my horn because I showed up at band class with a split lip, the bandmaster gave me a choice. "Quit boxing, or quit band."

It wasn't an easy decision, but I let boxing go for a while.

The best thing that happened to me that year was Elsie Simmons. She was my homeroom teacher, thin with gray hair, a kind smile, and complete dedication to her students. The class could tell she didn't feel well every day, but she never complained. She also made Army drill sergeants appear tame compared with how she ruled the roost. There was no nonsense in her classroom. We were there to learn.

She taught our spelling class and explained her expectations on the first day. "I grade in six-week periods, forty new words each week. To get an A, you make no mistakes for the period. Each word missed during the six weeks drops your grade one letter."

Surely she didn't really mean it. At the end of our first period, almost half the class received an F. I'd missed two words, *bureau* and *chauffeur,* and received a C for my efforts. She got my attention. I didn't miss any words for the rest of the year. I learned how to study. Spelling *bureau* and *chauffeur* in my sleep is no problem now.

I tried to stay out of trouble most of the time, but a kid needs to have a little fun. My last class before lunch was on the second floor, overlooking the entrance to the lunchroom. When the bell ending the period rang, kids made a mad dash out of the room, down the stairs, out the main entrance, and around the building to the cafeteria. On days when I had seventeen cents to buy lunch, they found me waiting first in line.

"How'd you get here so quick?" a classmate asked after I consistently beat everyone to the cafeteria entrance.

I hid a smile. "I run fast."

When it happened again, several of them asked how I got there first.

"I sit by the classroom door at the main entrance," a basketball player said. "Nobody can run that fast."

I shrugged and let them wonder.

A few days later, I had seventeen cents again and decided to eat lunch. When the bell rang, the students rushed for the door. When the teacher turned her back to erase the blackboard, I slipped out the open window and scooted down the fire escape. From there, it was only a dozen steps to the lunchroom entrance.

Unfortunately, someone saw me flying down the fire escape, and the word spread. I was forced to quit using that route before someone told a teacher.

As Christmas approached, my spirits rose, anticipating the holiday and a break from classes. My teachers seemed to become more like jailers.

Mrs. Simmons called me to her desk one afternoon. "Would you take this folder up to Mr. Steele's office? He's waiting for it."

"Yes, ma'am." I'd have a few minutes free of the classroom.

After leaving the folder with the superintendent's secretary, I stopped at the head of the stairs to gaze through the big window at freedom in the outside world. Turning back toward the steps, I marveled at the sight of the polished wood banister adorning the stairwell. It followed the turn in a graceful sweep as it descended to the first floor. We were forbidden to slide down it, but nobody was watching.

Why not? I looked both ways and sat on the banister. Raising my feet, I started to slide.

Navigating the turn was the hard part. It took perfect balance to avoid flying off the shiny rail to land on the stairs. Successfully through the turn, I felt the wind on my face as I picked up speed on the last straight-of-way.

A classroom door at the foot of the stairs flew open, and my math teacher, Mrs. Jones, backed into the hall carrying an armload of books.

This wasn't good.

I pushed off the banister to land on the stairs going much too fast to gain my footing. Mrs. Jones started to turn toward me as my feet clattered on the steps, trying to slow my descent and avoid falling. No such luck. I hit her head-on at full speed. She shrieked, and books flew in all directions to land with a noisy crash. I wound up sprawled on the floor amid the scattered books, trying to figure out what happened.

Mrs. Jones stood about five-ten and weighed a solid one hundred sixty pounds. She appeared to be angry. I knew I was in trouble when she grabbed the front of my shirt with one hand and lifted me to my feet to shove me against the wall. Her face appeared inches from mine. Her eyes threatened to bore holes through me as she pinned me flat against the hard tile, my feet barely touching the floor.

"What were you trying to do?"

No good answer came to mind. I felt faint. "I tried to stop."

"Don't you know the rule against sliding down the banister?"

"Yes, ma'am."

"If you ever try this again, I'll send you straight to Mr. Steele for a whipping you won't soon forget."

"Yes, ma'am."

Her voice hardened as she wagged a finger in my face. "When he's finished, you'll clean my classroom for the rest of the year."

"Yes, ma'am."

She released her grip so I could breathe again. "Now, help me collect these books."

Five months later, I finally gathered my nerve to slide down the banister again. Mrs. Jones was absent that day.

Shortly after our summer vacation began, Mrs. Simmons died of the cancer that afflicted her throughout the school year. She'd fought the disease while she taught our class to achieve their potential. Her dedication to her students and her profession left its mark on all of us. Her influence stayed with me. In addition to teaching me to spell, she taught me to ignore distractions and focus on whatever task I undertook.

She also taught me about caring for others.

The Road to Becoming a Sports Star

Starting my freshman year, I plotted to realize my dream of becoming a sports star. Grandpa hadn't let me play baseball on Sundays, but surely he wouldn't object to a school team.

During our first physical education class, a group of boys gathered in the gym for basketball practice. The coach let us shoot baskets while he wandered around looking for tall kids who showed potential. At five feet nothing and one hundred five pounds soaking wet, it's possible I evaded his notice.

Whoever caught a rebound would dribble to the edge of the circle and shoot. Never having played before, I didn't pick up on all the unwritten rules. After grabbing a loose ball, I dribbled out to prepare for a long set shot. Holding it for several seconds, I considered whether to use one hand or two to make the basket.

"Shoot the ball, dummy," a taller boy yelled.

I gave him a dirty look and resumed concentrating on making the shot. While I thought about it, a long arm reached out and slapped the ball away.

The tall boy smirked. "Stand and hold the ball, ya lose it."

Instinct took over. I dived for his ankles and dropped him on his rear. Moving quickly, I straddled his waist and snatched the ball. Looking down at his surprised face, I answered. "Try to take it from me again, and you'll get your butt kicked."

When I rose to take my time shooting the ball, nobody interfered.

Unfortunately, the coach had witnessed the incident. His long finger pointed me out, and he waved me to a far corner of the gym. "This practice is for boys who want to play basketball, not fight. Get out of my gym and stay out."

Banished, I wound up outside to join a group of boys playing sandlot football during the period. They played tackle without pads, and rules on roughing the passer or kicker weren't enforced. Our playing field was far from ideal. The sides were not parallel, and a row of steel posts bordering a driveway marked one sideline. The other was a sharp drop-off into a deep drainage ditch. A concrete sidewalk marked the goal line at the narrow end of the field.

Too small to play the line, I became a running back on offense and cornerback on defense. They only let a runt like me carry the ball because I was quick. I didn't know I was too little, and I wasn't smart enough to fall down when somebody hit me.

Our biggest and toughest lineman voiced his opinion. "Little, but gritty."

Since the gym was reserved for basketball practice, resentment among the football players ran high. Pride drove us to challenge the basketball team to a lunchtime football game. Believing they were superior athletes made them foolish enough to accept the challenge. The game was a spirited contest, and we scored on our first two possessions. The basketball players were bigger and quicker, but they weren't used to being hit. This game wasn't for sissies.

With time running out, one of the basketball stars ran a sweep and tried to race past my corner. Wasn't going to happen. As I forced him against the sideline, he sprinted with his head up, trying to blow past me. I met him low, with my shoulder below his belt and my arms around his knees. The ball continued forward, and he flew backward. My legs kept churning as I drove his backside into the rocks. We recovered the fumble.

A few sore spots from the collision bothered me, but I didn't admit it. Our all-state point guard missed the next three basketball games.

The coach gave me the benefit of his opinion. "You almost crippled one of our best players. I'd like to string you up on the nearest tree."

I survived the coach's wrath and soon learned to punt the football. Most kids didn't want the job because you'd get smacked after you kicked the ball and still had your right foot higher than your head. Rocks on the field left frequent prints on my backside when tacklers crashed down on top of me after the ball was gone.

A few weeks later, a horse stepped on the big toe of my right foot and broke it. Limping back to football practice, I didn't want to give up my place as a punter. Kicking with my left foot solved that problem. I lost a little bit of directional control, but my distance actually improved.

The football crowd asked the school to sponsor a team. Several townspeople even supported the idea. The answer from the school board came back no. It would cost too much, and we didn't have enough players to compete with the larger schools.

Tales of a Misspent Youth

One Saturday night, a board member passed a tavern in Hot Springs, where drinking was allowed. He spotted our basketball coach leaving a bar with a few noisy friends. We lived in a dry county, and most people took the liquor laws seriously. Others stretched them to the point of buying alcohol in a neighboring wet county or buying moonshine whiskey locally. In either case, they didn't drink it in public. Everyone agreed that frequenting a bar and drinking by a teacher was a bad influence on students.

The board met shortly after daybreak on the following Monday. The coach was fired, his desk emptied, and he was off the premises before kids showed up for classes.

Based on my previous experience with the coach, I failed to grieve.

In the spring, baseball practice started. Even if I made the team, I wouldn't be able to play in games because they were scheduled after school let out. Having no other way to get home, I had to catch the bus. The trip covered twenty-five miles of mountain roads. Our team needed another catcher during practice, so I jumped at the chance to play scrimmage games. After putting on the tools of ignorance, I crouched behind the plate—ready to command my territory.

The catcher is usually a big, tough guy who can block the plate on a play at home. I could catch the ball and throw out runners trying to steal. I didn't have any trouble getting in front of the base, but most runners could bounce me out of their path. Nevertheless, I managed to tag them and hold onto the ball more times than not.

My skills improved, and I considered staying overnight with a classmate so I'd be available to get in a game. Then, during batting practice, I lined a pitch over our short left field fence and into the woods. The pitcher delivered another strike. I connected, and the ball followed the first one into the trees.

The new coach walked up to me and held out his hand for my bat.

"What's wrong?" I asked.

He grinned as he handed it back to me. "Just wanted to see if you corked it."

Evidently, he didn't think of me as a power hitter.

That's when it began to soak into my thick skull that my chance of being signed by the St. Louis Cardinals was slipping away.

I resumed boxing without telling the bandmaster and managed to avoid another split lip. Several of us worked out during gym class, and a school carnival gave me an opportunity for fame. A boxing exhibition was scheduled as the feature attraction. Since I'd been doing well, the coach paired me with an opponent who outweighed me by at least fifteen pounds.

The stage at the end of the gym served as our ring. Jutting walls offered sharp corners, but the coach instructed us to stay away from them. Nobody anticipated that someone might be hurt.

The event attracted a large crowd. Competition was energetic, and the bouts drew loud applause. Spectators showed approval by throwing coins onto the stage. We threw the money in a box to be distributed evenly among the participants.

When my bout started, I discovered my opponent had better skills than I'd anticipated. Most of my time seemed to be occupied with defense. Since he was being so aggressive, it seemed certain he'd eventually tire. Then I'd have an opportunity to take charge and win the fight.

Careless for an instant, I gave him an opening. He tagged me with a hard right hand that spun me around, driving my head into a corner of the protruding wall.

Rebounding, I decided that defense wasn't going to earn me a win. I charged after him with fists flying. Solid punches to the body and head stopped him in his tracks.

His determined expression evaporated, and a look of surprise crossed his face. He stopped punching and retreated. Encouraged, I chased after him. He backpedaled and raised a glove. Then my vision seemed to cloud. How could I connect if he didn't stand and fight?

The referee grabbed me and stopped the bout. "Technical knockout."

Blood from a gash in my forehead streamed down my face and into my eyes. Spectators threw coins on the stage as they led me off to patch up my head. Yet another opportunity for stardom slipped down the tubes.

After the matches were concluded, the coach divided the coins. Each share added up to seventy cents. Hard to get rich that way.

My class picture announced my lack of success as a boxer. It wouldn't let anyone forget the embarrassing incident. The unsightly gash on my forehead was recorded for posterity in the school yearbook.

That picture advertised my lack of success. After some somber thought, I decided to forget about becoming a sports star.

Eventually, I came to terms with my inability to achieve fame on any of the high school teams. I wasn't eligible to buy a school letter jacket, and the wages for my boxing performance had been less than outstanding.

Maybe things would work out better if I started hitting the books.

A Loose Sole

At sixteen years old, Dan was a happy soul, a year older than me. We were in the same grade because he'd failed a year somewhere along the way. We'd been friends since the fifth grade. Poor as proverbial church mice, his family did little to encourage him to succeed in the classroom.

Back at our grade school, Dan had been the strongest and most daring kid there. Lacking playground equipment, we staged acorn wars for sport. Dan dominated the game. He could throw the tough green nuts harder and more accurately than anybody in the group. He wouldn't stop charging no matter how many kids threw at him or how many times he'd been hit.

At the high school, he was slow to make friends or mix with the town kids. "They're all stuck up."

Dan missed classes occasionally to work at home, and he had problems keeping up with schoolwork. He'd catch on with a little help, but he didn't show a lot of interest. Most of the time, he ignored the town kids. Some of them snubbed him because he wore work clothes to school and made no effort to cultivate the popular crowd.

I was often slow to come to his defense when other students made fun of him. Knowing it wasn't right, my reluctance to oppose the group kept me silent. Publicly siding with him might jeopardize my standing.

Dan made his mark on the playing field. He could throw a football fifty yards and hit his target on the fly.

His passing ruled the game. Gradually, he began to make friends with the football crowd. His classroom work showed faint signs of improvement.

"You need to study more," I'd tell him.

He'd just shrug and change the subject.

I had to respect Dan. I'd worked with him in the post woods. He did twice as much work as I could do on a good day. It wasn't just size and strength that made the difference. He planned ahead and attacked the job with urgency, never seeming to tire.

"How do you work so fast?" I asked him.

He shrugged. "Just peel each post faster than the last one."

Dan had problems in Mrs. Simmons's spelling class. She made a special effort to encourage him, but he fell behind. I offered to go over the list of words with him on the way home. That helped a little, but he frequently found an excuse to avoid it.

Some kids made fun of his clothes and his country ways, but he didn't seem to let it bother him. "They're just acting like town kids always act."

As winter approached, I noticed he skipped eyelets when he laced his brogans. The broken strings had become too short. They must have been the only shoes he owned because I never saw him wear anything else. Stitching on one of the shoes came loose, leaving open space between the sole and uppers. The gap grew longer each day, and his old gray socks showed through the crack.

A few kids remarked, but Dan just shrugged. I kept silent because defending him might embarrass me. Besides, I didn't have anything constructive to say.

Tales of a Misspent Youth

Dan finished tearing the stitches playing football one day. The sole tore loose completely from the shoe. Attached only at the heel, it flapped when he walked, threatening to trip him with each step.

Several kids laughed at him, and comments flew.

"Gets breezy, don't it."

"About time for a new pair, don't you think?"

"Going to get your feet wet when you step in a fresh cow pie."

The taunts got worse. Even some of the girls giggled at the way Dan threw his foot forward to prevent tripping on the loose sole as he walked.

Their comments overlooked an obvious fact. The worn-out brogan represented a serious problem for Dan. His parents didn't have money to buy another pair.

On the bus going home, his shoulders sagged, and he sat staring out the window. My lame attempts to cheer him up went unnoticed. His loose sole flapped down the aisle as he got off at home without speaking to anyone.

When the bus stopped to pick Dan up the next morning, he smiled and spoke to other kids as he marched to the back, looking for an empty seat. He sat down across the aisle from me and stuck out his foot.

"Take a look at this."

Baling wire wound around the toe of his shoe, holding the loose sole in place. The split was almost closed by several strands of tightly wrapped wire. The shoe made a clinking sound when he walked on the steel floor.

I nodded approval. "Looks like it works."

"More ways than one to skin a cat."

Kids at school noticed, too. His shoe became a joke. Some of the chatter didn't sound sympathetic. A lot of their remarks were downright rude.

"Those shoes are gone. Get a new pair."

"Looks like you found 'em at the garbage dump."

"Hillbillies fix everything with baling wire."

Girls pointed and snickered. The ridicule didn't stop.

As the day wore on, Dan lost his good humor. His smile faded. His lips compressed to a thin line. Downcast eyes avoided looking directly at anyone.

It wasn't hard to see these remarks hurt Dan. He pulled back into a shell and ignored the chatter around him. I wanted to stick up for him, but I didn't know what to say. To my shame, I said nothing and let the harassment happen without coming to his defense.

On the bus ride home, Dan sat stone-faced, looking out the window.

"Your shoe looks just fine," I told him.

He continued to stare at the passing countryside and left the bus without speaking to anyone.

The next morning, Dan didn't appear at his bus stop. He didn't show up all week. His sister finally told me he'd quit school. Some kids continued to make stupid remarks about his wired-together brogans. Others laughed as they recalled the funny spectacle.

Some of the boys mimicked the way he walked, throwing their foot forward as if trying to avoid tripping on a loose sole.

I just felt miserable.

A few weeks later, someone told me Dan was gone. "He left home to go work as a logger in the big timber out west."

Tales of a Misspent Youth

**

Years later, I got news of Dan. Hard work made him successful as a lumberjack, and he'd saved his money. A struggling supply store for loggers was put up for sale, and he bought it. His dedication and management skills turned the situation around. The store prospered, and he expanded the business.

Looking back, I felt sorry for the kids who had so much fun tormenting Dan. It hurt him at the time. Evidently, it motivated him to succeed. It also motivated me to think about how I would treat other people. Second thoughts about my failure to support him helped me develop resolve to stand up for my friends.

Dan accomplished more with his life than the majority of those who thought they were superior because the soles of their shoes didn't need to be wired in place.

"Bless your soul, Dan. You showed 'em."

Skill at pool is a sure sign of a misspent youth.

That Den of Iniquity

    Our school superintendent, Mr. Steele, disapproved of Gene's Pool Hall and advised all students to steer clear of its corrupting influence. The most influential bad examples—meaning boys to emulate—could occasionally be found inside its dim interior during school hours.

    Located at the end of a row of run-down buildings next to the highway, Gene's place housed three pool tables and a cooler where patrons could buy RC Colas or Moon Pies for a nickel. The north wall housed ball racks, a row of well-maintained cues, and chalk. The place smelled of tobacco smoke, unwashed bodies, and mold from the rotting structure.

    Gene kept a few illegal punchboards behind the counter. Customers could buy a chance for a dime, and the colorful board advertised the possibility of winning a large prize. However, I didn't personally know anyone who'd won much of anything. Rumor had it Gene would sell a pint of moonshine to people he trusted.

    Eight ball was the game the high school crowd chose. A few serious players displayed their skill at the snooker table. Townspeople frequented the place in the evenings, but most of them worked during the day. Boys cutting classes at the high school provided a good share of the

Tales of a Misspent Youth

daytime customers. Gene didn't object if they slipped away from school. He was glad to get the business.

A city ordinance required customers to be at least sixteen to enter such a disgraceful establishment, but Gene usually took people's word about their age. On one of my luckier days, I conned my way into the movie theater for the child's fare of a dime. After the movie, I passed for sixteen to get in the pool hall.

My grades might have suffered if I skipped classes, but I found ways to escape from an occasional study hall to check out Gene's place. Lacking money, I did a lot more watching than pool shooting. Nevertheless, it was a great place to hang out. Lots of interesting tales were spun while games were in progress. Older guys bragged about their conquests and revealed which girls were the best bets for a good time. I learned lots of stuff they didn't teach us in class.

Teachers never showed up there. The school board would have frowned on it. Churchgoers considered the place to be a den of iniquity. That aura made it even more attractive to high school boys.

Loser pays was the usual arrangement. I couldn't afford to risk it. It was a rare occasion when I had money for a game of pool. With my limited skills, it seemed likely I'd be a frequent loser. Guys like my friend, Oliver Olson, usually won. When your opponent paid for most of your games, it didn't cost much to play.

A few of the really daring players liked to live dangerously. If they lost, they'd make a side bet. "Double or nothing on the next game."

If they continued to lose, the debt skyrocketed. If they finally won, the debt dropped to zero. One of my unskilled friends lost a game for fifteen cents and ran up a debt of six hundred ten dollars and forty cents before he finally won. He probably exceeded his ability to pay when his obligation reached five dollars.

One dreary afternoon as a cold wind moved slate gray clouds across the threatening sky, boredom and a plausible alibi freed me from study hall. After slipping out the school's back door, I raced for the pool hall to spend five cents on a soda and listen to all the lies being told. When I entered, Oliver held court, running the table with the last half dozen balls.

The young pool shark was two years older than I was. He'd failed a grade when he was younger, so he was only one class ahead. The boy was a pool-playing addict, spending his lunch money and every other cent he could finagle at Gene's place. Since he didn't seem to care about grades, the superintendent finally notified his father that Oliver spent most afternoons cutting classes to frequent the pool hall.

He glanced at the crowd of watchers. "Who wants to pay my next game?"

A tall senior answered, "You're all talk. I'll beat your butt."

Oliver racked the balls and prepared to break when the door flew open and his father walked in. I immediately sensed trouble in Oliver's future. The crowd quieted as the big farmer stomped down the aisle. His reputation as a brawler in his younger days was well known. The room went silent when he slouched to a stop in front of his obviously nervous son.

He waggled a grimy finger. "Thought you was supposed to be in school."

Oliver laid his cue on the table and stuttered before responding. "I just got here. I only missed a study hall."

"Hear you spend lots of afternoons shootin' pool instead of going to class."

Oliver's adam's apple bobbed. He failed to find an answer.

Mr. Olson picked up the cue and tapped the handle against the table. "Get your ass back to school. Now! Don't let me hear you cut class to play pool again."

"Yes, sir." Oliver grabbed his jacket and made tracks for the door.

His father replaced the cue in its rack, nodded to the silent crowd, and walked to the front to speak to Gene. "Boy don't belong in here during school hours."

Gene's face paled. He nodded without speaking and watched Mr. Olson leave. I thanked my lucky stars my mother hadn't caught me in the pool hall. Five minutes later, I was back in study hall.

Several weeks passed after Oliver was caught. I avoided Gene's place. The weather turned cold, and a rare day of bright sunshine inspired thoughts of things I'd rather do than sit in a stuffy room reviewing my algebra assignment. After making up a good excuse to skip out, I headed for the pool hall.

When I walked in, Oliver banged the four-ball into a side pocket. Two tables were occupied, and a small crowd of onlookers provided friendly heckling as they watched. Oliver looked to be well on his way to winning yet another game.

I tapped him on the shoulder as I joined the hecklers. "Thought you quit playing."

"Just going to get in a couple of games. My old man won't never find out."

His opponent drove a ball into a corner pocket and, failing to find another cripple, left the cue ball trapped against the rail behind a small cluster. "Let's see you make something out of that."

Oliver sized up his options. "You was too chicken to try a shot of your own."

The sound of the front door crashing open to bang against an inside wall stilled the sparse crowd. Mr. Olson charged through the doorway and looked the place over. His boots carried the smell of cow manure. His threadbare overalls didn't look like they'd been washed for a week or two. He tipped his wide-brimmed straw hat to Gene and ambled back toward the pool tables.

Oliver stiffened, knowing he was in trouble. Worried about what might happen next, I shrank back into a corner and tried to become invisible.

The big farmer nodded to the group. "Howdy, boys." Then he reached out to select a cue from the rack along the wall. Sighting down the stick, he mumbled, "This'll do just fine."

Oliver stood facing the table, looking scared, when Mr. Olson swung the cue with a backhand motion. The long shaft struck the boy's back with a meaty thump, driving him face down onto the surface of the table. Mr. Olson proceeded to deliver a dozen more blows to Oliver's backside and legs while the boy lay helpless, writhing in pain.

When he'd dealt the final blow, Mr. Olson replaced the cue in the rack. Then he strolled to the front of the hall and stopped where Gene stood silent behind the counter.

Mr. Olson gazed at the hall's owner without speaking for a long moment. Nodding, he used two fingers to push his hat toward the back of his head.

His voice lowered as he leaned across the counter to stare into Gene's face. "If 'n I catch the boy in here again, I'll break every cue stick in the house, and I'll use the last one on you. Understand?"

Gene's answer came quick. "I'll be sure to keep him out of the hall, Mr. Olson. He belongs in school."

The big farmer nodded. "Sure hate to have to come back again."

"Won't be necessary, sir." Gene used a small towel to wipe sweat from his brow. "I'll keep him out."

Mr. Olson waved a hand to the crowd. "Y'all have a good day, y'hear." He smiled as he stomped down the steps, leaving the door wide open.

We helped Oliver off the table and tried to tend his bruises, but he didn't have time to tarry. "I gotta get back to school."

To the best of my knowledge, Oliver never showed up at the pool hall again. He dropped out of school at the end of the term. Said he was staying home to work on his father's farm.

Most of the boys continued to play when they found the opportunity, but my mind had been improved.

I steered clear of that den of iniquity.

Buck Fever

Deer season arrived the first week in December. Getting out in the woods to hunt might be the only excitement I'd have until Christmas vacation. Nearing the end of my first semester as a sophomore, I'd have to endure the monotony of algebra class until the holiday. I needed something to liven up my routine.

Eddie came up with a brilliant idea while four of us tossed a football around during our lunch break. "Let's go deer hunting at my farm on Saturday."

It took at least two seconds for Wally and George to agree.

They didn't beat me by much. "Let's do it."

That evening, I approached Uncle Bob. "Can I use your shotgun to go deer hunting at Eddie's place?"

Uncle Bob frowned. "That can be dangerous. Guys waiting on a deer stand all day tend to get buck fever."

"I've shot lots of squirrels," I said. "I know how to be patient."

"You need more than squirrel-sized patience for deer. Hunters have been known to shoot cows or horses or even people when they're too eager to get that big buck."

"I'll be careful," I promised.

Uncle Bob loaned me the gun and a half dozen rounds of buckshot. On Friday night, Wally, George, and I showed up at Eddie's place ready for action. We stayed up late telling tall tales and making plans for a successful hunt. The season opened at dawn on Saturday morning.

Tales of a Misspent Youth

We woke early with complete confidence we'd all get a deer.

A winter storm complicated our hunt with steady rain falling all day Friday. The bottom fell out of the thermometer by Saturday morning. After a quick breakfast of eggs with home-cured ham, we gathered our guns and started for the woods in darkness to reach our stands by daybreak. As we left the house, the temperature hovered at fifteen degrees with a brisk north wind.

With Eddie leading the way, we stumbled down a narrow trail through thick woods in the half-light of an approaching dawn. My fingers and toes soon began to tingle from the cold. Within minutes, we arrived at the south fork of the Ouachita River.

"How are we supposed to get across?" I asked.

"Easy," Eddie said. "Walk the foot log."

I slipped up to the riverbank for a better look. A tall sweet gum tree had been felled across the flooded stream, barely reaching the far side. Frigid water lapped at the shaky span. Ice crusted its surface.

Wally, George, and I exchanged skeptical looks. Bark had been worn from the slick tree trunk over time. This crossing appeared to be an unwelcome invitation to a December swim. It certainly didn't resemble a bridge. The cold wind would ensure we'd be stiff and awkward as we tried to balance on the long, skinny log. Swift water rushing beneath it would cause vertigo if we looked down. The ice-slick surface was likely to drop us into the river in any case.

I wasn't eager to try my luck. "Easier said than done."

Nobody volunteered to go first.

"You guys are a bunch of wusses." Eddie thumped his chest with a clenched fist. "I'll show you how."

He approached the seventy-foot tree trunk holding his rifle out in front. With a light step, he trotted across the treacherous span without a bobble.

He turned to smirk at us from across the swollen river. "Who's next?"

Nobody volunteered.

"You wimps act more like mama's boys than deer hunters." Eddie leaned his .30 caliber rifle against a tree and trotted back to rejoin us. Taking the guns from the other two aspiring hunters, he held one in each hand. Then he carried them over the rolling water as if he were strolling down a sidewalk in town.

With no rifles to carry, the boys dropped down on hands and knees to commence crawling. They slipped a few times but managed to stay on the log and mostly dry while making slow progress over the frigid water.

Eddie stood on the far bank, clapping his hands and howling with laughter. "You look like a couple of chickens climbing on their roost."

He continued to hoot and howl, making fun of the guys until they finally arrived safely on the far shore. Then he looked back at me. "Stay there. I'll come back for your gun. You can crawl over like your buddies."

His remark sounded like a challenge, and Eddie wasn't going to laugh at me. "I'll get there without your help."

Looking down at my borrowed twelve-gauge Winchester sent a little twinge of fear through me. My uncle would skin me alive if I dropped it in the river. Stepping up on the long, shaky pole, I hesitated while I

Tales of a Misspent Youth

found my balance. Then I looked out over the rushing water. The sheet of ice covering the span under foot struck fear in my gut. Gathering daylight made it look even scarier. Crossing with the gun might not be such a bright idea, but it was too late to chicken out.

I pushed off to maintain a slow but steady pace across the treacherous span. Eyes fixed on the far bank, I resisted the temptation to look down at the fast-moving stream. The feel of my shoes slipping on the ice made my gut queasy, but I kept moving. Biting wind buffeted my fear-chilled body, and I began to lose my footing as I neared the far bank. Panicked, I tried to break into a run for the last fifteen feet. When my foot skidded, I tumbled.

My left leg hooked over the slippery log as I fell. Grabbing at the slick timber with one hand, I lifted the shotgun high with the other. When I stopped moving, I was up to my neck in the cold water, but the gun stayed high and dry. Eddie trotted out to take my weapon, and I waded out of the cold water, past the thin film of ice at the edge, and up the steep bank. Freezing wind stung my wet skin as it penetrated my clothes. I began to shake.

"Find some pine knots, guys," Eddie yelled. "We need to keep him warm."

The boys used their hunting knives to shave off strips for tinder and built a roaring fire while I shivered. My shoes, socks, jeans, shirt and wool coat were soaked. Turning round and round like a pig on a spit, I stayed as close to the leaping flames as I dared. Pine tar smoke covered me. The black cloud brought tears to my eyes, and the pungent smell made me cough, but I wasn't about to move away from the heat.

Doyle Suit

The other boys fidgeted with anticipation and finally left me to search for deer along trails the animals frequented. I hugged my fire, regretting that I was missing my chance to bring home a big buck. Water from my wet clothes evaporated slowly in the heat. I coughed nonstop as the black smoke continued to choke me. Several times I had to leave the warm fire to gather more dead limbs to keep it burning. Hours later, my clothes had dried enough for me to leave the warmth and resume the hunt.

Unfortunately, the strong odor of wood smoke had penetrated everything and guaranteed that no self-respecting deer would come within a quarter mile of me.

Chilled, I waited in my still-damp clothing beside a game trail, hoping for a deer that was too stupid to stay away. A pair of rifle shots in the distance gave hope that a few of the shy critters must exist in these frozen hills. Ending the hunt and returning to Eddie's house couldn't come quickly enough.

After supper, Eddie loaned me some trousers and a flannel shirt while his mother washed the smell of burning pitch from my clothing.

The next morning, the log was ice-free, and we all managed to cross without incident. Eddie laughed at us anyway.

"I was hoping to watch another one of you mama's boys go swimming."

I settled down to wait in a screen of brush beside a well-traveled path. The temperature hovered near freezing, and the icy wind penetrated my still-damp coat. The sun climbed a cloudless sky, but the day didn't get much warmer. My fingers and toes felt numb, but I didn't stamp my feet for fear of scaring away the eight-point buck I hoped to find.

Later, a gray squirrel scampered out on the limb of a nearby oak tree. Since I hadn't found anything else to shoot, I was tempted. Shaking my head at the little critter, I muttered, "I'm saving my ammo for that big buck."

The wind carried sounds of distant voices and a couple of gunshots as the morning advanced. Midday passed. I shivered and waited, waited and shivered, expecting a deer to wander down the path and pass by my hiding place at any moment.

Suddenly a closer gunshot broke the silence. A jolt of adrenaline charged through me. Moments later, I heard something crashing through the brush and its rapid footfalls charging down the faint trail I'd chosen to guard. Dreams of a huge buck filled my mind as I clicked the safety off and steadied my weapon, pointing it at a big cedar guarding a turn in the trail. The deer would be about forty yards away when he raced past the tree.

Leveling my gun, I aimed at the open space in front of the dense evergreen, alert and ready to shoot. The pounding grew closer, and a vision of the big buck consumed me. He'd be trying to escape danger from the dogs behind him and fail to spot me as I waited in ambush. I even thought I could smell his fear. My hands trembled as I prepared for the opportunity to shoot. Judging by the noise, the animal had to be huge.

My nerves wound tighter as the deer drew closer. "I've got you, big boy."

A vision of the buck filled my head as it cleared the cedar. My heart threatened to leap from my chest as excitement consumed me. I shifted the gun to track its pace and make sure of my shot. My finger tightened on the trigger as it raced past the evergreen, and I saw its faded brown coat and stocking cap, its rifle pointed down the trail.

Releasing the trigger in panic, I managed to shift the gun. Hot on the trail of an imagined deer, the foolish hunter flashed by without even noticing me.

I sank to the ground and set the gun aside. My hands shook, and my breath came in short gasps as I waited for my racing heart to slow. The man must have been insane to run down a deer trail during hunting season.

I'd been certain it was a deer racing down the path. How had I managed to avoid pulling the trigger? Minutes passed before I was able to control the shaking.

After removing the cartridges from the pump-action shotgun, I waited for my group to gather. The hunter's crazy action and my imagination had almost resulted in tragedy. When the other boys finally showed up, I sat sprawled on the ground, leaning against a tree, anxious to quit the hunt.

Eddie laughed. "Look, guys. He got so bored, he took a nap."

None of us shot a deer, but the tales came quick and lively as we made our way back across the log to Eddie's house. The boys all had stories of almost seeing a deer and their plans to get him next time. I didn't add much to the conversation.

I'd heard hunters tell stories about buck fever for years, but I hadn't fully understood the power of imagination. I'd seen what I wanted to see, and I sent up a prayer of thanks that the foolish hunter survived my vision.

Buck fever almost killed the man.

Margie

Mother settled me on Margie's back. "You look like a cowboy."

The spirited little red yearling colt stood head up and alert in the middle of the gravel road in front of my grandparents' home. She wore neither a bridle nor a halter. I rested on her bare back while my mother supported me with one hand and caressed the playful animal's neck with the other. Margie seemed to sense that I was fragile cargo and accepted this indignity without moving.

At the time, I'd been two years old. The gentle colt was a year younger.

Thus began my long relationship with this noble animal. She was destined to become my loyal friend through good times and bad.

Margie earned the status of family pet from birth. Intelligent and friendly, she enjoyed keeping company with Ben, my youngest uncle. She followed him around the farm, always looking for attention or an occasional treat.

Ben had been twelve when Margie was born. The colt bonded with him, and he taught her a number of tricks as they grew up together. Her best performance was to buck on command. When her rider put a hand on the point of her right hip and applied pressure, she would start jumping. It wasn't too difficult to stay in the saddle when the rider knew it was coming. This performance offered a good way to show girls he was capable and fearless by staying on this wild and skittish creature.

Eventually, Ben became an Army Air Corps pilot and world traveler. Margie grew to be nine hundred pounds of compact and powerful Morgan mare.

The horse enjoyed most of the privileges claimed by Pudgy, our family dog. However, neither of them was allowed inside the house. The dog accepted this as the natural order of things, but Margie didn't agree to this exclusion from family life quite so easily. She would step up onto the front porch and wait to be invited inside. Her best friends stayed in the house. She grazed with the herd and got along well with other horses, but she seemed to prefer the company of humans.

The farm couldn't afford to feed animals that didn't earn their keep, so Grandpa pressed Margie into service as a draft horse. Paired with an evil-tempered and lazy, old black horse named Bones, she excelled at pulling our wagons and farm equipment. If the driver wasn't alert to keep her partner moving, Margie would lean into the harness to pull Bones' share of the load.

After Papa left the family for parts unknown, Mama brought the six of us to live with my grandparents. I was ten years old. The grown-up mare was even more impressive than the colt had been. With my family torn apart, I found myself in bad need of a friend. Margie filled that role to perfection.

I sidled up to Grandpa while we fed the livestock one evening. "Could I have Margie for my horse?"

Grandpa chuckled. "Several of your uncles have already laid claim to her, but you can ride her anytime you want to."

Margie would come to me in the pasture, and I'd climb aboard her broad back to hold onto her mane while we galloped around the farm. Pudgy would usually join our romp. Since I didn't bring a saddle or bridle, I learned to guide her with pressure from my knees and by voice commands.

Margie was a spirited runner, galloping as fast as her short legs would carry her. Gentle with children, she remained docile and walked slowly when a small child was placed on her back.

One summer afternoon, I left her tied to the fence by our front gate. A two-year-old cousin saw her and decided to go for a ride. The toddler slipped through the gate to wrap her arms around Margie's hind leg, attempting to climb on the horse. I froze with fear when I glanced outside. The tiny child clung to the horse's leg, her feet on top of the mare's hoof, scrambling to climb on. Dashing to the scene in panic, I snatched the disappointed child away.

The sensitive mare had remained motionless while the little girl clung to her leg. Even with horseflies nipping at her, she had refrained from stamping her hooves or swishing her tail to chase them away.

With hands on her hips, the little girl chastened me. "I ride Margie."

Relieved the child was safe, I lifted her onto the mare's back. Margie endured the little girl's thumping heels and yells of "Gitty up" without protest as I led her around the woodlot for the short ride.

Since our family raised beef cattle on open range, I rode Margie on numerous all-day searches to keep track of the herd. Grandpa only owned one saddle, and he used it when he rode Bones to join me on our quest. I'd toss a gunnysack on Margie's back for a blanket. The sun baked us as we rode, and it was usually a steamy day.

One summer afternoon, Grandpa dismounted from Bones to walk through a thicket of bushes and briars too dense for the horses to penetrate. "Those fool cows might be hiding in the shade to avoid the heat."

The mare's sweat had soaked through the makeshift blanket, and my soggy rear end became uncomfortable. Taking advantage of the dry saddle, I climbed aboard Bones to lead the mare on a detour around the thicket. "You can rest, Margie girl. We'll meet Grandpa on the other side of this jungle."

Margie's jealousy became apparent when she picked up the pace to overtake Bones. She pulled even, then turned her head to clamp strong teeth onto my leg and remind me I was being disloyal. Fortunately, the bite didn't draw blood, but the resulting bruise reinforced her message.

I tried to explain the situation to her, but I'm not sure she understood.

One Sunday, when I was fourteen, I rode Margie on a shortcut through the hills and across abandoned farmland to visit a school friend. The two of us spent several hours playing guitars and singing country songs until I noticed a black cloud approaching from the west. After hurrying to put the guitar away, I saddled Margie.

"Storm's coming. Might as well stay until it's gone," my friend said.

"I'll beat it home." Swinging onto the saddle, I nudged the mare into a ground-eating lope across the hills through uninhabited country.

Tales of a Misspent Youth

It soon became apparent I'd miscalculated. The black cloud closed in. Thunder like cannon fire boomed. Jagged streaks of lightning crackled across the sky. A sprinkle of rain overtook us. It quickly turned into a torrent. Margie maintained a steady lope as she slogged on.

We'd just entered a long stretch of deserted fields when things got worse. Heavy hail, some of it larger than an egg, bombarded the field at a furious pace, and there was no cover to protect us. Frightened, I reined Margie to a halt and dismounted. Seeking the best shelter available, I crouched beneath the mare's chest and neck for refuge. She turned tail to the wind and sheltered me while we waited for the storm to subside.

The saddle offered her some protection, but the splat of hailstones hitting her broad back made me cringe. She didn't move as I crouched low, the heels of my shoes resting on her hooves. Her body shielded me from most of the falling ice, but an occasional hailstone hit me a glancing blow. It hurt. Margie didn't flinch as I clung to the protection she offered. Minutes later, the hail moved on, leaving the ground littered with frozen white lumps. Heavy rain continued to soak us.

Worried about the mare, I ran my hands over her back and neck to check for injuries. After I remounted, she broke into a run and maintained a steady gait until we reached home safely and only a little worse for wear. I'd think twice before trying to outrun another storm cloud.

When I turned fourteen, I learned that Margie wasn't fond of gunfire. I shot a fox from horseback, and her reaction convinced me it hadn't been a wise choice. The fox died, and it was a close call for me. It took all my skill and a generous helping of luck to hang onto the gun and keep my seat in the saddle. After this experience, it occurred to me I might not want to consider a career as a bronco rider on the rodeo circuit.

Later, I encountered a rattlesnake. Forewarned, I dismounted to ground-tie Margie. "You're not gonna like this, old girl."

When I pulled the trigger, the mare almost jumped out of her skin, but she didn't go far. Score: would-be cowboy one, rattlesnakes zero, Margie showed progress in accepting gunfire.

From the time she'd been a colt, Margie loved to run, and I often raced her against my friends' horses. She adapted quickly to the idea of running as a competition. The spunky mare usually lost the short races, but she outlasted other horses at longer distances. Knowing when to quit wasn't in her makeup.

The spirited mare always stood ready to hear my troubles. She listened patiently when I told her about problems that bothered me. She'd fix me with a serious look and what I took to be sympathy. Her ears perked up, and she nuzzled me occasionally to let me know she cared. These sessions always left me feeling better. Good thing the horse never learned to talk. Some of the things I told her didn't need to be repeated.

When the sound of shotguns in our pasture broke the calm one Saturday morning, I grabbed my rifle and jumped on Margie, riding bareback without a halter. The farm was posted with NO HUNTING signs, and I'd planted wild grasses to attract several coveys of quail.

Topping the hill at a full gallop, I spotted three trespassers walking abreast, carrying shotguns. Waving my rifle, I shouted at them. "Any of you guys know how to read?"

Three well-dressed men looked irritated. One responded, "We're just shooting quail. We always hunt around these parts."

As I guided the mare with my knees, she approached by a zigzag pattern. Margie knew the drill for herding cattle, and she applied it to herding trespassers. My rifle waved over my head. Hopefully, it looked threatening. "You saw the sign when you climbed my fence. You don't hunt here."

Margie continued to quarter as she advanced. I stayed out of shotgun range and waved the rifle to encourage the hunters to leave. All three of them started slow, but they speeded up to a fast trot before they reached the fence.

Years later, after graduating from high school, I moved away to work in the city, and another generation gained custody of the loyal mare. I had an opportunity to ride her again when she was twenty-six. This time, I carried my two-year-old son in my arms. She conducted herself like a gentle lamb as we rode slowly around the farm.

I was nearing thirty when Margie was turned out to pasture with a herd of cattle on my cousin's farm. Age had robbed her of the ability to do hard work. She would come to the fence to greet people when they stopped by to visit. I rode her one final time as she approached thirty-five. She appeared to remember an earlier time, breaking into a full gallop when I put one foot in the stirrup. After I found a seat in the saddle, it took a firm hand to rein her in.

Fields of tall grass kept the loyal mare fat and happy until she died a natural death at age thirty-seven.

To this day, I mourn the passing of my special friend. The sight of horses always takes me back to fond memories of my faithful companion.

A Better Job

After I finished my junior year of high school without two pennies to jingle in my pocket, something had to give. As a senior, I'd need a lot more money, and my brothers were getting older. Their needs ate up more of the family budget. I'd made a few dollars selling vegetables and pigs. Temporary work on neighboring farms and the post woods had helped, but I needed a better job to pay for my final year of high school.

Mama had worked in Hot Springs before she married. The town was only twenty-five miles away, and that appeared to be my best chance to find a job. Uncle Frank and Aunt Marie lived there and offered me room and board for four dollars a week and my help with family chores.

The opportunity was too good to pass up. My brothers would pitch in to do my share of farm work during the summer.

When I arrived, Aunt Marie tacked on a couple of conditions with my rent. "You'll have to help Uncle Frank tend our garden. We grow most of our food."

Chores had always been a normal part of life. "I can do that."

"What about laundry? I'll wash and iron your clothes because you need to look neat on a job. In return, you can iron my kids' clothes. They're not so particular."

That didn't sound like a lot of trouble, and four dollars was a lot cheaper rent than I'd find elsewhere. "You'll have to show me how."

I was sixteen when I arrived at Frank and Marie's house the first weekend of summer vacation. An early bus took me downtown to the employment office on Monday. I walked in to find a lone clerk presiding over the empty room. His downcast eyes didn't bother to acknowledge my entrance.

I took a deep breath and stepped up to the counter. "I'm looking for a job."

He gave me a bored glance without bothering to stir from his chair. "There ain't no jobs in Hot Springs."

Not discouraged, I hit the bricks to look for work along Central Avenue at Bathhouse Row. Then I worked my way south, stopping at each place of business. "I'm looking for a job."

Nobody wanted to hire me, so I kept walking. When I reached the intersection with Ouachita Avenue, I turned west. The sun had already started its downward arc. I didn't even have a nibble yet. The repeated answers of no began to weigh on me.

After another hour of asking and a dozen more rejections, I entered Stuart's #10, a small chain grocery store. Still hopeful, I approached the cashier. "Could I speak to the manager?"

Moments later, a lean middle-aged man with a crew cut burst out of a back room and charged up the aisle to meet me. "I'm Joe Hardin. What can I do for you?"

I introduced myself and got to the point. "Looking for work."

Tales of a Misspent Youth

He folded his arms and gave me a critical onceover. "What do you know about the grocery business?"

"Nothing," I said. "But I grew up on a farm. I know how to work."

His head snapped up, and he grinned. "You're hired."

Mr. Hardin gave me a quick tour of the store and explained he owned the franchise. I needed to report early the next morning, and I'd earn fifteen dollars a week for working six ten-hour days. My duties would consist of stocking shelves, delivering groceries on a bicycle, and cleaning the store.

The pay wasn't good, but I didn't have much choice. If I turned the job down, I might not find a better one. Working at the store wouldn't leave me time to look for another job.

I soon learned that everyone working there made a lot more money than I did. When Mr. Hardin had a spare moment, I approached him. "I'm learning how to do the work. Don't you think I deserve more money?"

He pursed his lips and gave me another critical look. "I can raise your pay to eighteen dollars, but you'll have to come in a half hour earlier and learn how to set up the produce displays."

I needed the money, so I didn't hesitate. "Fair enough."

Setting up the fruit and vegetable counters wasn't as easy as it looked. Mr. Hardin wanted it done his way. "Cull out spoiled produce. Tear off wilted leaves. Make sure you sprinkle the fruits and vegetables to keep them crisp."

He taught me to make attractive arrangements and explained that I had to complete the job before the store opened. Produce must look clean and fresh and arranged in a certain order. Damaged goods would be destroyed.

I caught on quick and did the job without supervision after a few days. My only bad experience was releasing an imprisoned bumblebee when I opened a crate of lettuce. The vengeful creature didn't seem to appreciate his time in captivity, and I had a couple of tender spots on my arm and neck for a few days after he vented his displeasure.

My long hours ruled out much of a social life. By 6:00 a.m., I'd be up getting ready for work. On days we tended the garden, we'd already worked for more than an hour before the rooster crowed. Chores added to the length of my workdays. Ironing the kids' clothes consumed another hour or two each week. At least I could rest on Sundays. I managed to watch a few movies at the Roxy Theater, and Uncle Frank took me fishing on Lake Catherine. During the week, I didn't have time for recreation.

Hot Springs was filled with interesting characters, and many of them showed up at the store. Apartments lined the streets along the approaches to West Mountain adjacent to the store. They housed tourists from every corner of the country. Our cashier was a snippy, overweight woman who tried to dress sexy. She was always looking for ways to get someone else to do her work. She didn't seem to like me and used some crude and colorful language to express her opinion. Her chin lifted, and she looked down her nose when I approached. I avoided her as much as possible.

Some of the salesmen who delivered merchandise spun a variety of tall tales and kidded me about being a naïve country kid lost in the big city.

Tales of a Misspent Youth

Our sign painter was my favorite character. Gus was a homeless wino who would work for the price of a bottle of muscatel. He made whitewash illustrations and price lists on our front windows. Gray-haired and rail-thin, the old man looked shabby and not always clean, but he was a talented artist who did our windows several times each week. Always polite, he spoke in a soft voice and proved to be a good storyteller and my friend. Mr. Hardin frequently refused to pay him in cash. Instead, he invited Gus into his backroom office where he kept a hotplate for himself. Gus would receive a decent meal. It might have been the only good food he had during the week.

Soon after I took over the produce display, the talkative guy who delivered our fresh vegetables quizzed me. "How much is old tightwad Joe paying you?"

I swelled with pride when I told him. "Eighteen dollars a week."

He laughed. "Don't you know you're worth a lot more than that?"

A couple of days later, I approached Mr. Hardin. "I'm learning about the grocery business. Don't you think I deserve more money?"

He frowned. "I just gave you a raise. I'll think about it."

I turned seventeen that week, and Mr. Hardin hadn't said anything more. On Friday, I asked again. "What did you decide about my raise?'

"I could use help behind the meat counter. I'd have to teach you how to cut the meat, and you'd need to come in earlier to help me set up the counter. I'll raise your pay to twenty-two dollars."

I agreed, and my first assignment was to empty all the refrigerated cases, crawl inside, and scrub them down. The smells of rotted meat and ammonia fumes competed to see which would kill me first, but I survived. Mr. Hardin taught me how to carve slices of ham and pork chops, cheese, lunchmeat, and chicken. Scraps went into the grinder to mix with hamburger. Fresh red meat was mixed with the scraps to make the display look better. Learning to cut steaks came later. Mr. Hardin soon found other things to do and left me alone in the meat department.

Within a few days, our regular customers began referring to me as the butcher, and I took pride in trying to live up to their expectations. A few boneheaded mistakes slowed my progress, but I eventually learned to manage the counter with occasional help from Mr. Hardin.

When salesmen delivered sides of beef and pork, I'd talk to them and pick up tips on how to process the big carcasses. They showed me how to break down the large pieces of meat into chunks we could sell to customers. I learned to use the meat cleaver, sharp knives, and grinder without losing any fingers. Before long, I was doing most of the work in the meat department.

Eventually, a salesman asked, "How much is that cheapskate paying you?"

When I told him, he laughed. "Looks like he saw you comin'. A butcher should make double what he's payin' you."

After I cornered Mr. Hardin once more and pointed out my new skills, he agreed to pay me twenty-five dollars a week.

Tales of a Misspent Youth

Most of my salary went into savings, but paying for lunches and room and board took a good chunk of it. Bus fare cost twenty cents each day. A ticket cost me fifty cents when I stayed in town to watch a minor league baseball game. If the game finished late, the last bus had made its run and a three-mile walk took me home. Every dog along the route yapped and threatened to eat me as I trudged down the deserted streets. The skill displayed by athletes on the local team convinced me I didn't have much chance of playing for the Cardinals.

My savings account wasn't growing fast enough to get me through my senior year, so once again I waylaid Mr. Hardin. "I need to make more money."

He threw up his hands as he laughed. "Tell you what. We're surrounded by apartments. Lots of tourists come here for the bathhouses and the lakes, and there are no other stores close by. We might develop a good milk and bread trade if we opened on Sunday. Think you could work another day?"

"Yes, sir."

"You'd have to run the store by yourself."

"I can do that."

He grinned as he shook his head again. "Time will tell whether or not we have enough business to justify staying open. You'll be making thirty-five dollars."

My workweek was already seventy-five hours long, and keeping the store open on Sunday added another twelve.

The extra money would boost my savings. Sunday trade started slow, but it grew each week. I stayed busy and managed to handle the job without help. Work dominated my life. What the heck. I didn't have a social life anyway.

As the end of summer neared, Mr. Hardin made me an offer. "I could use part-time help during the winter. You could make some money and finish high school here in Hot Springs."

"Thanks, but I want to graduate with my class."

A few days later, Mr. Hardin called me back to his office with another request. "The wife and I haven't had any time off for the past year. We'd like to visit our son in Oklahoma City. Think you could manage the store for three days while we take a short vacation?"

"Sure." I felt about a foot taller.

When they prepared to leave, he gave me the keys. "Use your own judgment in handling problems that come up, but don't let vendors sell you anything. You can sign for purchases to restock the shelves, but don't buy any new merchandise."

"Yes, sir."

"One more thing. Don't cash any checks. No exceptions."

"Yes, sir."

When I opened the doors the next morning, the jitters attacked me. The other clerks acted frosty when I cruised the aisles to verify that everything was clean and displayed properly. Richard and Calvin were both older than I was, and Calvin was supporting a wife. Each of them made a better hourly wage than I did. They appeared to resent my being left in charge. I couldn't change their minds, and I couldn't afford to spend time worrying about it.

Tales of a Misspent Youth

Our forty-year-old cashier flashed me an evil glance when I passed the register. "Joe must've been out of his mind, leaving a dumb kid in charge of the store."

I retreated to the meat department and took care of my normal work. A couple of quiet walks through the aisles reassured me everything was running smoothly. When salesmen arrived, I bought what we needed to replenish the shelves. Greeting our regular customers and helping people find things came naturally.

Shortly after lunch, the cashier called me to the front. Mr. Hardin's friend, Mike, waited by the cash register. Both hands stuffed in his pockets, he fidgeted and bit his lip.

"Hi, Mike. What can I do for you?"

"The bank refused to cash this for me. Joe always cashes my checks."

"I'm sorry. He told me not to accept checks."

"He always takes mine."

"He told me no exceptions."

Mike grumbled under his breath as he stomped out of the store, but he returned just before closing time. "I'm really in a tight spot. Nobody wants to cash this check, and I need the money now."

"I'm sorry. Mr. Hardin told me absolutely not to do it."

Mike's shoulders sagged, and he muttered to himself as he left.

Three days passed quickly. The store was busy, without any major emergencies. The cashier eventually calmed down, but she still didn't treat me like I was a real human being. Nevertheless, I breathed a sigh of relief as I made one last inspection of the store and locked up after the third day.

When I arrived the next morning, Mr. Hardin and Mike waited for me by the cash register. Mr. Hardin said, "You should have cashed Mike's check. He was in a jam and needed the money. I already did it this morning."

Mike scowled at me. He stood with his arms crossed, eyes appearing to pin me against the wall.

I looked at Mr. Hardin. "You told me no checks."

"Yeah, but Mike's different. I always cash checks for him."

"I did what you told me."

Mike lifted his eyes to the ceiling and stalked out the door.

Mr. Hardin grunted as he turned away. He wandered around the store, strolling down each aisle, verifying that everything was in place before returning to the meat counter. "Everything looks good."

I wasn't sure whether or not I was in the doghouse, but I took the comment as a positive sign.

At the end of the week, I said goodbye to everyone and looked forward to going home and starting my final year of high school.

Mr. Hardin shook my hand. "I'm thinking about taking over the meat department in a large supermarket across town. It has terrible management, and is losing money. If you'd like to manage it next spring, I'd pay you fifty dollars a week. You'd have six months to get it shaped up. Show a profit, and you'll have a raise. If it is still losing money, I'll fire you."

"I'll think about it."

Tales of a Misspent Youth

After a few days to consider his offer, I made up my mind. *Sure hope I can find a better job than this when I graduate.*

The Big Bang

Activities kept me busy during my imprisonment in high school. Not having transportation to play varsity sports, I concentrated on sandlot football and became a one hundred twenty-pound catcher for the baseball team's practice squad. Playing tuba in the band and maintaining good grades saved me from getting into serious trouble for my frequent transgressions. I'd been an officer in the Future Farmers of America and even served a term as class president, but being an enthusiastic thespian became my favorite activity.

In our senior class play, I took the role of a fearless Texas sheriff who won the sweet young bank clerk and nailed the bad guy. In the climactic scene, the villain robbed the bank and escaped with the money, leaving our heroine tied to a chair.

The script called for the sheriff to catch the villain and defeat him in an offstage shootout. After a gunshot, the sheriff would appear onstage, smoke trickling from his shotgun's barrel, to rescue the fair maiden. Uncle Bob loaned me his pump-action Winchester to use as a prop. Our cast didn't even consider using a toy weapon. What could be more realistic than an actual shotgun?

Practice was fun. I even tried chasing the girls without much luck. They weren't that easy to catch and didn't seem to be overly impressed with my charms. However, we all remained friends and learned our lines as the date for our performance approached.

Tales of a Misspent Youth

During rehearsals, we had a problem with sound effects. Nothing we tried resembled a gunshot. We even made blank cartridges by removing the powder and shot, leaving only the primer. When I fired the blank, the resulting pop was too feeble to be heard past the front row.

"A cap gun with wet powder makes more noise," the bad guy said.

I scratched my head. "We need something a lot louder."

We tried smacking pieces of wood together. That made a lot of noise, but it didn't sound like a gunshot. We all searched, but no one managed to find a left over firecracker.

I brought the problem to our play director's attention. "We can't find a realistic sound effect for a gunshot."

"Don't worry about it," she said. "The audience will understand. It's just a high school play. Whatever you come up with will work just fine."

Just fine wasn't good enough for me. I needed something that made people think it was a gunshot, and the director's answer seemed to have left room for me to be creative. The male members of the cast got their heads together to brainstorm the problem.

The stage stood at one end of the gymnasium. For the play, chairs would fill the floor. One of the boys pointed out the large oak tree, twenty feet from our dressing room window. It gave him an idea. We discussed it at length, and everyone agreed we'd found the best possible solution.

On Friday night, the gym was crammed full for our performance. Even the bleachers were filled. The play proceeded without a hitch. Nobody forgot their lines, and the entire cast sparkled. As the final scene approached, I opened a back stage window facing the big tree. Its broad trunk looked huge from the window. It would easily contain the shot pattern of a live round from close range. I'd need to aim carefully because another school building stood behind the oak. After loading the borrowed cartridge in my Winchester, I took a deep breath and waited for my cue.

As the end of act three approached, the villain exited the stage with his sack of money and grinned. "Wake 'em up."

A quick look verified that no one was outside. I stepped back from the open window so the shot would be heard better and fired a live round directly into the tree trunk.

The noise that a twelve-gauge cartridge makes when fired inside the cavernous gymnasium defied belief. When I squeezed the trigger, it sounded like a bomb had exploded, reverberating into every corner of the open building. My ears rang from the violent indoor detonation. After I hesitated for a long moment to recover from the concussion, I stumbled onstage carrying the sack of loot, smoke curling from the barrel of my trusty weapon.

The heroine—tied in her chair—appeared to be terrified. The director occupied a seat front row center, her face ashen, mouth and eyes wide open. The audience looked on in shocked silence. The entire gymnasium was still.

I untied the heroine, and the two of us recited our closing lines. By the time the cast ran onstage to take our bows, the crowd had recovered sufficiently to provide a scattering of subdued applause. Not being sure how my "simulated" gunshot had been received, I made a quick bow and bolted from the stage.

An outdoor gunshot wouldn't have disturbed most of those present, but an indoor explosion that resembled cannon fire in the gym may have frightened a few of our less hardy patrons.

Nobody asked me how we accomplished the sound effect.

Apparently, nobody wanted to know.

"Twenty Dollars" was originally published by The Spring Hill Review, *July 2005.*

Twenty Dollars

My senior year of high school started in the fall of 1951. The biggest immediate problem facing boys my age was the possibility of being drafted and sent to fight the war in Korea. I had another year or two before the draft threatened to change my life. The Army didn't pay much, and I needed to make money to pay for college after I graduated.

Hard times still held a firm grip on the mountains, and many of my friends dropped out of school to work on family farms. My mother did much of the hard labor at ours so I'd be able to attend school. I'm not sure I appreciated it properly at the time, but making an effort to succeed was the least I could do.

At school, I sang in the chorus and garnered all-state honors in band. Love of music stuck with me despite the annoying fact that my talent was barely mediocre. Performing in school plays was fun, but my proudest accomplishment was being a Beta Club (honor society) member all four years.

Trouble continued to follow me, but good grades and participation in school activities shielded me from consequences for most of my shenanigans. Our vocational agriculture instructor let me go with a reprimand after catching me pitching pennies during class time despite his previous instructions to knock it off. My math teacher failed to follow up on her threat to kill me after I slid down the forbidden banister to flatten her at the foot of the stairs. Another disaster was avoided when the principal intervened to save me from the basketball coach when I put a hard tackle on his all-state guard during a sandlot football game. The battered young athlete suffered significant bruises that sidelined him for the next three weeks.

Savings from my summer job paid most of my expenses as a senior. However, after buying school clothes, my class ring, a few lunches, and other necessities for the family, the money evaporated.

The Beta Club made plans to attend the state convention in Little Rock. They would spend two nights in a hotel, attend meetings and workshops, and finish with a dinner dance. Since my school entered a candidate for state president, our sponsor requested that the entire club attend the convention to support her. Having already spent my savings, I told the sponsor I couldn't make the trip.

She proved to be a resourceful woman and didn't give up easily. A few days later, she had a solution to my problem. "A businessman in town wants to support the Beta Club. He's agreed to pay your expenses. You can make the trip with us."

Surprised, I mumbled a quick response. "Let me think about it."

Such a tempting offer was hard to refuse. My friends would all be there, and our sponsor wanted full participation. I wanted to go, but accepting the gift didn't square with the self-reliance I'd been taught at home.

Allowing a stranger to pay my way for an activity which wasn't vital to my education made me uncomfortable. My family managed to survive on a tiny income, but we didn't ask for gifts from strangers.

The decision wasn't easy, but it would be wrong to spend money I hadn't worked for. After struggling with the problem overnight, I gave the sponsor my answer the next morning. "I can't accept the gift, but if you'll tell me who offered it, I'll ask him to loan me the money."

She sent me to see the owner of the local hardware store.

During lunch break, I walked into town to find him hard at work. After a moment's hesitation, I approached the merchant. "I'd like to attend the Beta Club Convention, but I don't have money for the trip. Twenty dollars should cover my expenses if you'd loan it to me."

He opened his wallet and handed me two ten-dollar bills. "Are you sure that's enough to cover everything you'll need?"

"Yes, sir," I answered. "Thank you. I'll repay you when I graduate and get a job."

Our club attended the convention and had a grand time, staying at a downtown hotel—my first taste of this kind of luxury. Being careful how I spent the money allowed me to get by with twenty dollars. Little Rock was the largest city I'd ever visited, and we all took in the sights. The tall buildings and crowds of people impressed me. My chapter took a leadership role, and our candidate was elected Beta Club State President.

After the first day of business, I rushed to try out the hotel pool and its ten-foot diving board—taller than I'd ever attempted. After posing for a moment at the end of the high board, I gathered my nerve to dive. Springing off the end, I jackknifed to start my downward plunge. As I launched myself, a yellow, two-piece bathing suit filled by a gorgeous blonde caught my eye. My head entered automatic tracking mode and turned to gawk at her as I hit the water. The impact wrenched my neck. My body veered right and surfaced quickly. My neck hurt for the next week.

During one of the next day's meetings, I recognized the blonde in the yellow bathing suit. She was even prettier than I remembered. That's when I let my mouth overturn my better judgment. I introduced myself and made a request. "Will you save me a dance tonight?"

She awarded me a smile. "I'm Carla. I'd be happy to save you a dance."

That evening, Carla showed up at the ball wearing a dress that appeared to cost more money than I'd seen all year. Turned out to perfection and graceful as a fawn, she danced like she'd had a lifetime of lessons. Boys flocked around her.

Thoroughly cowed, I avoided the young princess, trying to hide in the crowd. It didn't work. She found me and forced me to claim my dance.

"You promised." She tossed her blond curls and held my gaze.

Finding no graceful way to avoid what I'd requested, I ignored my sprained neck and led her to the floor.

When we danced, Carla displayed diplomacy as well as grace. She tolerated my lack of skill and maintained a smile as I plodded through a Glenn Miller classic using the box step without variations. Happy to survive without stepping on her toes, I thanked her and fled the scene, never to see her again.

After graduation, I found a series of temporary jobs as store clerk, construction laborer, carpenter, and mechanic's helper. It took me almost a month to accumulate twenty dollars to repay my debt. I bought a money order and mailed it with a note of thanks to the generous merchant who had volunteered to pay for my trip.

During more than four decades in the business world, I made numerous choices involving large sums of money. Still, one of the better financial choices I ever made was my decision to borrow and repay twenty dollars.

Wheels of My Own

A huge smile covered my face as I walked off the stage after graduating from my small town high school. Even saying goodbye to friends who would scatter couldn't dampen my enthusiasm. School had been a long grind, but I stood ready to conquer the world. A good-paying job during the summer and college in the fall would be next. A scholarship to play in the band would help me afford tuition. Nothing would stop me.

One detail nagged at my self-esteem. My family hadn't owned an automobile since Papa left us. I'd never admitted to my friends that I didn't even know how to drive. Getting wheels of my own became my second priority, right behind going to college.

Hot Springs had yielded me a job the previous summer. I returned to try again.

An auto supply house hired me as a tire salesman. The job paid almost a dollar an hour. The manager started me in the shop, learning to change tires for the big trucks hauling logs from the mountain ridges surrounding the town. I did well at the labor involved, but nobody taught me to offer assistance to customers and make sales.

I didn't sell many tires.

At the end of two weeks, the boss called me into his office. His gruff voice delivered a blunt message. "I just hired an experienced salesman. I'll have to let you go."

Being fired left me devastated. All the good summer jobs were taken. It would be a scramble to find work of any kind. A series of menial one-or two-day stints allowed me to pay rent and survive, but I wasn't able to save for college.

I finally found work selling men's clothing in a department store during their summer sale. It didn't pay well, but it promised to last six weeks. I was glad to get it. Selling men's clothing came easy. My short-lived job at the auto supply store had taught me one valuable lesson. Don't wait for someone to tell you what to do. If I presented a friendly and helpful attitude, people would respond.

A slender girl with striking brown eyes and dark hair caught my attention shortly after I started work. Cathy worked in the women's department, and I made a point of finding a way to meet her.

"Hi there."

She smiled. "You must be the new guy in men's wear."

We chatted for a few minutes, and I was hooked. "Would you like to stop for a Coke after work?"

She cocked her head and pursed her lips like she was thinking about it. Then she nodded. "Sure. I'd like that."

It didn't take long to figure out I had a problem. Cathy was nineteen, two years older than I was, and surely more sophisticated. I wanted to ask her for a date, but I lacked a car to take her places. I couldn't think of any way to spare money to buy one.

A few days later, she solved my problem by letting me know she didn't mind driving so we could do something together. I treated her to a hamburger dinner, and she drove us to the top of West Mountain where we parked to watch the city lights. Our friendship developed quickly. I'd have been in a happy fog if I hadn't been so self-conscious about not owning a car. I never once hinted I hadn't learned how to drive.

We left work one evening to drive across town for ice cream, and she found her car parked in tight, front and rear. Barely a foot of space was left between bumpers. I slipped into the passenger seat to watch as she attempted to escape. The car pointed downhill, and she had difficulty with the stick shift on the steep grade. As she depressed the clutch, her car crept forward, bumping the vehicle in front. The other cars had left her almost no room to maneuver. She shifted into reverse and turned the wheel sharply. When she accelerated to gain a few more inches of room, the front wheel jumped the curb. Her right front fender smacked a telephone pole.

Cathy speared me with an angry look and threw her hands up in frustration. "Would you move this stupid car for me?"

"Sure." Unable to admit I couldn't drive, I faked it and slipped behind the wheel.

I rode the clutch and brake to inch forward and backward in the restricted space. The transmission protested with loud grinding noises when I failed to coordinate the gearshift and clutch, but I eventually gained enough room to escape.

After a few anxious moments, I reached Central Avenue and drove us across town during rush-hour traffic. The streets were filled with summer tourists poking along sightseeing and with impatient locals speeding to get home. My first driving lesson ended without adding more scratches to her car. When we arrived at Walgreens, I parked and rushed to open the door for her, limp with relief that good luck had saved me.

Cathy didn't comment on the ride across town, but she took the wheel when we left the soda fountain.

Befuddled by the charming girl, my priorities evolved. I needed a car to assume my manly role and date Cathy in style. Not being able to pick her up made me feel like a second-class citizen. Nothing appeared to be more important than impressing the girl.

My Uncle Frank worked as a mechanic at the local Chevrolet dealership. He found me a clean-looking 1936 Ford sedan on their lot. It had a V-8 engine, milled heads, glass-pack mufflers, and it had been lowered all around like a hot rod.

I had to have that car.

After Frank talked to the manager, they allowed me drive it away for a fifty-dollar down payment. Being a minor, I signed an illegal note to pay the balance in three monthly installments of twenty-five dollars each. My savings weren't nearly sufficient to pay for college anyway, but I had wheels. A parent's signature was required for my driver's license, and Mama wasn't available. I solved that problem by driving without a license for three weeks until I turned eighteen.

Cathy appeared to be impressed when I picked her up in my sixteen-year-old car. We ate hamburgers and drove to the top of West Mountain. I was in love.

Shortly before quitting time the next day, Cathy approached me in tears. "Don't go to your car after work. My boyfriend, George, found out about us. He's waiting for you outside."

Her boyfriend? That was the first I'd heard about a boyfriend. It felt like a brick had been dropped in the pit of my stomach.

"I can take care of myself."

She shook her head. "You don't understand. George is twenty-five. He's a big, tough weightlifter with a terrible temper. He means to hurt you."

"George may get more than he bargained for." I sounded braver than I felt.

Cathy pleaded, but I refused to listen. She was still crying when she returned to the women's department. An hour later, I left work and headed for my car.

The Ford waited on a quiet side street near the store. My eyes searched all the other vehicles as I made a cautious approach to my parking spot.

A burly man with a crew cut sat behind the wheel of an old Plymouth sedan parked across the street from my older Ford. As I drew closer, he loomed ominous with an ugly expression on his face. He spotted me in his rearview mirror, but he didn't appear to be certain I was the competition he intended to destroy.

After swallowing my fear, I approached the Plymouth from the rear. "Your name George?"

His unshaven face darkened. "You been goin' out with Cathy?"

"Yeah."

"Stay away from her, or I'll break your neck."

I moved behind the driver's door so it wouldn't hit me if he shoved it open. If I planned to get out of this in one piece, I couldn't let him get on his feet. I'd have to hit him hard when the door opened. "I'll stay away when Cathy asks me to go."

He must have figured out my plan because he stayed in his seat. "Ain't goin' to tell you but once."

"I heard you the first time." I stepped back when he started the car and peeled rubber as he drove away. He didn't bother to look at me again.

The next morning at work, I found Cathy arranging a rack of dresses. "How about going to a movie with me tonight? *Sailor Beware* is playing at the Roxy."

She started to cry again. "I can't see you anymore. George and I plan to get married in the fall."

Speechless, I retreated with a heavy heart. However, it wasn't all bad news. At least I wouldn't get beat up by George.

Three weeks later, I turned eighteen and passed my driver's test. The sale ended, and my job ended with it. I went back home to find work as a carpenter's helper in a nearby town, building a fairgrounds pavilion. The foreman started me carrying two-inch x twelve-inch oak timbers and nailing them in place as floor joists. Then I built pens for cattle and hogs. The job lasted two weeks. The first car payment took a big chunk out of my savings.

When I got home after losing that job, our elderly neighbors, Billy and Mae Miles, asked me to drive them to a funeral on Sunday afternoon. I agreed and filled the tank with gasoline on the way to the cemetery. It felt disrespectful to call them Billy and Mae, but that's how they wanted to be addressed.

After the service, we started home with Billy sitting up front and Mae in the back seat. When I approached the turnoff from the blacktop highway, I noticed a Continental Trailways bus top the hill a quarter mile behind me moving fast. I gave a hand signal for a right turn and slowed for deep ruts in the dirt road as we entered. The car proceeded at a crawl as I tried to minimize the bumps.

When I glanced in the mirror, all I saw was the bus. The driver hit the brakes, and the big tires tried to grip the asphalt and skidded. The little Ford had nosed into the narrow lane with the back bumper still at the edge of the pavement when the bus hit behind my car's rear wheels. It sounded like dynamite. The world started to spin.

The impact took off about two feet of the rear end of my car like it had been cut with a knife. The back bumper bowed out about a foot, and the front end of the car shot upward. The fuel tank split open, spraying the full tank of gasoline onto the pavement and gravel shoulder. The car spun like a top down the edge of the highway. Sparks flew as the damaged bumper dug deep gashes in the asphalt and gravel. I felt myself being tossed around the interior of the car, collecting bruises. The Ford came to rest on its side in the ditch about thirty yards from the intersection.

I lay in the wreckage momentarily stunned. When I tried to move, all my limbs responded. "Are you all right, Billy?"

He let out a low groan from where he was pinned beneath me in the wreckage. "Think so."

I tried to look back and saw only mangled sheet metal and a tumble of broken seats.

"Mae. Are you all right?"

She didn't respond.

I climbed out an open window and helped Billy to exit. He looked shaky.

"Mae. Are you hurt?"

Still no response.

Reaching inside, I pulled seat cushions out of the wreck to search for Mae. She lay doubled over at the bottom of the pile, unconscious. The afternoon sun beat down on us, and the smell of gasoline filled the air. The back end of the car had been demolished, and Mae appeared to be badly hurt. I crouched over the open window, afraid to touch her, watching raw gasoline trickle down the ditch from the split tank.

An automobile braked to a stop beside the wreck, and a lady ran toward us. "Is anyone inside?"

"She's hurt." I pointed to the mangled interior.

The lady pushed me aside. "We have to get her out of there."

I protested. "We might hurt her worse if we move her."

"I'm a nurse. We can't leave her there in this heat. She'll suffocate. The gasoline could catch fire."

I trembled in fear as the two of us lifted the unconscious Mae out of the mangled vehicle and carried her to the shaded porch of a nearby farmhouse. Nobody was home. The nurse stayed with me as we waited almost a half hour for an ambulance and the highway patrol to arrive.

The ambulance took Billy and Mae to the hospital. I refused to go. The patrolman examined the wreckage, and then he asked me several questions. Next, he questioned the bus driver and some of the passengers. I watched him measure the distance from the point of impact to the parked bus. Skid marks showed it hadn't steered to avoid the collision.

Tales of a Misspent Youth

The driver of a stopped car approached the patrolman. "The bus passed me down the road a ways. He was doin' at least eighty-five miles an hour."

While the investigation continued, I took stock of my condition. My right knee hurt, and other bruises became apparent. Small cuts on my chin and forehead were bleeding but not serious. I discovered I'd been walking around with a huge rip in the seat of my trousers. A borrowed safety pin relieved my embarrassment.

When the patrolman returned, he put his notebook away. He glanced at the wreckage and turned back to me. "You're free to go. I've placed the bus driver under arrest. He was replacing a stalled bus, two hours behind schedule, and he was obviously speeding. The bus isn't even licensed to operate in this state."

"What about Mr. and Mrs. Miles?" I asked.

He straightened and wiped sweat from his brow. "Mrs. Miles should survive. Continental Trailways will have insurance. Mr. Miles should get a lawyer and make sure they collect for the damage they've suffered. The company should pay for your car as well."

The next day, Uncle Bob loaned me his truck, and I drove Mama to visit Mae in the hospital. Her right arm was broken in several places, and she suffered a concussion, plus a half dozen broken ribs. Insurance company lawyers had already visited her. While she was under sedation, Mae signed a waiver of liability in exchange for the company agreeing to pay her hospital bills and awarding her $1,500 in cash. She recovered eventually but was unable to resume the farm labor they depended on to live.

I'd wait six months before the insurance paid for my car.

My whole body hurt the next morning. It took several days until I was able to move normally. A hard look at what my new wheels had done for me was depressing. Billy and Mae never blamed me, but I felt guilty about the accident. The girlfriend who inspired me to buy the car married an ugly muscle man who looked like a loser. My money was gone and the car demolished. College was out of the question. With no car to drive, I still had two more payments to make and no job to earn the money.

My situation didn't look promising.

It felt like my graduation had happened only yesterday. I'd made some big plans, but the naive optimism had disappeared. My expectations for a bright future dimmed considerably.

Something positive needed to happen soon.

Intrusion of the Real World

I'd turned eighteen with no car, no job, and no prospects. Dejected, I mulled over my situation during the middle of the hot 1952 summer, broke with more car payments due. The family was barely hanging on, and my mother's health was failing. Even worse, my girlfriend had jilted me for an older man. Dreams of success after my high school graduation faded fast. Starting college was out of the question, and Hot Springs, Arkansas, offered little hope for the future I'd planned.

My only prospect appeared to be going somewhere I could get a good-paying job, so I asked the clerk at the employment office where that might be.

He actually lifted his head far enough to look at me. "Caterpillar is hiring in Peoria, Illinois, and Boeing is hiring in Wichita, Kansas."

"Thanks." I checked the map. Wichita appeared to be closer to home.

My fourteen-year-old brother, Jason, loaned me fifty dollars he'd earned by pretending to be eighteen to get a job with the county. They put him on a crew to cut trees and brush encroaching on gravel roads through the mountains. Two weeks later, he'd been fired after someone snitched about his true age. The informant probably wanted his job.

A twelve-dollar bus ticket took me to Wichita. After an all-night ride, I arrived shortly after dawn with less than thirty-eight dollars in my pocket. A precious dime bought me a copy of *The Wichita Eagle* and a listing for a room to rent. I paid the landlady seven dollars for one week, left my suitcase, and visited the Boeing Airplane Company personnel center. I'd been told they paid good wages.

Spurred by the war in Korea, Boeing built jet bombers for the Air Force. Uncle Sam wanted more of them quickly, and the company needed workers to man their huge assembly line.

A recruiter called me to his desk and made notes as he listened to the list of my lack of qualifications.

Sensing he wasn't impressed, I squirmed in my chair. The only way to get experience was to get a job. "I like airplanes, and I'd like to learn more about them."

He raised his eyebrows. "You don't have any skills, so we'll have to put you through training. A class for tool and die makers opens next week, but you'd have to pass an aptitude test."

My response was immediate. "I'd like to take the test."

An hour later, he handed me a printed page. "Congratulations. You're in. Report on Monday for paid training. You'll need to bring all the precision tools on this list."

I sensed disaster. "How much do they cost?"

"You can buy them used at a pawn shop for about seventy-five dollars."

A lump formed in my throat. "I don't have seventy-five dollars."

He frowned. "You can't start the class without tools."

I needed a job, and tool and die makers were in demand. Without tools, it wasn't going to happen.

Tales of a Misspent Youth

Thinking back to problems I'd faced during my misspent youth, I realized I'd never accomplished anything by failing to try. Desperate, I searched for a way out. "Do you have any other tests?"

He rubbed a hand through his thinning hair. "We're hiring trainee draftsmen."

The word frightened me for an instant, until I convinced myself he didn't intend to draft me for the Army.

"That test is even harder. You'd need about thirty dollars for tools, but you might be able to start training without the full set."

After a moment's thought, this possibility sounded even better. Tool and die makers earned good money, but drafting might offer a better future. "I'd like to take it."

Two hours later, I'd aced the second test and been scheduled to start training. Evidently, paying attention during plane geometry class paid off.

The friendly manager at a drafting supply house explained what I'd need to start training. "The minimum you can get by with is a precision scale, triangles, protractor, a circle template, compass, a drafting brush, pencils, and trigonometry tables. You can buy additional tools as you need them."

I invested seventeen dollars in drafting equipment and planned to walk a few miles to and from classes. However, my money wasn't going to last until payday. Something had to give.

When I returned to my room, I approached the landlady. "I found a job at Boeing, but payday is two weeks off. Could you wait until then for next week's rent?"

She bit her lip and frowned. "The last time I did that, the man moved out, and I never collected the rent."

My voice choked. "I pay my debts."

She puffed her cheeks and exhaled. "I'll trust you until payday."

Walking to classes made me hungry, and fifteen-cent hamburgers sustained me for two weeks. The landlady awarded me a happy smile when I paid the rent.

By January, I'd bought a 1941 Chevrolet and rented a house near the Boeing plant. A friend at work offered to haul my family's belongings in his pickup truck, and I moved my mother and younger brothers to Kansas.

None of them ever needed to accept another welfare check.

We lived on my salary until Mama found work and contributed to the family coffers. After I settled into my job, I earned a few promotions and a leadership role.

Boeing redesigned the wings for their B-52 bomber to provide integral fuel tanks and an improved structure. Engineers did the basic design, and my group was tasked with producing hundreds of drawings to define part of the new wing.

My supervisor called me to his desk. "I need lead men to manage the work. You'll be in charge of producing the drawing package for the outboard thirty feet of the wing. A dozen draftsmen should be able to meet the schedule. You'll need to coordinate with design groups and make sure your people stay on schedule and stay busy."

My prospects had improved. I was earning good wages and working overtime. I'd completed my freshman year of college in night school, and Boeing gave me a significant job. Being responsible for a big chunk of detail design work appeared to be a good omen for my future.

Mama's and my savings made the down payment on a larger house. We became homeowners and moved to a better location.

The country was at peace. Only a few young men were being drafted as 1957 dawned. I'd almost stopped worrying about that possibility. A month later, I received a letter from my draft board. I knew trouble was brewing when I read the heading. *Greetings*. It appeared that President Eisenhower required a few more able young bodies to augment our military forces. I had thirty days to settle my affairs and show up for induction into the U.S. Army.

I went peaceably when the draft board indicated that, otherwise, the Army would come and get me.

When I left, Boeing gave my performance an overdue compliment. They assigned a graduate engineer to replace me. I reported to Camp Chaffee, Arkansas for basic training to serve my country.

Your Father's Peacetime Army

Two months of basic training at Camp Chaffee introduced me to sharing my room with thirty-one other recruits and meals with several hundred. I got acquainted with a few bunkmates the first evening. Then a sergeant marched us all to the barbershop for our military haircuts. Without hair, we became strangers again.

Duck walking through police call each morning before breakfast was an energizing new experience. The entire unit lined up to pick up trash on the ground surrounding our barracks. The sergeant's cheerful voice still rings in my ears when I think about it.

"Move out, men." His voice boomed loud enough to split the fog. "If it's not growing, pick it up. If it moves, salute it."

We moved out across a field in a squat. Invariably, a recruit would miss a scrap of trash, and the sergeant would gently proceed to admonish him. He bellowed. "Take your left hand and grasp your right ear. Now, take your right hand and grasp your left ear. Now, young soldier, you'd better pull your head out of your ass."

When we marched to the chow hall, we were confronted with an eight-foot tall chinning bar. Our field first sergeant explained its purpose. "Each recruit will perform three pull-ups before being permitted inside the mess hall. Those who fail can stay here and practice while the rest of us enjoy our meal."

Tales of a Misspent Youth

About a dozen overweight recruits were left to struggle with the challenge while we ate. They were simply too heavy to lift their weight.

When the time allotted for eating had almost expired, the sergeant would yield. "Out of the goodness of my heart and military regulations, you men can proceed to the chow line."

When they'd filled their trays, the sergeant stood beside them. "Time's up. Feel free to eat as much as you can shovel down between here and the garbage cans."

They had only about fifty feet to walk, so it was unlikely any of them gained weight. After a couple of weeks everyone managed to do their pull-ups.

We spent a lot of time learning to fire and care for our M-1 rifles. Recruits were required to field strip and clean them daily. This was an easy task since my misspent youth taught me to shoot before I turned fourteen, and a semester of ROTC at Wichita University taught me more about maintaining the rifle than a recruit needed to know.

The city-born soldier in the next bunk didn't catch on quickly enough. He drew the wrath of our instructor.

"You need to get better acquainted with your weapon." The instructor gave the young soldier a sympathetic glance while he broke the rifle into about a dozen loose parts. "Put these under your bottom sheet and sleep on them tonight. You'll be more familiar with your piece by morning."

The barracks sergeant verified the parts stayed in place for the night, and I lost sleep because of the tossing, turning, and cursing from the next bunk.

Another recruit evidently made someone unhappy. He spent an entire Sunday afternoon standing on the orderly room steps, facing our barracks. Every sixty seconds, he'd tuck his hands under his armpits, flap his elbows, and shout, "I'm a big-assed bird."

I didn't go close. It might have been contagious.

After three weeks of unrelenting harassment, the first sergeant lined us up in formation during a refreshing Saturday morning rain.

"Great training weather, men." He pounded his chest. "Great training weather. Any of you recruits have a civilian driver's license?"

Dozens of hands shot up, and he selected the four volunteers nearest him. The remaining recruits were assigned menial tasks to alleviate their weekend boredom. Six of us wound up in a storeroom dusting bottles on the shelves. A coal stove at one end of the long room took the chill off the damp air. After a few minutes of dusting, my companions gathered by the stove, warming their hands and shooting the bull. Being a suspicious sort, I chose a convenient shelf at the opposite end of the room and continued my task.

Minutes later, a sergeant walked in and spotted the gathering. "Come with me." He led them out into the rain.

I spent a warm and dry morning wiping the same row of clean bottles a few hundred times, taking care to look busy each time a sergeant walked through.

The volunteers with driver's licenses made repeated trips past my window, slogging through the red clay mud, pushing wheelbarrows filled with rocks. I'd learned a valuable survival skill. This enlightening scene always inspired caution when I considered volunteering for anything. During chow, nobody could figure out how I had the only dry uniform in the outfit.

Tales of a Misspent Youth

Nearing the end of our cycle, my company was granted the privilege of carrying a field pack eleven miles and camping out in two-man pup tents for field training. A steady rain lasted for the entire week. After raising our tents, we dug individual prone shelters for protection in case someone started shooting at us. The task became more complicated when a light plane made repeated passes over our camp and bombarded us with tear gas.

A sergeant charged through the camp roaring, "Don your gas masks. Keep digging."

I strapped on the ugly and uncomfortable mask but never quite understood all the fuss. I'd plowed fields behind a team of mules that fouled the air with much more potent gas than the puny stuff the airplane released.

During our bivouac, we were treated to a forced crawl through deep mud, carrying our rifles as we slithered through barbed wire barriers in the infiltration course. They taught me to lie on my back and push through the mud with the heel of my boots. The barrel of my weapon tucked under the rim of my helmet protected my face from the wire. An upwards glance at the bright tracer rounds mixed in with machine gun bullets flying above us encouraged me to keep my head down. I could tolerate this inconvenience, but I got a bit upset during our outdoor lunch. It rained so hard the hot dog floated off my tray before I could eat it.

I'd signed up as a candidate for officer's candidate school when I arrived, but somewhere during that muddy bivouac, I decided I'd prefer to serve my mandatory time and resume civilian life.

Eventually, nine weeks of basic training passed and the Army sent me home on leave, my uniform sporting a sharpshooters badge and no stripes on my sleeve.

Missing officer' candidate school? Probably a good decision. I'd probably have wound up as a second lieutenant, commanding an infantry platoon in Viet Nam.

Fort Belvoir

After basic training, the Army, in its infinite wisdom, sent me to an engineering school at Fort Belvoir, Virginia, for advanced training. One hundred fifty soldiers checked in, but the school could only accept seventy-two trainees. I was number one hundred forty-seven to sign in and wound up in a casual company, awaiting assignment to a working unit.

Our nation's capital was only a short bus ride away from the fort. On my first night in the casual barracks, about a hundred troops awaited passes to go to town. I planned to take this opportunity to visit Washington, D. C.

A young lieutenant walked in at 1800 hours, carrying a clipboard. He had a different idea about how we should spend the evening. "This place looks like a pig sty."

We all stood at attention as he climbed on a raised post at one end of the big open room and reached up to wipe a finger across the top of an overhead heating duct. "The dust is a quarter-inch thick here. No passes will be issued until this barracks shines. I'll be back in two hours to inspect it again."

It was obvious nobody had given this place a thorough scrubbing in months, probably years for the top of that duct. It didn't seem fair we'd been tasked to correct a situation that happened long before we got there.

A corporal who had the misfortune of being stuck with us shrugged. "Reckon I'm senior man. We're not going anywhere until the lieutenant is happy. Get to it."

Everyone started cleaning while I stood in the aisle and studied the situation. Removing the thick layer of accumulated dust from that overhead duct would be a big job, and we wouldn't finish until it was too late to leave the base. We needed a plan. A raised post that allowed someone standing on it to reach the top of the duct stood at each end of the long room. The lieutenant had already checked one. I approached the corporal with a possible solution to our problem.

After hearing me out, he laughed. "It's worth a try."

I grabbed a bucket of water, a sponge, and a handful of rags and climbed on top of the second post. Fifteen minutes later, everything within reach of my perch was shiny clean.

When the lieutenant returned, he found a freshly scrubbed barracks. Donning a white glove, he marched straight to the second post and reached up to wipe the top of the duct. The glove was clean when he withdrew it, and he didn't bother checking anywhere else. Ninety-five percent of the duct was still covered in its thick layer of accumulated dust.

The lieutenant glanced around the barracks once more. "Good job, men. Anyone who wants a pass to go off post can stop at the orderly room."

I savored a small triumph as he left the building.

The next morning, we fell out in formation to receive duty assignments. The prospects didn't look good. The scuttlebutt was that ninety percent of us would wind up armed with a pick and shovel in a construction battalion.

Tales of a Misspent Youth

My only hope of escaping this disagreeable outcome would be to volunteer for one of the few remaining assignments.

A sergeant announced they needed three men to become military policemen. That didn't sound like anything I wanted to do, so I took a chance and waited. Later, he announced an opening for a company clerk and added a condition.

"You need to be able to type for this job."

That sounded better. My hand flew up. Ten minutes later, I was back in the ranks. They gave me a typing test, and my fifteen words per minute typing speed hadn't impressed anyone. When they needed three jeep drivers in the headquarters motor pool, desperation motivated me to volunteer again. My hand went up once more, and the sergeant selected me to become a jeep driver at the regimental headquarters.

The company motor sergeant came for us, and we gathered our gear. On the way to our company, the sergeant offered another possibility. "My dispatcher is completing his tour of duty, and I'll need a replacement."

By the time we arrived at the motor pool, I had the job. I'd learn to type in my spare time.

It didn't take long to figure out how the unit worked. The motor sergeant usually took off before 1500 each day to go home and grab a slug of Jack Daniels while he watched TV. The assistant motor sergeant was an athlete who could catch the 100-mph breaking ball the pitcher on the post softball team threw. He was usually gone in pursuit of the U.S. Army championship. That left the dispatcher to run the motor pool.

Two weeks later, the motor sergeant presented me with another challenge. "We're scheduled for an inspection at the end of the month. See to it our maintenance records are up to date and our vehicles are spotless when the inspection team arrives."

When I checked for the maintenance records, they didn't exist. Not willing to accept defeat, I manufactured six months of completed forms for our sixteen vehicles using different pencils and altering my handwriting. Some I laid on the shop floor and drove a jeep over them for added authenticity. A few wrinkles and grease stains later, our records were complete. Thorough washing and a little fresh paint to cover rust spots prepared our vehicles.

We passed the inspection with flying colors. The commendation our motor pool received was icing on the cake.

My company commander visited the dispatch office during the afternoon and stopped at my desk. "Good job."

I never learned if he knew how we passed, but I was pleased to know I'd saved the company from a bad situation. Gaming the system had been the only way to get it done.

During the summer, our workload increased, and I was forced to take a driving assignment after completing my morning paperwork. Being the dispatcher gave me first choice of which one. I chose a deuce and a half truck and hooked onto a trailer carrying an experimental new plastic-bodied water tank. A new design gasoline engine generator went along for the ride. An engineer rode with me to monitor how the equipment held up as I drove on varied road conditions. We packed a lunch, took a map, and explored Eastern Virginia for three weeks. We returned to the motor pool each day by 1500 so I'd have time to log the other drivers in as they completed their day's work.

The unfortunate motor sergeant took care of my morning dispatch chores.

NCO Rescue

Heavy rain drummed on the barracks roof when the charge of quarters kicked my bunk at 0230 hours. I shook my head to clear the cobwebs. "What's wrong?"

"The NCO Academy is bivouacked along the creek, and their camp flooded in this rain. The entire class for noncommissioned officers is wading in a foot of water."

I raised up on one elbow. "Why tell me?"

"Someone has to rescue them. You're the dispatcher, so haul a driver out of bed to go get them."

I dropped a reluctant foot to the floor. "Crap. Somebody's gonna be mad."

"That's their problem."

The positive attitude that got me in occasional trouble kicked in. "Guess I'm already awake. Might as well do it myself."

After pulling on my fatigues and boots, I signed out a deuce and a half truck to rescue a bunch of dumb-assed sergeants who didn't know how to set up a camp that wouldn't flood when it rained.

The olive drab truck rumbled to life, and I made my way through sheets of falling water in the deserted streets. The task began to look scary as I left the paved road and started down the steep hill toward the flooded creek. Heavy rain left a sea of soupy clay mud. I navigated the sharp turns with caution as the clumsy vehicle crept down the narrow track.

After rounding the final curve, the headlights illuminated a scene of total chaos. The creek spilled a quarter mile out of its banks. A foot of surging water covered the camp. All the tents had collapsed, and their equipment lay waterlogged. A large crowd of soaking wet NCOs huddled together, awaiting rescue.

I jumped from the cab into the flood to find the NCO in charge.

A scowling staff sergeant splashed up to stand in my face. "I'm Sergeant Worley, in charge here. Where the hell you been?"

His attitude took away some of my sympathy for his plight. "I came soon as they called."

"Can't you see we're in trouble here?"

I pushed back my cap. "We need to get your equipment on the truck. The men will have to ride on top."

After loading all the ruined gear and mud-soaked tents, we hooked their five hundred-gallon water trailer behind the overloaded vehicle. Twenty-three men struggled to find a place to perch atop the mess. The senior sergeants climbed into the cab with me. All of us were caked in river muck.

I shifted into all-wheel drive and the lowest compound gear as we eased through the floodwater and started up the treacherous hill at a crawl. The vehicle made slow progress, advancing a couple of yards then sliding back one. The trailer threatened to jackknife when we lost ground. The sergeants offered numerous *helpful* suggestions on handling the truck as I fought the wheel and accelerator.

I finally responded. "Listen, Sergeant. I'm having enough trouble herding this truck. I don't need any more advice to distract me."

A couple of dirty looks suggested my remark hadn't been prudent, but silence reigned from my front seat passengers.

In places, I could add power and advance. Others required the lightest touch to prevent the wheels from spinning and losing ground. The tight curves proved to be the most critical challenges. My emotions alternated between panic and triumph and back again as the truck made fitful progress up the hill. After what seemed an eternity, the ground leveled before us, and I breathed a sigh of relief. The rain slacked, and a gray dawn greeted us as the truck found a paved road.

I turned in at the academy with a feeling of pride. A tall black master sergeant stood on the steps of the orderly room to watch the truck grind to a halt in the middle of the parade ground.

The gaggle of NCOs grabbed their personal gear and jumped from the vehicle to head straight for their barracks. None of them stopped to say, "Thanks for the ride."

Sergeant Worley jumped from the filthy cab and pointed to a low building beside the cleared area. "Spread the tents over there to dry, and stack our equipment by the building. Leave the water trailer by the shed in back."

I stared in disbelief. "Is that all, Sergeant?"

"When you're done, you can return to your unit." He disappeared into the barracks.

My temperature rose. I was only a lowly private, but I'd left my bed in the middle of the night to rescue this sorry lot. I'd worked as hard as anyone to load the truck, and I'd sweated blood to maneuver their clumsy cargo up the muddy slope. I did everything they asked, and they deserted me without a word of thanks. While the NCOs were enjoying their hot shower and a solid breakfast, it would take hours for me to unload their gear and clean the truck. The vehicle had to be spotless when I returned it to the motor pool, and I'd already missed out on chow. In addition, the motor sergeant would be unhappy that I'd saddled him with the task of dispatching the drivers.

"I don't think so."

My determination firmed as I approached the orderly room. When I entered, the master sergeant stood beside his desk facing me. He looked like he'd just stepped from a recruiting poster. When I looked down, a muddy pool of water on his clean floor surrounded my boots. The sergeant regarded me in silence. Black NCOs were rare in 1957, and I'd never met a black master sergeant. The creases on his tropical worsted trousers looked like they might cut if you touched them. His polished shoes reflected the image of my face. Rows of medals adorned his chest, nestled beneath the blue combat infantryman's badge above.

He nodded a greeting. "I'm Sergeant Carter, supervisor of training. What can I do for you, Private?"

I cleared my throat. "Sergeant, I missed half a night's sleep to rescue these men. I loaded their gear, made sure they were safely settled on the mess, and did some damn good driving to get them out of there. They left me to unload while they showered. Nobody even said thanks. I've missed chow, and I'll spend two hours cleaning the truck after I unload their mess and leave here. I don't think it's right."

Sergeant Carter wrinkled his brow, and then he smiled. "Go stand by your truck to supervise the unloading. When it's empty, my class will be happy to clean it. Make sure they do a good job."

Stunned, I turned to leave. "Thank you, Sergeant."

I watched him enter the barracks. Thirty seconds later, doors flew open and half-dressed NCOs raced to unload the truck. When it stood empty, they attacked the mud with rags and hoses. Feeling vindicated, I watched their progress and offered helpful advice. Inside the cab, Sergeant Worley crouched on the floor, cleaning the interior with a damp rag.

I pointed to the side of the seat. "You missed a spot, Sergeant."

Restraining my satisfaction at the expression on his face proved to be a challenge. Was it possible I'd not completely outgrown my misspent youth?

A half hour later, the truck gleamed. As I passed the orderly room to leave the academy, Sergeant Carter stood on the steps. With my right hand gripping the steering wheel, I leaned out my window to wave and throw him a left-handed salute.

"Thanks, Sergeant."

He touched his cap with the swagger stick. "Carry on, soldier."

**

As the summer waned, the company commander called me to the orderly room. "I have to release five men for overseas assignment. You're included. Four will stand guard at the East German border. One goes to Paris as a VIP chauffeur at Supreme Headquarters Allied Powers Europe. That's SHAPE. You get first choice."

An entire second expired while I made up my mind. "I'd prefer SHAPE, sir."

Ten days later, I boarded the troopship, *USS General Buckner*, in New York Harbor. It would be my first trip outside the United States.

During the voyage to Germany, I shared a large amidships hold with two hundred-forty men, our bunks stacked four deep. Everyone was assigned to on board duty. I drew permanent KP. It wasn't too bad, though. We were given free run with the ship's stores for snacks. I ate a lot of ice cream.

Everyone seemed to spend their off-duty time playing poker. Being broke, I found a game where they limited the stakes to a nickel. Careful playing and long hours eventually earned me twenty dollars. Feeling lucky, I entered a dollar-limit game on deck. Fifteen minutes later, my stake had disappeared.

I was broke again.

Supreme Headquarters Allied Powers Europe

Fourteen days on the round-bottomed troopship rolling and pitching across the Atlantic brought me to Bremerhaven, Germany. An all-night train ride delivered me to Paris, and the 42nd Car Company sent a vehicle to collect me at the *Gare De L'Est*.

The company first sergeant gave me the onceover when I reported. "I'm Sergeant Manson. How long since you've had a haircut?"

"Three days, Sergeant, before I left the ship."

"Get another one and report to the CO. If you don't have money, I'll loan it to you."

"I have enough money for a haircut."

Thirty minutes later and freshly shorn, I reported to Lieutenant Small.

He looked up from a personnel file and returned my salute. "You have a clean record, and your previous CO recommended you. You'll join our taxi platoon."

"Yes, sir."

I stowed my gear and reported to the dispatcher. "What does the taxi platoon do?"

"Two-star generals and up rate a car and driver. Everyone below that rank calls us for transportation on official business. I'll dispatch a car from your platoon. You'll take them where they need to go. Lieutenant Small is an exception. As company CO, he rates a staff car and driver. You don't want that job."

"Why not?"

Tales of a Misspent Youth

"Everyone calls this company the 42nd Fender Benders. We have the worst accident rate in the U.S. Army, and Lieutenant Small is paranoid. He'd make your life miserable."

After learning my way around Paris, I hauled officers and staff people around the city, picked up visitors at the airport, and drove senior officers to social events during the evening. Any spare time was spent cleaning and waxing my vehicle.

When I'd gained a few weeks experience, the dispatcher assigned me to drive Brigadier General Andrews to an event at the home of René Coty, the President of France. "You'll have a long evening. The general likes to party. He won't leave until they're ready to throw him out."

After I dropped General Andrews off at the main entrance, the *gendarmes* directed me to park on a street two blocks away and gave me a number they would call when the general prepared to leave.

Bored and figuring I had lots of time, I wandered down to the *gendarmerie* where music was playing. A group of the French police and international chauffeurs were singing country western songs to the accompaniment of an American driver playing the guitar. Someone handed me a glass of hot mulled wine, and I settled in to enjoy the party.

An hour later, another driver grabbed me. "They've been calling your number."

I sprinted to my staff car and rushed to pick up an unhappy general.

As I drove away, he growled. "What the hell happened? I've been waiting for a half hour."

"They called out numbers in French. I must not have understood."

He grumbled a bit and let the matter drop. I chalked up a stroke of good luck and a valuable lesson learned. I didn't do that again.

My new assignment wasn't bad. I enjoyed getting acquainted with Paris. I could soon find my way from the *Tour Eiffel* to the *Arc de Triomphe* to the *Place de la Concorde* and back to the headquarters. On weekends, I frequented the bars around the *Etoile* and began to put together bits and pieces the language.

A few weeks later, the dispatcher stopped me as I returned from a run. "Lieutenant Small wants you to report to the orderly room."

My nerves fluttered as I entered his office. *What had I done wrong?*

The lieutenant eyed me. "I've selected you to be my new driver. You'll set the example. Your car will be the cleanest, most highly polished vehicle in the company."

"Yes, sir."

"You will scrupulously follow all military regulations and set the standard for driving skill and military courtesy in this organization."

"Yes, sir." Thus began my life in purgatory.

A typical run would elicit a string of comments from the martinet who now ruled my life.

"There's a spot of mud on the left rear tire."

"You didn't wait for a proper gap in traffic before pulling onto the highway."

"You should have avoided that bump."

"I felt the car lurch when you shifted gears."

"Look out for that bicycle!"

"Anticipate the possibility before one of those crazy Frenchmen cuts you off."

Sometimes, he didn't even pause to catch his breath between observations on how I could improve my performance.

Lieutenant Small visited the headquarters several times each week. On our first visit, I stopped at the main entrance, ran to open his door, snapped to attention, and saluted as he stepped from the vehicle.

He pointed to the walk thirty yards short of the entrance. "Park there and wait for me to exit those doors. By the time I descend the steps, you'll be front and center, standing at attention, saluting, with my door open."

"Sir, parking there is prohibited."

"Is something wrong with your hearing?"

"No, sir. I'll do as you say."

Ten minutes later, an MP walked up to my window and pointed to the parking lot across the street. "Move this car, soldier."

I raised my hands in a gesture of helplessness. "My CO ordered me to park here."

He gave me a dirty look and left. A few days later, we repeated the scene.

I parked there once more and rolled down my window when a tall light colonel strolled up to my vehicle eyeing me with a skeptical smile. "Why the hell are you blocking the main entrance to SHAPE, soldier?"

"Sir, my CO, Lieutenant Small, ordered me to park here to wait for him."

The colonel's smile disappeared. "I'm the provost marshal here. Move your vehicle to the parking lot. When

Lieutenant Small returns, have him report to Colonel Clark."

"Yes, sir."

When the lieutenant returned, he waited several seconds for my arrival. As I pulled away, I caught his eye in my mirror. "Sir, Colonel Clark..."

He leaned forward to glare at me. "I saw Colonel Clark. In the future, you'll park in the lot where you belong."

"Yes, sir."

A few weeks later, the Army replaced our olive drab uniforms with spiffy new green ones. We were granted a one-year phase in, and that would be beyond my expected tour of duty. More than half my salary went home to help my family. The uniform cost more than the pay I drew each month, so I didn't buy one.

Lieutenant Small immediately announced a Saturday morning inspection. He walked down the ranks, peering at the troops, the sergeant beside him taking notes. I kept my gaze above the crown of his cap as he looked me over. When the lieutenant left, the sergeant called out the names of those who had failed. My name was among those called.

Failure meant restriction to base. I quickly figured out the cause. By some coincidence, troops wearing a green uniform passed. Those wearing olive drab didn't.

Back at the barracks, my platoon sergeant dropped the other shoe. "The weekly inspections will continue until the entire company passes."

I spent the next four Sundays in the mess hall, pulling KP for guys who could afford to pay ten dollars to avoid the fifteen-hour ordeal. Another half hour was needed to wash off the stink. Then I bought the green uniform.

The weekly inspections ended.

On a rainy Saturday morning, Lieutenant Small called me to the orderly room. "My wife wants to go shopping. Use my civilian car, and take her to the stores. You can carry her packages."

"Sir, you refused me permission to have a civilian driver's license."

"Are you having another hearing problem? Use your military license."

This didn't sound legal, but I couldn't think of an alternative. "Yes, sir."

I followed the woman as she shopped for hours, carrying packages and being treated like a slave to the princess. When she finished, I drove her home and started back to the base. Three miles short of my destination, the car sputtered and stalled. I was out of gas, and steady rain continued. With no way to avoid it, I walked a half mile to the nearest service station, left my watch as a deposit on a can, and bought two liters of gas.

Rain soaked my dress uniform as I plodded through the mud. When I'd emptied the can in the gas tank, I drove back to the station to return it. Gasoline was fifteen cents a gallon on base and seventy-five cents on the French market.

After counting my money, I told the attendant, "Fill it up. I'll need a receipt."

Back at the base, I dripped water on Lieutenant Small's clean floor when I reported, "I ran out of gas, sir, and filled the tank at a service station. Here's your receipt."

He almost leaped from his chair. "You what?"

"I bought gasoline, sir."

His lecture on how stupid I'd been to waste his money lasted at least ten minutes. I thoroughly enjoyed the experience, but he didn't look happy as he repaid me. My relationship with the CO went downhill after the incident.

The strain of trying to keep Lieutenant Small happy began to weigh on me. As we left the headquarters several days later, I made an attempt to improve my lot. "Sir."

He looked up from the back seat to face my rearview mirror. "Yes?"

"Sir, I appreciate the recognition you've given me by selecting me as your driver, but I'd like to request reassignment to the taxi platoon."

Silence reigned in the back seat for the better part of a minute before the lieutenant answered. "I'm sorry you don't like your job, private. But you're in the Army, and you'll do as you're damn well told."

"Yes, sir."

After considering my plight overnight, I chose a course of action. Shortly after noon, the dispatcher told me Lieutenant Small wanted to go to the headquarters. After a brief check to make sure my vehicle was spotless, I picked him up.

After a long wait for a sufficient break in traffic, my car crept onto the highway and accelerated to a snail's pace. Cars swept around us with horns blasting. Lieutenant Small looked confused and impatient. Two dump trucks careened by with loud horns protesting my presence, but I held to my stately speed.

Lieutenant Small leaned forward. "Speed up. You're going to get us killed."

Tales of a Misspent Youth

"Sir, I'm driving as fast as I consider safe given the weather and traffic conditions." More cars blew past us with horns blaring.

"Speed up, dammit."

"Would you put that order in writing, sir? I don't feel safe driving faster." I'd decided to hit the next telephone pole after I had the order in my pocket.

Neither of us spoke for the remainder of the trip. I actually increased my speed by about five miles per hour as we returned.

Thirty minutes later, the dispatcher called me to his shack. "You've been reassigned to the taxi platoon."

**

The following week, the dispatcher called me again. "Air Vice Marshal McGregor's driver is taking leave next week. You'll fill in while he's away."

The AVM lived on a motor yacht moored across the Seine River from the *Tour Eiffel*. He'd been a spitfire pilot in the Royal Air Force during the big war and came to SHAPE as a senior British officer second only to Field Marshal Montgomery. I felt intimidated when I picked him up Monday morning. His ten-year-old daughter, Anne, accompanied him.

"Drop me at the office and take Anne on to school. Here's the address. Then you can report to my secretary for the day's schedule."

I started through the *Bois de Boulogne* cautiously, trying to shift smoothly and avoid bumps.

The AVM leaned forward in his seat. "Step it up a bit. Don't want to be late."

"Yes, sir." I increased my speed slightly.

The next two mornings, he admonished me again to drive a little faster. I was already driving faster than my Army speed limit and hesitated to exceed it by too much. During the day, I ran errands for him and picked up visitors from the airport. His daughter found out I was learning French and volunteered to tutor me while I drove her to school. She turned out to be a good teacher. My rudimentary French improved.

Thursday morning, as we started across the *Bois* again, the AVM fidgeted, and a loud roar emanated from the back seat. "Dammit, I don't have all day to get to work."

He had my attention. I floored the gas pedal.

When the speedometer reached seventy, he roared again. "That's enough."

"Yes, sir." I reduced speed slightly and continued. After we reached the *autoroute,* I increased my speed to seventy again. The US Army speed limit was fifty.

When we arrived at SHAPE, the AVM paused to ask me a question. "Did you enjoy this assignment so far?"

"Yes, sir. Very much."

Two hours later, the dispatcher called me to his shack. "You've been assigned as VIP chauffeur for AVM McGregor."

The AVM commanded respect. I gave him my loyalty and worked my tail feathers to the bone.

Colonel Price, a U.S. Army bird colonel and the AVM's aide, told me I was his fourth driver in less than a year. He'd fired the first three.

Later, an air force colonel waved me to a stop as I left the headquarters to take Anne to school. "Why is a child in your car, soldier?"

"I'm taking the AVM's daughter to school, sir."

He stepped back and waved me on.

When I checked in at the office later, Colonel Price motioned me into his office.

"I saw an American officer stop your car earlier. What did he want?"

"He wanted to know why I had a child in the car, sir."

Colonel Price cocked his head. "In the future, if anyone asks you anything about your activities with the car, your answer is you're on dispatch to the AVM. If they wish to know more, they should ask him."

"Yes, sir." This could open up new possibilities.

AVM McGregor proved to be a considerate boss. His wife was pleasant, and his daughter a delight. I shopped for him in the American PX and drove him wherever he needed to go quickly and safely. In return, he made sure I had extra time off and kept me out of trouble.

A number of drivers gathered at the PX for coffee call during the afternoon, and I stopped by when possible. It didn't take long for my platoon sergeant to react.

"You don't have any business here. You work for a Brit. You're driving a government vehicle. Is this trip authorized?"

"I can't discuss my duties, Sergeant. You'll have to ask the AVM."

I took a little verbal abuse, but nobody ever called.

One afternoon, I parked the staff car at the PX in a spot reserved for military police. While I was inside drinking coffee, a French civilian driving a U.S. Army truck cut a corner too sharp. His rear wheels mangled the back bumper and quarter panel of my car. I filled out an accident report and presented it to Lieutenant Small.

He looked up from his desk with brow wrinkled and lips drawn tight. "What were you doing at the PX?"

"I was dispatched to AVM McGregor, sir, and I'm not allowed to discuss my duties. You'll have to ask him."

The lieutenant dropped the matter and ordered my staff car repaired.

He continued to search for an excuse to court martial me, but as long as I kept the AVM happy, I was out of his reach.

Then I met a charming French girl named Alice, and we explored Paris together. Within three months, I asked her to be my wife.

Life was good.

Lieutenant Small glared at me. "You're too irresponsible to get married, and you don't make enough money to support a wife. I'll not allow you to live off post."

"Yes, sir."

Three weeks and thirty-eight pages of military and state department paperwork later, Alice and I were married in a beautiful old church on the *Avenue de la Grande Armee* in Paris. Her family and friends plus a few of my army buddies attended. Since I lacked sufficient rank to have a wife in Paris and didn't make enough to support one, the Army refused to pay for off-post quarters for her.

Since I needed dependable transportation, I got a civilian driver's license, and we bought a little Renault Dauphine on credit. Working Sunday KP for ten dollars a day helped pay the rent. Alice knew a group of French lawyers, and I provided them with Scotch whiskey from the PX. The profits kept us from starving.

Knowing I had limited leave time, the AVM arranged to maximize my time off. Once each month, I'd drive him to work on Friday. He'd grant me the rest of the day off and catch a ride home with another officer. I'd pick up Alice and drive to her family's village near Strasbourg for the weekend. A one-day leave on Monday followed, and I'd avoid being AWOL by calling the charge of quarters before midnight on Tuesday, letting Uncle Sam know I was home. That gave me a five-day vacation for one day of leave.

On a rainy Friday afternoon, I'd been out of telephone contact and arrived at the headquarters a few minutes before the AVM normally left the office.

He raced from the entrance and dived into the back seat. "I have ten minutes to get to the *Palais de Chaillot.* Move it."

The *Palais* was eleven miles away in downtown Paris. Heavy rain and rush-hour traffic made the challenge more difficult. "Yes, sir."

The Chevy peeled rubber, and I speed-shifted to second gear. Still accelerating, I blew past the MPs at the main entrance and ran the stop sign. I rocked the wheel hard right, and executed a power drift as I entered a small break in traffic with the accelerator on the floor. At the entrance to the *autoroute*, I slammed the shift lever into third gear, passed a car on the ramp, and cut directly to the inside lane. The speedometer topped out at ninety-five.

Spray made visibility poor, but I spotted Lieutenant Small's old sedan chugging along at about forty in the outside lane. I'd be in trouble if he identified me, so I swerved into the center lane to cover his old clunker in a sheet of water. Reducing speed slightly when we left the *autoroute* for surface streets, I slid to a stop at our destination with fifteen seconds to spare.

The next morning, the dispatcher sent me to report to Lieutenant Small. I came to attention on entry and sensed the executive officer enter and stand behind me. The lieutenant read my rights under Article Fifteen of the Uniform Code of Military Justice.

Then he fixed me with a threatening stare. "How fast were you driving?"

"Sir, I'm not allowed to discuss my duties while I'm dispatched to the AVM. You'll have to ask him."

"The AVM was reading the newspaper. He couldn't possibly know your speed."

I stood frozen at attention, saying nothing.

The lieutenant slapped both hands palm down on his desk. "You'll return to live in the barracks and forfeit your off-post allowance. You'll relinquish your civilian driver's license and attend remedial driver's training at night. If a future violation occurs, I'll convene a court martial and assess stockade time. Dismissed."

Worried, I retreated to SHAPE and told the AVM's secretary I needed to see him. If this punishment stood, I'd be unable to support my wife. The secretary ushered me in.

"Sit down." The AVM indicated the chair in front of his desk.

"I'm in trouble, sir." I explained my problem.

"That's a bit of a sticky wicket." He hit the intercom button. "Send Price in."

A moment later, the colonel strolled in and gave me the evil eye. "What the hell did you do this time?"

The AVM explained. "He got into a spot of trouble yesterday. See what you can do for him."

I followed Colonel Price to his office and told my story. He wanted details.

"How did you get in this much trouble this quick?" He shook his head and motioned me to sit on the corner of his desk. "I might need to ask some questions."

Then he dialed Lieutenant Small.

From my perch, I heard both sides of the conversation as Colonel Price suggested the possibility of leniency for me.

"Sir, I'm responsible for safety," the lieutenant said. "There's no reason to consider leniency."

"The AVM is happy with his performance. He's always been dependable, efficient, and trustworthy."

"He endangered the life of everyone on the road."

Colonel Price settled back and offered a different perspective. His technique made drill sergeants look like amateurs at getting a point across.

Lieutenant Small stood his ground for a few minutes. "The man's a menace!"

Colonel Price's communication skills finally penetrated after he explained that a bad decision might be career limiting for the young officer.

The lieutenant began to waffle. His answers changed. "Yes, sir," "No, sir," and "What else can I do to make the AVM happy, sir?"

When I returned to the motor pool, the lieutenant had requested my presence at my earliest convenience. My misspent youth reared up and led me astray again. I let him wait for almost an hour before it became convenient.

He displayed a friendly smile when I entered his office. "Stand at ease. I've had good reports on your performance for the AVM, and I've decided to remove all punishment. I'll submit a commendation for your outstanding work."

I stood silent, my face blank.

"Please let the AVM know you're in good standing here. If he has any concerns about your treatment, tell me what we can do to reassure him."

I maintained my blank expression. "I always try to be dependable, efficient, and trustworthy, sir."

He dismissed me.

Three months later, I requested a six-month extension of active duty to allow Alice more time with her family before dragging her off to America. She was pregnant and wanted her parents to see the child.

AVM McGregor completed his assignment and returned to the UK to be knighted by Queen Elizabeth, receive his third star and lead Fighter Command for the Royal Air Force.

He left his successor with a request to look after me.

**

AVM Bowling didn't have the warm personality of AVM McGregor, but he was a considerate boss. He continued the policy of stretching my leave time, and I served his needs to the best of my ability.

When I completed my tour, the army allowed Alice space available on a troopship for transportation to the

United States. That meant a probable wait of three months after I returned home. I needed to buy a commercial ticket for her and our infant son.

AVM Bowling balked. "We can do better than that."

After three weeks of finagling and arm twisting, Alice had been assigned a seat beside me on the C-54 transport returning me to the United States. She would be the only dependent on board. Relieved of the need to buy a ticket for her, I traded my year-old Renault for a new one and shipped it to New York.

Two days before we were scheduled to leave, I was called into the office of a U.S. Air Force colonel. When I reported, he pointed to his wastebasket. "Your orders are in there. I don't work for your AVM. Your wife is not authorized to accompany you. It's not going to happen."

We had a problem.

After thanking the colonel for his kindness and consideration, I retreated to consider my options. Alice and I finagled to scrape up money for her ticket by selling a few items and borrowing from her family.

I took the military flight back to the United States.

After my release from active duty in Fort Dix, New Jersey, I met Alice at the airport in New York. We picked up our new car and counted our money. Together, we had almost seventy dollars. The new car had a block under the accelerator pedal limiting its speed to thirty-five mph until the five hundred-mile maintenance was performed. At least I was a civilian again.

We took the Pennsylvania turnpike and headed west.

An Accidental Engineer

The three of us arrived at my mother's home in Wichita, Kansas, at 0400. We'd driven all night because we didn't have money for a motel. The needle on the gas gauge was bouncing against the empty mark when our little Renault pulled into the driveway. Mom sheltered us until I could afford to rent an apartment.

I needed a job.

Fortunately, Boeing rehired me the next day. We rented a one-bedroom flat, bought a bed on credit, and relatives donated furniture for us to move in. I still have the damaged card table I bought for two dollars to use as our dining table. Then we settled in to live frugally and save money with my salary of more than triple what Uncle Sam had paid me. After a few classes in night school, the company gave me the opportunity to lead a group of draftsmen. My job felt secure.

That feeling turned out to be a bit optimistic.

Boeing lost several contracts and reduced the work force in Wichita from 35,000 employees to an eventual 2,500 survivors. Imminent layoff appeared certain.

An opportunity to transfer promised to rescue me. NASA awarded Boeing a large contract to design and build the first stage of the vehicle that would take astronauts to the moon. The company sent a team to Huntsville, Alabama, to pick up the job from Werner Von Braun's NASA team and start work on the Saturn V rocket.

Tales of a Misspent Youth

My group in Wichita was laying off draftsmen each week. Only seventeen of an original crew of one hundred-twenty remained.

I approached my boss, Carl Caldwell. He insisted on being called "Mr." unless you belonged to the select group that did yard work and washed his car on Sundays. "I'd like to interview for the space program."

He frowned as if something trivial had been requested. "I can't release you until you finish the job you're working on."

I'd have had a better chance if I'd washed his car. "The recruiters are only here this week. Then I'll be laid off."

He shrugged. "Guess you'll have to take your chances."

Later that day, I applied for a job as a contract employee elsewhere. They accepted me. My notice to Boeing followed immediately.

Mr. Caldwell's face turned red. "I'll not recommend you for rehire. You're being disloyal, failing to complete your assignment."

That's when the personnel department decided I could interview for the space program. The recruiters gave me a promotion and a temporary assignment at NASA in Huntsville. The Boeing team stayed six months to transition work on the huge booster rocket.

When I joined the project, management failed to note my status as a draftsman. Everyone appeared to assume I was a design engineer.

After three days, reading procedures manuals, I found a few problems that were not being addressed and started work on something that looked interesting.

280

Burning midnight oil, I bought a couple of textbooks to study structural design and stress analysis at home. For the next few months, I created preliminary designs for tail fin structure and engine fairings on the huge vehicle. My confidence soared when NASA accepted my work.

Six months later, I reported to the Boeing plant in New Orleans, Louisiana, where we would manufacture the giant rocket. Management assigned me to supervise a group of draftsmen. I wasn't happy, but I accepted the position. We built a team that excelled. I saw people doing challenging design work and felt like I'd been stuffed in my cage.

**

After a few months, my old boss, Mr. Caldwell, reported to me for training. "The company laid me off in Wichita. Since I'm within a year of retirement, they allowed me to complete my time here."

I quelled an impulse to gloat. "Welcome aboard, Carl. NASA uses different drawing standards, and we need someone to write a new procedures manual."

He frowned. "I've never written a manual before."

I kept my expression blank. "If you have problems, I'm available to help you. I'm sure you'll do fine."

A piece of advice I'd heard somewhere came to mind. *Be nice to people on your way up. You may meet them on your way down.*

For several frustrating months, I marked time doing my job and coveting the work I'd done at NASA.

Frustration drove me to approach my boss. "I'm capable of competing with designers. I'd like a promotion to design engineer."

He leaned back and scratched his head while he thought about it. "You're capable of doing the work, but you don't have a degree. Program management will have to approve."

A week later, he called me in his office. "Your reclassification was approved by the director, but the engineers' union refused to accept you. There'll be no promotion."

"Why?"

"You don't meet their educational requirements."

It took a moment for me to control my voice. "Thanks for trying."

Three days later, my resume went in the mail. Three weeks later, McDonnell Aircraft Company hired me as a design engineer. My family moved to St. Louis, and I started the new job.

After an initial stint designing small mechanisms and developing a bilge pump for the F-111 escape capsule, the company sent me to the F-4 fighter program as a structures designer.

The job lasted two hours.

I'd stowed my belongings and sat at my desk, trying to decide where to start, when my new boss called me to his office.

"Say something in French."

The request surprised me. *"Qu-est-ce que vous avez envie d'y entendre?"*

He shrugged. "Guess you do speak it. You don't work here anymore."

I reported to advance design. McDonnell adapted a French short takeoff and landing airplane to American specifications with rights to market it in the Western Hemisphere. I translated technical documents into English and did structural and fuel systems design. Serving as a translator during meetings and working with the French engineering team became a valuable learning experience.

The program suffered when a U.S. Air Force pilot crashed our prototype on a runway. He reversed the propellers eighteen feet short of the ground for touchdown. The airplane dropped like a rock. The crew was unhurt, but the airplane was severely damaged. We weren't immediately sure it could be made flight worthy again.

The boss called another engineer and me into his office. "They're shipping the fuselage back to St. Louis. You two will design repairs and make a few modifications while it's down."

Operating from a shop balcony, we designed repairs. An elite group of mechanics frequently installed our designs the same day. Looking toward military sales, we designed a larger aft door to accommodate paratroopers. That change required major structural modifications. We added an interlock to prevent the propellers from reversing until the wheels were on the ground. The French crew repaired the broken landing gear, wings, and propellers. I learned a lot from their chief engineer. Six months later, the aircraft flew again.

When we failed to sell it, I moved on to a team proposing an anti-submarine aircraft for the Navy. My initial task was consulting technical specialists and turning their conflicting advice into drawings of candidate configurations for our proposed airplane. As we zeroed in on a configuration, our small group needed someone to define the four crew stations.

It sounded like fun. "I can do that."

The job required learning a new skill set. It also offered a chance to work with pilots and senior officers, attend military schools, and fly training missions on patrol aircraft. Five days on an aircraft carrier and a flight on an S-2F airplane was a blast—after I'd survived the catapult launch and arrested landing.

We lost the competition, and I moved on to other projects. The freedom to dream up new aircraft configurations challenged and inspired me.

Twenty-five years after Boeing hired me as a trainee draftsman, I earned my college degree at night school.

I posed a question to the boss. "Don't I get a raise?"

He gave me a cross-eyed look. "What the hell for? You got a raise last fall."

Later, I worked with Air Force and Marine Corps pilots, developing cockpits for a new generation of fighter planes. The chance to meet senior military and government leaders from the United States, Great Britain, Spain, Italy, and Sweden expanded my horizons and taught me new ways to approach problems. Several of these contacts became friends.

The ability to work with customers contributed to making me a crew systems manager. A rewarding aspect of that role became hiring and training newly graduated engineers. An added bonus was pride in watching them grow and develop skills.

An intelligent and supportive wife raised our children. When the kids started high school, she took a job and contributed to the family coffers.

Looking back at a satisfying career, several events influenced my direction. NASA supervisors failed to understand my status. Rejection by Boeing's engineers union and fluency in French opened doors for me to use my creative talent elsewhere.

I also credit learning to overcome hardship during a misspent youth. Hard times challenged us, but it made good training for survival in the business world. I never met a boss or customer more difficult to deal with than the father who deserted me when I was ten years old.

My mother's steadfast example inspired optimism and perseverance. She kept our family together and fed until we all graduated from high school. Her unceasing work and love of family instilled determination and faith in our abilities.

Forty-four years of a challenging career passed quickly. I was privileged to meet and work with people who were smarter and achieved more than I did. Whenever possible, I learned from their examples.

What Happened Next?

Now retired, looking back on those years brings satisfaction.

Alice and I take pride in our children and grandchildren. We celebrate each display of character, initiative, and good judgment as we watch them grow. Hopefully, we set a good example and curbed the temptation to offer unsolicited advice.

Picking cotton at age six introduced me to the demands of work. My grandfather's example taught me truthfulness and fair play. Attempts and failures with projects to make money during childhood instilled persistence. Good teachers taught me respect for learning. Good neighbors provided a supportive community.

I can't take credit for many conscious decisions that influenced my working life. Chance provided opportunities. I only needed to take advantage of them.

I'm still learning.

Lacking seventy-five dollars to buy tools paved the way for me to become an engineer.

Becoming a spinner of tales just happened.

About the Author

Doyle Suit is a retired engineer with forty four years of experience in aircraft and spacecraft design. He is the author of numerous articles and stories published in magazines and newspapers. *Tales of a Misspent Youth* is his third full-length novel. He is a dedicated duffer who enjoys golf. Other favored activities include sailing, travel, gardening, playing guitar, and singing country and bluegrass music if nobody is listening and time spent with family. He is active in Coffee and Critique, Saturday Writers, and Ozark Creative Writers groups.